D0571633

The MAGICIANS OF ELEPHANT COUNTY

The
MAGICIANS
OF
ELEPHANT COUNTY

WRITTEN AND ILLUSTRATED BY
ADAM PERRY

HARPER
An Imprint of HarperCollinsPublishers

Library of Congress Cataloging-in-Publication Data

Names: Perry, Adam, date. author, illustrator.

Title: The magicians of Elephant County / Adam Perry.

Description: New York, NY : Harper, an imprint of HarperCollins Publishers,
    [2018] | Summary: "Amateur magicians Duncan and Emma are forced to come
    clean to police about their involvement in their small town's biggest
    disaster, which all started when they discovered that legends about the
    local witch might actually be true"-- Provided by publisher.

Identifiers: LCCN 2018004922 | ISBN 9780062795359 (hardback)

Subjects: | CYAC: Magic tricks--Fiction. | Witches--Fiction. |
    Magic--Fiction. | Humorous stories. | BISAC: JUVENILE FICTION /
Fantasy & Magic. | JUVENILE FICTION / Humorous Stories. | JUVENILE
FICTION / Action & Adventure / General.

Classification: LCC PZ7.1.P44766 Mag 2018 | DDC [Fic]--dc23

Typography by Jenna Stempel-Lobell

18 19 20 21 22   PC/LSCH   10 9 8 7 6 5 4 3 2 1

❖

First Edition

To Andrea, my co-magician

In an effort to understand the events that occurred this fall in Elephant County, we have pieced together the written accounts of the people of interest, Duncan Reyes, age 11, and Emma Gilbert, age 12.

We compared their versions with other eyewitness testimony and crime scene evidence.

Though there are some minor inconsistencies between their statements, we believe this to be the most accurate representation of what really happened.

Attempts have been made to organize these documents into a cohesive narrative, and it is our hope that you will leave with a better understanding of the matter.

It goes without saying that everything contained in these files is strictly confidential and must be handled with extreme sensitivity. Due to the level of damage to private property and the high costs associated with the repairs, the public is understandably interested in the details of the case. However, we believe the truth would pose a danger if released.

For now, our top priority is creating an alternate credible narrative and figuring out what happened to the children after we interviewed them.

The current location of Duncan Reyes and Emma Gilbert remains unknown.

DUNCAN AND EMMA, MAGICIANS

EMMA

Let me be clear about something—I am *not* Duncan's assistant.

Assistants lie in a box while a handsaw is going through them and magicians bask in the applause and glory.

That's not me. No way.

My mom told me that I don't have to be the quiet one in the dress who is chopped apart, put in cages, or blown to bits in an explosion. Forget about it.

Duncan and I are co-magicians, and if anything, he is *my* assistant.

I met Duncan the first day of kindergarten at Elephant County Elementary, and he was the most annoying, obnoxious, and stinky kid in the class.

It was hate at first sight.

He was short, with dark curly hair and skin the color of wet sand. His breath smelled like pretzels. He asked everyone in the class if they'd be his friend. He followed us around all day like a puppy, his big brown eyes blinking constantly behind his dorky square glasses.

It was super pathetic.

I asked the teacher to make him leave me alone, but she

said I had to learn to get along with others. So I took pity on him, which is good because Duncan has a way of growing on you, kind of like chicken pox. You know, you hate him at first, but then he wears you down and you finally just accept that he's going to be around for a while. Plus, scratching him feels pretty good.

Then, in second grade, Duncan started doing magic.

That's where it all went wrong.

DUNCAN

The first time I disappeared, I had the whole town looking for me. My picture was on the evening news and three police officers came over to our house. Mom was crying pretty hard. I didn't feel good about that, but there's no point doing a trick if you don't commit to it.

Earlier that day I had constructed a box with a tilted mirror that made it look completely empty when viewed from a certain angle, and I stayed curled in a ball inside it until that evening. You want to see mad? Pop out of a box in a room full of cops and your sobbing mother and say, *Ta-da! Here I am!*

Not good.

I learned that day never to use magic for evil. Sure, it's fun to cut off and reattach your thumb in front of a bunch of kindergartners, but the lasting emotional trauma they'll have isn't worth it.

Or so they tell me.

My name is Duncan Reyes, and I am a magician.

Magic is my life, and with the help of my assistant, Emma, it was something I planned to do forever.

But I'll give it all up if you'll forgive me. I'm so sorry about what happened, and I'll work the rest of my life to pay everything back.

And I never meant to hurt anyone, especially her.

EMMA

I admit, I thought Duncan's magic act was stupid at first, and the tricks he did were super obvious. Removable thumb, cut-and-restore rope, pen through a dollar bill, cups and balls—that kind of stuff. I could figure out how he did them in about five seconds. He was terrible, and I enjoyed how sad it made him when I guessed exactly how a trick was done. But I think that made him work harder, because soon he started to get good.

Like, *really* good.

I was impressed, and a little jealous of the attention he got. Duncan practiced all the time, and before I knew it, I was practicing with him. Anything to get out of my house and away from my sisters, who thought magic was the most embarrassing thing ever.

Duncan wanted to be just like Quinton Penfold. I'm sure you know about him from all his TV specials. He's pretty much the most famous magician, and does the biggest and corniest tricks ever. Duncan wanted to look like him, talk like him, and be famous like him. He was obsessed. Every year, Quinton hosts the Elite Magicians Convention in a big city, and all the best acts perform and share magical secrets with up-and-comers. Our plan was to create an act so good that everyone would freak out and my parents would be impressed and pay for us to go.

By fifth grade, we had put together a whole routine, and had decided to show it off at the Fall Talent Jamboree.

It was supposed to be our big break. It took place in the high school auditorium on a pretty awesome stage, with lights, a food stand, and stadium seating.

I waited in the audience while Duncan stayed backstage in his tuxedo and red cape (that used to be his blankie—don't tell him I told you that). We had to suffer through Jose Ruiz's off-key rendition of "Three Blind Mice" on the trombone, this third-grade girl's choreographed dance number, and Sammy McGovern's attempt at stand-up comedy. He just told jokes he found online and made fart noises. Some talent.

Finally, Principal Howell came onstage and said, "All right, for our next act, please welcome Duncan Reyes, magician extraordinaire, to the stage."

Duncan walked through the curtain, chest out, with a big smile on his face. Music played from the speakers.

"Magic," he began, "is something that can show you the world in amazing new ways. It can make things appear out of nowhere"—he clapped his hands and in a puff of smoke, flowers appeared—"and it can break the laws of physics." He ripped off his cape (blankie) and made it float between his hands.

Small applause.

"But magic wasn't meant to be done alone. I need a volunteer."

I raised my hand and waved it around.

"You there," he said, pointing to me. "Please come to the stage. Have we ever met before?"

"No," I yelled. "Never."

People in the audience laughed. My sisters hid their faces in their hands, as if that would make anyone forget we were related.

"You can't do magic in those kind of clothes," Duncan said. He held his cape in front of me. When he dropped it a moment later, I had done a quick change into the exact same tuxedo he was wearing.

The crowd roared. Like I said, no dresses for this girl. No way.

We continued with the show, doing a straitjacket escape, disappearing scarves, and the teleportation box that transports anything you put into it to a separate box across the stage. I can't say how it's done, but I will say that buy-one-get-one-free coupons come in handy.

It went pretty great, and by the end, the whole auditorium was cheering for us.

Evan Sanderson ended up winning the Fall Talent Jamboree, but that was only because he's the most popular kid in class. I don't believe for a second that his guitar playing was that good, but all the other girls go crazy when he smiles at them.

After the show, my parents said, "That was really cute, Emma," and my sisters were like, "Can't you just act like a normal girl?"

Whatever. No Elite Magicians Convention for us.

We decided we would practice even harder and put on a show that would blow everyone away next time.

Well, mission accomplished. No one is *ever* going to forget our second appearance at the Fall Talent Jamboree.

We really brought down the house.

I wonder how long it will take to rebuild the auditorium.

DUNCAN

I work hard for my magic. Every trick I do has taken days, weeks, sometimes months to master. I've studied all the greats, and I know most of the secrets.

If I see a magician on TV cut a person in half, I know how that's done.

Straitjacket escape. Simple.

And if a lion disappears from a cage and reappears in another cage halfway across the room, I have a pretty good idea how that's done, too. I'll give you a hint: two lions.

I learned everything from an old stage magician named the Amazing Zuggarino. I call him Zug.

He retired years ago and owns Zug's Magic Shop in town. It's small, dusty, usually empty, and located in the bottom section of an old house. He has a window display with a giant top hat and wand, and the first time I saw it I begged my mom to let me go in. That's when my life changed forever.

Zug was standing at a small felt-covered table at the front of the store where he demonstrates tricks to potential buyers. He's really good, and makes everything seem real and mystical.

He saw me, smiled, and shoved a pen through a dollar bill. It went clear through, no doubt about it, and when he pulled it out the dollar was unharmed. I felt like my world had been turned upside down. My stomach fluttered, my knees went weak, the room spun around.

"It's just a trick," he told me.

Sure it was.

The kit to learn the trick cost twelve dollars, which Mom didn't have. You might as well know now, we don't have a lot of money, and I feel bad for picking up such an expensive hobby. My mom works hard at the salon, and Dad sends her some money each month, but it's not enough to buy every little thing I want. I get presents for Christmas and my birthday, but that was too long to wait.

I *had* to have this trick now.

If I could fix holes in dollar bills, who's to say I couldn't make them appear out of nowhere? The trick would pay for itself in no time. Then I'd buy my mom whatever she wanted.

I saved for two weeks to get it. I went door-to-door to neighbors' houses and did yard work. I helped Mrs. Mendelson carry in groceries. I admit, I even swam for pennies at the bottom of the fountain in the park.

Finally, I laid the money down on Zug's counter and received a small plastic bag with the instructions and necessary props (a dollar bill and a pen, believe it or not). Zug took me into a creepy back room decorated with cobwebs and skull candles and demonstrated how the trick was done.

It took me two seconds to figure out I'd been conned. Hoodwinked. Ripped off. I was devastatingly, outrageously, horrifyingly angry.

The trick was just a gimmicked pen that was cut in half and held together with magnets. Before you shoved it through, you palmed the top half off and then concealed the rest of the pen with your other hand. If you did it fast enough, with one quick motion the two pieces snapped together and it looked like the pen had pierced the dollar.

You want to know how to get twelve dollars from a sucker? Sell him a magic trick.

I'm not proud of this, but I cried. Zug pulled a string of seven colorful hankies out of his sleeve and I sobbed into them.

Zug felt so bad for me that he refunded my money and offered to let me help around the shop. He said he couldn't pay me, but he *could* show me how to do tricks and put together an act of my own.

That's how Zug and I became friends. After school I would go over to his shop and sweep the floor or clean the windows, and he would show me tricks. I would watch as he created impossible illusions, soaking it all in.

Each trick was amazing, and every time I was convinced that *this* couldn't be faked. *This* must be real magic.

But then he would reveal the secret. For every levitating pencil or switcheroo container, there was a thin piece of string or a false bottom. It was a disappointment.

One day, Zug grabbed me by the shoulders, looked into my

eyes, and said, "Duncan, magic tricks are meant to bring joy and mystery to others. That's why you do it. There is no *real* magic. It doesn't exist."

Yeah, Zug's a liar.

EMMA

So you're probably wondering what all this has to do with the case.

I mean, that's why you're reading this, right? You want to know how two kids could get involved in one of the worst series of events ever recorded in our town.

Well, considering we were told to give the complete account, starting at the beginning, I thought it was important that you understood a little bit about me and Duncan.

Because this story is about *us* as much as it's about *her*. And at the beginning, we didn't know much about the witch.

THE WITCH

DUNCAN

When Zug told me there was no such thing as real magic, I believed him. No one was going to fool me again, especially not with a story about some silly old witch.

The legend of the witch is well known in Elephant. People say she's immortal. They say she eats children. They say she curses cashiers that don't let her use expired coupons.

Sure.

So what if there was a creepy house on West End Avenue?

And so what if it was old and splintery, with chipping white paint the color of graveyard bones? Who cares that the dying shrubs look like the hands of zombies bursting through the ground, curled and grabbing? Yes, it howled like a tortured cat at night, but that was all a dumb coincidence. The wind from the field must have hit the shutters at *just* the right angle.

Everything had a rational explanation.

Mom told me to be careful around that house. The legend of the witch is so old that even she heard the stories when she was my age, back in ancient times, almost twenty years ago.

Everyone in town thought the witch's house was haunted, but I'd read enough books and seen enough movies to know that every town has at least one scary old person who lives in a creepy house that all the schoolchildren think is dangerous and rotten. Inevitably, it turns out they're just a nice and misunderstood weirdo and all the kids end up drinking lemonade on their porch at the end.

I was certain that was the case, and that anyone that thought she was a *real* witch was an idiot.

EMMA

Oh, she was a real witch. Absolutely. Positively. No question.

Duncan doubted it, but I always knew.

He used to say she was just misunderstood, but the witch was *not* misunderstood. She has always made it perfectly clear to everyone that she should be left alone. I mean, just look where she lives: 66 West End Avenue is the dictionary definition of a *haunted house*. We call the place "Misery Manor," mainly because that's what the sign out front says.

One time, Mia Colón's dog wandered onto the yard and pooped and the witch turned it into a frog. True, it turned back the next day before Mia could show anyone, but she said she spent all night rubbing the poor frog's back, begging it to bark.

I've heard that the witch waits at the window, looking for people to curse, and that if you look her in the eyes, your brain will melt.

They say that if you chant "the Elephant Witch" five times in front of the bathroom mirror, she'll clog your toilet.

I can confirm that one to be true.

DUNCAN

No one in town knew much about the witch. She was unlisted in the phone book, and legend has it that when some curious children tried to find out her real name at the courthouse by pulling the deed to her house, the paper burned up in their hands as soon as they touched it. Yeah, right. For five bucks, I could buy some flash paper from Zug's shop and do the same thing.

Before this whole mess, I'd never seen the witch in the flesh. The closest I came was seeing her silhouette through a window one night. It made my whole body go cold, but that was probably the breeze blowing down the street.

My mom says she saw her at the grocery store, wrapped in a black shawl.

"Why didn't you talk to her?" I asked. "I'm sure she's just an old lady that likes bingo."

"Well, even if she *isn't* a witch, it's obvious she doesn't want to be bothered."

I wish I had taken mom's advice and left her alone. But really, what happened next wasn't my fault.

It was Tommy Wilkins's.

TOMMY WILKINS

EMMA

I don't know when Tommy Wilkins started to think he was the coolest thing in school, but I suspect it happened in second grade when he had an uncontrollable growth spurt and was at least four inches taller than anyone in the class. You should see our class picture from that year. He looks like a towering beast that's come from the mountains to eat the children.

By the start of sixth grade, Tommy was taller than our teacher and wider than a trash can (with a similar smell).

All the girls laugh at Tommy behind his back. The way he lumbers around, all angry and drooling, is pretty funny.

He usually picks on the smallest and skinniest boys in school, which makes Duncan his number one target. Most of the time it's harmless and funny. And trust me, I like seeing Duncan get put in his place as much as anyone, but sometimes Tommy crosses the line.

The day this all started was one of those times.

We were three weeks into sixth grade, and Duncan and I were sitting at our own table in the corner of the lunchroom, alone. That was nothing new. Even my sisters try to sit as far away as possible. Our friendship didn't make much sense. I'm a girl, he's a boy. I'm cool, he's not. My family has a lot of money, and his house is the same size as my detached garage.

Duncan had already scarfed down half of his sandwich while I carefully cut my meat loaf, making sure each chunk was the proper size for digestion. He was shuffling his deck, working on new ways to force a card. Forcing a card means that when he asks you to pick one at random, he already knows what it's going to be. Duncan would be mad that I told you that because of the Magician's Code, which is a long and complicated document we found on the internet, printed out, and signed. It's very important, and states that we can't tell any non-magician how a trick is done. But that doesn't matter anymore. I'm done with magic after this. Duncan can sue me if he wants.

A shadow appeared over our table.

"Hey there, Dunk Dunk," Tommy sneered. "What do you got there?"

"Cards," Duncan said. He tried to stash the deck in his backpack, but Tommy grabbed his wrist. Zug had just given them to him from his personal collection, and they had a special finish that made them extra smooth to handle.

"Oh, *cool*," Tommy said. "I think magic is awesome. Can you teach me how to do one of your little tricks?"

"Sorry, Tommy, but I think your fingers are too stubby to handle the cards."

I slid my plate away from Duncan. I'm not psychic, but I could foresee Tommy shoving Duncan's face into my potatoes.

Tommy set his tray down at our table, next to Duncan, and a nasty grin appeared on his face.

"Can I sit down, *buddy*?" he asked.

"Err . . . sure," Duncan said.

"Come on. I really want to learn a trick. I feel like we've had a bad start this year, Dunk Dunk. You always seem to be avoiding me."

"My name is *Duncan*."

"Do you remember kindergarten, Dunk Dunk? We used to be friends."

"Yeah."

"What happened? Why aren't we friends anymore?"

"I don't know. We've grown apart, I guess."

"You've grown upward," I added, "probably because of a chemical spill at the lake."

"Quiet," Tommy said, pointing his fork at me. "I want to be your friend, Dunk Dunk. Then you can stop hanging out with a girl."

"How would hanging out with *you* change that?" Duncan asked.

The table of girls behind us giggled. Tommy's eye twitched. This wasn't good.

"Let me see those cards," Tommy said.

"No."

"I'm not asking anymore, Dunk Dunk. Give me the cards."

"All right, Tommy," Duncan said, smiling. "But first, how about I show you a trick?"

DUNCAN

Tommy started to convulse, leaning back and taking in large gulps of air until he let out a fake sneeze, spewing spit and bits of food onto my sandwich.

"Sorry, Dunk Dunk. Feeling a little sick, I guess."

"No worries." I pulled out the deck and shuffled. First the riffle, then the overhand shuffle, then the Argentinian Mix-Up. I made sure to leave the three of hearts near the bottom, then did a final false shuffle. "I have something that might make you feel better. You're going to pick a card, and then I'm going to find it."

"Boring," Tommy said. "I've seen that one a million times."

"Not the way I do it."

I fanned the deck out, flashed a mysterious grin, and said, "Pick a card, if you dare."

Emma covered her eyes. She doesn't handle high-stress situations well.

"Pick *one* card?" he asked. "Why don't I just take the whole stupid deck?"

He lunged for the cards and I pulled back.

"Tell you what. If I can't find your card, I'll *give* you the deck. How does that sound?"

"Good," he said.

I knew he was going to take the deck either way, and I could ask Zug for another one, so I was really just hoping to humiliate him enough that he'd leave me alone for a while.

He pulled a card and showed it to everyone.

By now I had drawn a little bit of a crowd. The girls at the next table had circled around, and Tommy's friends Wilson Howard and Juan Perez stood behind me in a threatening way.

I cut the deck at a random spot.

"Put it back," I said. When he laid the card down, I slid the three of hearts on top and did another false shuffle. I fanned the deck and noticed that the seven of diamonds was next to the three of hearts. That was his card. The hard part was done.

"Now I'll use my magic abilities to find your card."

I wiggled my fingers over the deck and then dipped my pinkie into Emma's mashed potatoes. She gave me a nasty look.

"All right, Tommy. Now think really hard about what card you had. Picture it in your mind. Chant its name over and over."

Tommy squinted, the pain of mental exercise obvious on his pudgy face.

I rubbed the glob of mashed potatoes on the back of the seven of diamonds, slipped it on top, and pushed the deck against his forehead.

"Think hard, Tommy. Think harder than you've ever thought before. Not too hard, though. You don't want to hurt yourself."

Tommy growled.

I pulled the deck away. The seven of diamonds was stuck to his face, right between his eyebrows and buzz cut hairline.

Kids around the table shrieked with laughter.

"Everyone quiet," I said, winking at my audience. "No one say a word."

I flipped through the deck and pulled out a card, waving it in the air.

"Is your card the three of hearts?"

"No!" Tommy screamed, standing up and howling with laughter. "You're the worst magician ever, Dunk Dunk!"

He faced the onlookers, seven of diamonds still stuck to his forehead, and said, "Duncan can't even find my card! It was the seven of diamonds. He's an idiot! It was the SEVEN OF DIAMONDS!"

The audience went wild, clapping and laughing at Tommy's big stupid face.

Then he stole my deck.

EMMA

Sarah Shufflebotham told me Tommy got the whole way through math and halfway through social studies before the teacher asked him what he was doing with a card stuck to his face. She says the class howled and his cheeks turned bright red. He tore the card up and sat with his head on the desk for the rest of the class.

Oh, Tommy. When will you learn?

But Duncan really should have known better. You don't humiliate a kid like Tommy without expecting some kind of revenge.

As soon as school let out, we ran around back, hopped on our bikes, and headed toward Zug's shop. We didn't even get out of the parking lot before Tommy cut us off on his big mountain bike, with Wilson and Juan right behind him.

"Where you going, Dunk Dunk?" Tommy said.

"Yeah. Stick around," Wilson said. He was a short kid, with a weaselly face and greasy hair.

"What do you want?" Duncan asked.

"I thought maybe we could have a party," Tommy said. He reached into his backpack and pulled out a handful of ripped paper, throwing it into the air and letting it rain on us like confetti. There were hearts, clubs, diamonds, and spades on the pieces.

Duncan's new deck.

Duncan's eyes narrowed to little slits and his nostrils flared. He bent down to pick up the pieces and threw them in his bag.

"It's a shame your mom's too poor to buy you another one," Tommy said.

Big mistake. You can make fun of me, and you can make fun of Duncan, but his mom is off-limits.

Duncan jumped off his bike and lunged at Tommy. It was a cute attempt, but Tommy wrapped his meaty arms around Duncan's neck and pinned him down.

"You're magical, huh?" Tommy asked. "How'd you do the trick?"

"I can't tell," Duncan choked. "Magician's Code."

"Code? Tell me how you did the trick. Now."

"I can't," Duncan said. "It . . . was *real* . . . magic."

His face had turned red and tears had begun to stream down his face.

"Real magic?"

"Yes."

"You have *real* magic powers?"

"Yes."

"Then I have a great idea."

It was a terrible idea.

DUNCAN

Sure, Tommy had me in a headlock, but that was only because I intimidated him. I'm trained in advanced straitjacket escape and I could have easily gotten away from him at any time. I just wanted to minimize the bodily harm I would inflict on him.

Tommy dragged me back to the front of the school, where kids lined up for their buses. Principal Howell blew a whistle and directed cars around the parking lot. Tommy eased up on his hold and wrapped his arm around my shoulder so we looked like best buddies. Principal Howell smiled at us.

"Listen up!" Tommy yelled when we were in the center of a large group of students.

They stopped and looked, probably expecting a fight. Tommy resumed his choke hold.

"Duncan tells me he's got *real* magical powers. I'm going to give him a little test to see if that's true."

More kids circled around us.

"You know the witch, Dunk Dunk? If you're really so magical, you'll ring her doorbell. What do you think of that?"

"Hrphhh blurrr mrrbrrrshhh?" I asked.

"What?" He released my head from the clutches of his odorous armpit.

"I said, how will that prove anything?"

"Because if you're *not* magical, she'll turn you into a cockroach or something. And if you *are*, then you can defend yourself."

That didn't make any sense to me, but I have to admit that I was a little relieved. I just had to ring some old lady's doorbell and this whole thing would be over and everyone in school would think I was really magical? Sign me up.

It could have been the best thing for my career since false thumbs.

I was wrong about that.

MISERY MANOR

EMMA

We rode our bikes in a snaking line to Misery Manor, following Tommy and his friends. Other kids followed behind us, announcing the news of Duncan's test to everyone they saw. I rode my bike next to Duncan's and begged him not to set foot on that horrible old lady's yard.

"She'll kill you," I said. "Grind your bones, eat your flesh, drink your blood."

"There's nothing to worry about," Duncan said, his eyes glowing behind his glasses. "She's not a witch. Trust me. You know there's no such thing as *real* magic."

"You need to believe me," I begged him. "Just this once, trust *me*."

"Emma, after I do this, no one will make fun of us ever again."

"It's not worth it, Duncan," I said. "They might laugh at you and call you a chicken, but at least you'll still be alive. I won't think you're a chicken, and my opinion is the only one that should matter."

"We'll both be laughing about this in a few minutes,"

he said, patting me on the back. "Aren't you a little old to be believing in witches, anyway?"

I wanted to kick him off his stupid bike.

We arrived at the witch's street. Her house stood at the end of the neighborhood like a tooth with a cavity. Not a single light was on and the trees in her front yard were already bare, a few weeks earlier than the others on the street.

As we got closer, the temperature dropped. The bright sunny day changed to an overcast gray, windy and harsh.

I shivered and hugged myself, half for the warmth and half for the comfort.

Our group stopped in the street, leaving a ten-foot barrier between us and her yard.

"Here we are," Tommy said, grabbing Duncan by his shirt and ripping him off his bike. He pushed him toward the witch's house. "Go ahead. Ring the doorbell."

Duncan stood, facing his audience, a born entertainer. He stepped backward, getting closer and closer to the witch's yard until the heel of his left foot touched her yellow grass.

"Leave your helmet on," I begged him.

He took it off and threw it at me, ran his fingers through his hair, and bowed.

"The forces of evil may scare you, but they are no match for me. Dark spells, haunted houses, and evil old ladies do not intimidate a magician of my stature. As a demonstration of my power, I will ring the witch's doorbell and return, *unharmed*."

Some children clapped.

"Quit talking and ring it," Tommy said.

Duncan bowed again, milking the attention as long as he could, and whispered, "With pleasure."

DUNCAN

I took a full step onto the yard and turned around to smile at Tommy. He was hiding behind one of the tall, twisted oak trees in front of the witch's house and peered around it to watch. Emma covered her face with her hands, peeking through her fingers as the rest of the kids knelt behind their bikes for protection.

I stepped slowly, as if I was on a narrow bridge above a lake of lava. I held my arms out, shook violently at times, and pretended I was pushing away a force field.

"The aura is strong," I said. "It's . . . hard to . . . get through it. I must keep . . . pushing . . . with my magical powers."

Dead leaves crunched under my feet.

I made it to the stone walkway that led to her front door and stopped. I put my hands on my knees and panted, pretending to be exhausted from the effort.

Her house was fifteen feet away. There was a cat inside, watching me from behind a window with old, wavy glass.

"I see . . . a feline . . . observing my movements," I said. "I can feel its spirit . . . and . . . it used to be . . . *human.*"

Some kids gasped. This was the best day of my life.

Closer to the house, I began to smell something rotten, like sewage and old eggs.

"The smell . . . ," I said, "it . . . reminds me of . . . cooked brains and fingers . . . with barbecue sauce."

More gasps behind me, and the smell was getting worse with each step. I could barely breathe.

Even though I didn't believe the lies I was telling, I knew I wanted to get out of there. Something felt *wrong* about that house, and it made my bones feel cold and my brain feel like mush. But I had to keep going. I couldn't disappoint my audience.

The porch was in front of me, covered with splinters. Bent nails stuck up on each step. I moved carefully, approaching her front door. The cat jumped from its perch and I heard strange sounds inside, like howling and laughter.

I closed my eyes and breathed in a few times, trying to stop my imagination. She wasn't a real witch. She *couldn't* be a real witch.

Next to the door was a small white doorbell encased in a metal lion.

I pushed it.

There was a loud BING BONG DING DONG inside the house and Tommy squealed with laughter.

Before I could run to the safety of the street, Tommy yelled, "Wait there, Duncan, you're not done yet!" and the rest of the kids applauded.

"I did it!" I yelled back, trying to make my voice sound calm even though my heart was beating really hard. "I rang it. I'm done!"

Emma still hid her face.

"You can't just ring it and run," Tommy yelled. "Stay up there for a whole minute. See if she shows up."

I was trapped. I couldn't go back now, or this whole thing would be for nothing. I should have known it wouldn't be that easy.

"Start counting," I yelled, and my voice had a definite, hard-to-miss quiver.

He began. "Sixty, fifty-nine, fifty-eight, fifty-seven . . ."

A light switched on in the house. Someone moved inside.

". . . fifty-one, fifty . . ."

The walls creaked, like the house was a living, breathing thing.

It felt like Tommy was counting in slow motion, like time had stopped moving. My head hurt, and my vision was getting cloudy.

". . . forty-one, forty, thirty-nine . . ."

"Count faster!" I yelled.

Suddenly, all of the windows opened and black smoke billowed out. There was a clumping sound inside, like a giant beast had been awakened.

No such thing as real magic? I needed to have a serious talk with Zug when this was over.

". . . thirty-one, thirty . . ."

The front door opened, hinges squealing, and the blood drained from my face.

The silhouette of a small woman appeared through the smoke. Her voice cackled, "Who is it?"

Tommy stopped counting.

I looked behind me and saw the other kids on their bikes, riding away. Tommy followed close behind, his hulking frame hunched over his handlebars. Emma was still there—my only friend, the only one whose opinion *should* have mattered to me.

"What do you want?" she asked with a scratchy voice. She had a strange accent, like nothing I had heard before. She stepped through the smoke and into the light. She wore sandals and a blue sundress, covered in a repeating pattern of flowers. Her skin was green and bumpy, like pancake batter that wasn't stirred long enough. Her hair was black and thinning and stuck together in matted clumps. Her nose was like a shark fin that hung over a mouth full of sharp green teeth. But it was her eyes that I remember best, those terrible yellow eyes with the little black pupils, darting back and forth at me and the crowd of children fleeing down her street.

She was a real witch. Everything I believed was a lie.

She moved closer and I stepped backward, tripping over a loose board and falling. My backpack hit the porch and books and papers and torn pieces of playing cards spilled everywhere.

"You horrible, horrible children. I tell you to stay away and you never lis—"

She stopped, bent down, and picked up the ripped corner

of a five of hearts with her long, warty fingers.

"Well, look at this. Are you a *magician*?" she asked, spitting out the word like it was an insult.

I tried not to stare at her horrible face. She smiled at me, her eyes evil and mad.

"Yes," I squeaked. "But please don't hurt me."

I shielded my face, hoping that whatever spell or curse she cast wouldn't be too disfiguring.

The house moaned and creaked.

"Not a normal prankster, I see. How did you find me, *magician*?"

"I'm n-not a real m-m-magician," I stuttered. "Just little tricks. I can't . . . do real magic. Not like you."

"Like me, eh? Well, I won't give it to you," she growled.

"Give what?" I asked. I didn't understand, and my head hurt so bad.

"Not without a fight. Even if we all have to die. And wouldn't that solve all the problems?"

"Please don't kill me. *Please*," I begged. I was too young to die. I hadn't even seen an R-rated movie yet.

She bent down, putting her awful face an inch from mine and whispered, "Go."

She stood and screamed and smoke billowed from the door. Wind whipped and howled, and the torn pieces of my deck swirled around us.

I didn't understand what she was saying, but I didn't want to wait around and find out. I jumped down the front steps and ran across the lawn. Emma was cowering with her bicycle behind a tree and I ran past her, faster than I ever have before.

"Wait!" she yelled. "Duncan!"

I wasn't listening. I grabbed my bike and hopped on, racing down the street and turning left where I should have turned right, toward the woods at the edge of town, away from the witch and everything else.

· EMMA ·

Duncan pedaled faster than I'd ever seen before, through neighborhoods and straight toward the forest. Our town is surrounded by wooded mountains, and we're kind of plopped in the center, like a big asteroid landed on Earth and buildings sprang up around it.

If you stand on top of the tallest building, all you would see is trees, trees, and more trees. There's a river that separates us from the closest town, with a highway bridge about a half mile long over it. I'd guess that most people who lived in the state all their lives had never even heard of Elephant County.

That was before, of course.

Our town is called Elephant because of a giant boulder located in the middle of town that looks exactly like an elephant. Well, more like a slightly deformed, lopsided elephant with tiny ears and no tusks.

My dad says when frontiersmen were scouting the country, they saw the boulder in a clearing, thought it was a giant monster elephant, and wasted all their ammo trying to kill it. You can still see the bullet holes. They must have felt real silly when they realized it was a rock, and named the town that very day, building it around that mammoth gray monument. It's about as long as a school bus and two stories tall.

I think it's a neat story that sometimes the thing you're most scared of can be nothing more than a harmless rock.

"Duncan, wait up!" I yelled, but he acted like he didn't even hear me. He rode past the old factory and over the small metal bridge next to the abandoned railroad tracks, toward the gravel path that led to the woods. He was in his own little world, focused, never looking back, never checking for cars as he pedaled faster and faster away from the witch's house.

When the ground became too bumpy with roots, he hopped off his bike and ran, eventually stopping at a tree and sitting down, knees pulled up to his chest, face white, eyes darting around the forest.

He jumped when he saw me and I approached him slowly, sitting down and resting my head on his shoulder.

"It's okay," I said, though I didn't know if that was true.

Finally, he said, "We're all going to die."

A little melodramatic, sure, but at least he wasn't making fun of me for believing in the witch anymore.

"What did she say to you?"

"She says she won't give it to me."

"Give what?"

"Don't know."

"Wow. Then what?"

"That we're all going to die."

"I told you not to go there. Do you believe in her now?"

He nodded.

We sat in silence for a while, staring at the trees and listening to the wind. I think Duncan was in shock. He stared into the distance, hardly blinking.

The sun began to set, igniting the sky into orange and pink. There was flapping overhead, bats probably. Then a shadow passed over us.

I jumped, but when I looked up, there was nothing there.

DUNCAN

I don't remember the rest of that afternoon, really. I only remember sitting, thinking, shaking.

My head hurt.

When I closed my eyes, I saw the witch's eyes, bright and yellow, staring into me.

I could feel my brain rearranging itself, trying to make sense of what happened.

Emma showed up and put her head on my shoulder.

Normally, I would have hated it, but that day it was all right.

A good night's sleep and I'd try to forget the whole thing, maybe even convince myself I had made it all up.

It was just a dream. A bad, bad dream.

EMMA

We were *supposed* to be at Zug's shop that afternoon, practicing our routine for this year's Fall Talent Jamboree. It was Tuesday, and the show was Saturday night, and we still had a lot of work to do to finalize our performance.

We had been working on our routine all summer. One day back in June, Zug took us to his storage space and showed us some of the tricks he had used in his touring days, back when he was the Amazing Zuggarino.

His storage space was packed to the ceiling with boxes and posters of a young, thin Zug in a tuxedo and cape. There were antique posters of old magicians—Thurston the Great with devils on his shoulders, Robert-Houdin with his magical orange tree, Harry Blackstone making a woman levitate, and, of course, Houdini in chains. Zug had a lot of the standard things you've probably seen a million times—shackle escapes, vanishing cabinets, birdcages, a box you could stick a person in and shove swords through, and piles of other tricks that wouldn't fool anyone over ten years old.

Duncan gravitated right away to a big trick in the corner called the Water Torture Chamber. It was a box that was six feet tall and three feet wide, with glass panels on all of the sides.

It looked really scary, but there was a trapdoor at the top that made it easy to get out of.

"No," Zug said. "Not that one. Too dangerous."

But we've already established that you can't reason with Duncan.

"This will be the showstopper," Duncan said. "Mix this with the straitjacket for the finale and I'll win the whole thing."

"*We'll* win," I corrected him.

"Sure, sure, we, we."

I wanted to punch him.

"So, you'll be in the water chamber. What will I do?" I asked.

"You can hold the curtain over the chamber while I get out of the straitjacket."

"That's it?"

"No. You can also lift the curtain when I'm out of the trapdoor."

I growled at him.

"Too dangerous," Zug repeated. "It leaks. And the trapdoor gets stuck."

"We can oil the door," Duncan said. "And patch the holes."

"It's really heavy and hard to move," Zug said. "You'd have to rent a truck."

"I still have some birthday money left," I said. I kind of liked the idea of him getting stuck inside.

And that was that—the Water Torture Chamber would be

part of our show, and our fate was sealed.

So when we didn't show up at his store that afternoon, Zug must have called our parents. As soon as we made it out of the woods, a police car blinked its lights and drove beside us.

"Hey! Hey there!" the officer yelled, leaning out of his window.

It was Officer Ralph.

"You scared your mom," he said to Duncan. "She thought something might have happened to you."

Duncan didn't even look over.

"He's fine," I said. "We had a long day."

"You should have called," Officer Ralph said. He stopped the car in front of us and got out. "For all she knew, you may have done one of your little tricks and blown yourselves up. Come on, I'll take you home."

He put our bikes in the trunk and we crawled in the back of the police car.

"It's to the slammer with you, ya dirty scoundrels," Officer Ralph said, trying to be funny. We were in no mood for jokes.

Ten minutes later I walked into my house. Jenna was practicing her gymnastics routine on a mat in the living room, and Anna was in the kitchen, mixing things together for dinner. Molly was swatting at toys in her bouncer and squealed at me.

"Don't worry," I announced. "I'm home. Safe and sound."

Dad looked up from his laptop at the table and said, "Oh. Hey, Emma. I didn't realize you weren't here."

Ms. Reyes called the police and this was the reaction I got. I felt so special.

OFFICER RALPH

DUNCAN

You should probably know that my parents were never married. They were young when I was born (Mom actually had me several months after high school graduation), and they could never really make it work.

Do you remember that time I "disappeared" in the box and those police officers showed up at my house? Well, Ralph was one of them. He and my mom really liked each other, and he stuck around. Talk about a trick gone wrong. If I hadn't disappeared, Mom never would have called the cops, Ralph never would have appeared at the front door, and we would have lived happily without him, just the two of us, never having to hear his bad jokes or terrible singing.

I didn't say a word to Ralph the whole ride home. We pulled up in front of my house and I waited for him to let me out.

"So you want to tell me what happened tonight?"

"No."

"Are you getting picked on again?"

"Nope. Everyone loves me."

He sighed. I knew I frustrated him, but I kind of liked it.

My mom had been waiting at the window, and she opened the door and ran into the yard, her arms out for a hug. Normally I would have resisted, but I really needed it that night.

"Duncan! Where have you been? You were supposed to go straight to Zug's shop after school."

She looked tired and I felt bad for worrying her.

I didn't want to tell her anything. I wanted to act brave and tell her I was fine, but there was a catch in my voice and she never would have believed me.

"She . . ." I couldn't take it anymore. I started to cry.

She looked at Ralph and he shrugged.

"What's wrong?"

"She . . . she's awful. And they made me do it, Mom. I didn't want to go."

"Who? Made you do what, Duncan?"

My face was red and hot and I wanted Ralph to leave.

"Come in. I have dinner ready. Sit down."

My head was feeling a little better by the time she brought out the roast chicken and mashed potatoes, but I still felt bad, like something was broken inside me.

"Tell us what happened," Mom said.

There was no use stalling. Mom and Ralph were staring at me, quietly chewing, so I might as well tell them everything.

"I saw the witch."

Mom stopped chewing. Her mouth hung open and some green beans fell on her plate.

"Where?"

"At her house. Tommy made me ring the doorbell."

"You *rang* her *doorbell*?" she asked, as if the words were foreign to her. "The *witch's* doorbell?"

Ralph started to laugh.

"What witch? You mean that old lady down on West End Avenue? That's what this is all about? *Please.*"

Ralph was from a big city and thought he was smarter than most people in Elephant. He hadn't grown up with stories of the witch and thought they were all superstition. I would have agreed with him before, but that afternoon had changed everything.

"She's a horrible old woman, Ralph. And she's dangerous," Mom said, rubbing my hand.

"The only thing she's a danger to is a jar of prunes."

"What did she say to you?" Mom asked, looking at me with scared curiosity that would become standard over the next couple of weeks.

"Not much. Her skin was green and her eyes were yellow. Smoke came from the house and—"

Ralph burst out laughing again. "You have some imagination, kid!"

"And then what?" Mom asked.

"She said we were all going to die."

"What?"

"And then I ran."

"He's joking," Ralph said. "Don't you see? This is another one of Duncan's tricks."

"It is not!" I yelled.

Mom shot Ralph an angry stare.

"When you finish dinner, go upstairs and do your homework. You can watch some TV when you're done."

That's when my blood went ice cold and my food started crawling back up my throat.

"What?" Mom asked.

"My backpack," I said, grabbing the edge of the table and re-swallowing my food, "I left it on her porch."

EMMA

Duncan wasn't on the bus the next day, and by that time the whole school knew what had happened. Tommy spread the story to anyone that would listen, conveniently leaving out the part where he had fled for his life at the first sign of the witch.

Throughout the morning, Tommy ran through the hallways with Wilson and Juan, stopping at lockers and telling kids how *he* had seen the witch and rescued Duncan from her dangerous claws.

"Don't know if the poor guy will be here today," Tommy said at Carla's locker, enjoying the attention from the students that gathered around. "He was pretty freaked out. I think he wet his pants."

"That's not true!" I yelled. "You're lying!"

Wilson wrapped his arm around my shoulder, his weasel eyes blinking ferociously.

"Ah, how do you know?" he asked. "Lots of excitement. I saw you hiding behind a tree."

"Well, I saw *you* racing down her street and screaming like my little sister. *You* were the biggest chicken there."

56

I tried to walk away, but Juan jumped in front of me, spreading out his arms to block me.

"You better be quiet if you know what's good for you," he whispered.

Juan was shorter than me, with chubby red cheeks and mangled hair that looked like it had been cut by his mother during a sneezing fit.

"Is that a threat?" I asked, readying my foot for my trademark shin kick.

Juan looked over my shoulder and gasped, his mouth open and cheeks puffing up and then deflating.

The hallway went quiet.

Duncan had arrived, walking toward the office, Ms. Reyes by his side.

I ran toward him, wrapped my arm around his shoulder, and whispered in his ear, "You brought your *mom*? Everyone's talking about you today, Duncan. You can't bring your *mom* to school."

"Hi, Emma. How are you?" Ms. Reyes asked.

"Fine, thanks. *Great* to see you here!"

I leaned back in and said, "People will think you're a baby."

"I have bigger problems."

That was true.

Duncan and his mom turned into Principal Howell's office.

DUNCAN

Two hundred thirty-seven dollars and sixty-two cents.

That's how much money it costs to replace math, social studies, vocabulary, and geography textbooks. Total rip-off. I wouldn't pay five dollars for any of it.

"That's half a week's work," Mom told me. "I can't afford that, Duncan."

I felt really bad, but what was I supposed to do? Go back to the witch's house and ask her for my bag? No way.

Mom told Principal Howell to wait—we would see if it turned up somewhere. Then she called Ralph.

"Leave it to me," he said. I could hear him laughing through the phone. "I think I can handle knocking on a sweet old lady's door and getting a backpack."

"Great," Mom said.

"On one condition. Duncan goes with me over lunch. I want him to see that there's nothing to be afraid of."

Did I mention that I *really* didn't like Ralph?

"Fine," Mom said, her voice shaking a bit. "I'll let his principal know. But let him stay in the car."

Mom left and I went to class, hiding in the back row.

Tommy, Wilson, and Juan found me on my way to the next period and announced, "There he is! Duncan Reyes, the magician that was too scared to stand on the witch's porch for a minute."

I was in no mood to talk.

"Look at me! I'm Duncan, I'm so scared! Oh, I hope the old witch doesn't hurt me," Tommy said.

Emma walked toward us.

"Oh yeah? Then why don't you stand on her porch?" she asked.

"Just let it go," I whispered. "You're going to make it worse."

Tommy's face got red and I thought he might smack me across the face.

"I'm not afraid of the witch," he said.

"You were more afraid than anyone else there!" Emma yelled. "You three were the first to run!"

"*Quiet*," I whispered.

"You better shut up," Tommy said.

"You wouldn't even step on her front lawn," Emma replied. "Your legs were shaking. *Chickens*."

She started clucking like a chicken and Tommy hit a locker and walked away.

"You shouldn't have done that," I said.

"What's the worst he can do?" she asked.

EMMA

It turns out, the worst Tommy could do was *way* worse than I thought.

A VISIT WITH THE WITCH

DUNCAN

Ralph picked me up before lunch in his police car. I made a big show about getting into the back seat, raising my arms in surrender in case anyone was watching. If the other kids didn't think I was magical, maybe they'd at least think I was a dangerous criminal.

We coasted out of the parking lot and onto the main street. It had been sunny when we left school, but as we got closer to her house the sky darkened and it started to drizzle in what I now assume was *not* a coincidence.

Ralph turned on to West End Avenue and parked in front of the house.

"Couldn't you just give Mom the money to replace my books?" I asked. "It'll be a lot easier than messing with the witch."

"Come up with me, Duncan. Everything's fine. You'll see," he said.

"Mom said I could stay in the car."

He sighed and adjusted his belt, making sure his gun was still there. A crack of lightning ripped through the sky and he jumped a little.

By the time he reached the front porch, I was hunched as low as I could get in the back seat. I peeked out the window. Ralph knocked on the front door and turned to smile at me.

There was no response.

He pushed the creepy lion doorbell.

No smoke came from the door. No fire. No screams. Nothing.

He rang again and waited.

The door finally opened and a small figure stood in the entrance.

I couldn't see her face, just the shadow of motion in the dark house.

"Afternoon, ma'am," Ralph said. "I'm Officer Neale, how are you?"

If she responded, I didn't hear it. Neither did Ralph because he leaned in closer.

She said something that was too quiet for me to hear.

"Excuse me? No, ma'am, I don't have a warrant. This is just a friendly visit. I wanted to ask you if—"

She continued whispering.

"No, I am not a troublemaker, ma'am. I am a police officer, and I would appreciate your cooperation. I'm here because a local boy claims that he lost his backpack in this area and I'm wondering if you happened to see it?"

His voice got higher, which meant he was frustrated. I make him do that a lot.

I pressed my face against the glass, trying to get a look at her.

For the briefest moment I saw her eyes, small circles that glowed with evil.

"Yes, that's him," Ralph said, pointing. "He's in the car. Come out, Duncan, say hello. You'll think this is funny, ma'am. He's a *magician* and has this vivid imagination. He seems to think that you are a WAAAAAHHHHH—"

In an instant, Ralph went flying twenty feet in the air and hung upside down, floating near the top of the witch's house. He let out a high-pitched scream that I would have found hilarious on any other day.

His belt and gun fell to the ground, morphing into a snake and rabbit that sat confused for a moment and then disappeared under a bush.

"What's going on?" Ralph screamed, flapping his arms in the air as if he were in a swimming pool and could just push his way down. "Let me go! I'm a police officer!"

The witch stood on the porch, her hands raised high.

She stepped out of the shadows, but that day she looked like a normal old lady, short and a little plump with long and thick gray hair. She wore a loose-fitting sundress, and rows of bracelets dangled on her wrists.

Then green scales crept down her arms and up her neck and her hair turned a dark shade of black. Warts and scars sprang up along her skin and her smile was full of jagged fangs. Her eyes turned a horrible shade of yellow as she walked across her yard, getting closer and closer to me.

"You again," she screamed. "The little *magician*."

The car doors were locked, but that didn't make me feel any safer. I slipped down off my seat and curled into a ball, hiding my head under my hands.

"Please don't kill me, please don't kill me," I screamed.

A tornado-like whir of wind swirled around the car and cracks of energy escaped in the air. A shadow came over me and then everything stopped.

Dead silence.

I looked up, slowly, and there she was, her horrible face leaning in toward the glass.

My body shook and I thought I might throw up. Her eyes locked with mine and I couldn't look away, like I was in a trance. Her face was angry, but also sad, and I just wanted the bad feeling in my stomach to stop.

"Magician," she said. "Never come back here again. Never."

"I won't!" I yelled through the glass. "I really won't!"

She lowered her hands and everything stopped. The spell was broken and Ralph floated to the ground and landed gently on her lawn.

She walked toward her house, slowly changing back into a normal old woman.

Ralph brushed himself off and got in the car, started it, and drove away.

He called my mom and left a message, saying, "Hey, I just stopped by the house and that sweet old lady says she doesn't have Duncan's backpack. He probably left it somewhere else.

I'll keep an eye out. Love you."

The only other thing he said the entire ride back to school was, "My annual review is next month. Never mention this to anyone."

EMMA

"There he is! The *amazing* Dunk Dunk!" Tommy announced as Duncan entered the cafeteria shortly before the end of lunch.

Duncan had that dazed look again, like he was staring through the walls and into some secret place no one else could see.

"Did you get it?" I asked.

"Get what?"

"Your bag, dummy."

He sat next to me and jumped a little, snapping back into reality.

"Bag? Bag? Oh, no. No bag. Didn't . . . get . . . bag . . . because . . . floated . . . and then . . . snake and rabbit . . . fangs . . . all the fangs . . ."

"Can we get some cold milk over here?" I yelled. "This boy has gone crazy!"

Tommy strutted over and slammed a fresh milk carton in front of Duncan. Wilson and Juan circled behind us.

"How ya' doing, Dunk Dunk?" he asked, speaking in a calm and gentle voice that reminded me of my mom's therapist.

"I'm . . . fine . . . everything . . . great."

Duncan took a swig of milk and grimaced as he swallowed.

"You know, all that talk about me and my friends being chickens sort of hurt our feelings."

Wilson and Juan moved in closer. There was nowhere for us to go.

"You need to be more careful with your words, Emma," Juan said.

"People could get the wrong idea about us," Wilson said.

"And we wouldn't want people believing lies, would we?"

"The truth is the truth, boys," I said. "If you're not scared of the witch, there's only one way to prove it."

"How?" Tommy asked.

If we ever wanted them to leave us alone, we needed to embarrass them in a huge way and show the whole school how scared they really were. I stood on my chair and cupped my hands around my mouth.

"Wow, Tommy! You're going *inside* the witch's house?" I yelled, loud enough for the surrounding tables to hear me. "Wilson and Juan, too? That sure is brave of you."

Duncan recoiled and coughed, dribbling milk out of his nostrils.

Juan and Wilson went pale and looked at Tommy, who paused as the slow-moving gears clunked in his brain.

"Going inside the house?" he asked.

Kids started cheering.

His eyes lit up and he smiled a big stupid grin. He turned to the cafeteria and raised his arms.

"Yeah! We're going *inside* the witch's house tonight!" Tommy announced. "Spectators are welcome."

The cheering continued, getting louder.

"And Duncan and Emma are coming with us," Tommy added.

I really should have seen that coming.

Duncan's eyes rolled back in his skull, and he would have fallen off his chair if Wilson hadn't caught him.

"No . . . no . . . we can't," Duncan whispered.

"Don't worry. They'll never do it," I said. "And it will prove to the whole school that they're a bunch of wimps. Trust me, it's a great idea."

INSIDE THE HOUSE

DUNCAN

It was a horrible idea, but at least I can finally say it: *this part was all Emma's fault.*

Sure, Tommy shares a lot of the blame, but it was Emma's big mouth that started the whole thing.

I would have been fine never setting foot on West End Avenue again, and I would have erased the sight of the witch from my brain if I could.

Maybe they'll chicken out, I thought. *No way they'll go inside her house.*

Mom was working that night, so I made myself dinner in the microwave. A freezer-burnt burrito and macaroni and cheese was a pretty crummy last meal, but it's all we had. I had just finished when the doorbell rang, and I looked out the front window to see half of the class on my front lawn. Part of me thought Tommy wouldn't show, but here he was, with an audience. I was going to die with everyone watching.

I opened the door.

"You coming, Dunk Dunk?" Tommy yelled. He was wearing a black hooded sweatshirt and carrying a metal baseball bat. Wilson had a bandana wrapped around his face and swung a large stick back and forth, and Juan was wearing hockey pads and a big winter hat with earflaps.

"What's that stuff for?" I asked. "We're not going to hurt her, right?"

"Hurt *her*?" Tommy asked. He sneered at Wilson and spit on the ground. "This is for *our* protection."

"Come on, Duncan," Emma said, shivering in the cold fall air, "let's just go."

The class started to chant my name, and I grabbed the house keys and locked the door behind me.

"So what's our plan if they don't chicken out?" Emma asked as we jumped on our bikes and pedaled up the hill over Oak Lane.

"Plan? I don't have a plan. This was your idea," I said. "What's *your* plan?"

She reached into her pocket and handed me two smoke bombs.

"I found these in Zug's desk. These guys are bigger than us but they're slower, too. We'll go inside for a second and then slip out. Full-view escape."

"Great," I said. "We're going to die."

We crossed Virginia Avenue and turned down Ridge Drive, riding all the way to the entrance of West End Avenue. The street was filled with shadowy movement. Kids hid in bushes and behind trees as we coasted down the street. Not a single light was on.

The sun was setting and Misery Manor was silhouetted

in gold light. The air smelled worse than before, like garbage and dead leaves. The whistling wind howled through the trees.

"Be safe," Sammy McGovern whispered from inside a bush.

We got closer to her house, each step feeling like a walk to our doom.

"You ready for this?" Tommy asked, smiling as we approached her yard. The witch's house was dark except for one flickering candle in an upstairs window.

As my foot touched the grass, I felt a tingle travel up my leg, all the way to my neck.

I headed toward the front door but Wilson grabbed me.

"Not that way," he said, pointing to the side of the house. "Follow us."

We crouched over and ran in a line. Tommy stopped under the side window and tried to open it. It was locked.

"Well, we tried," Emma said. "No one can say we didn't. Let's go home."

Tommy shook his head, pointing to the back of the house. The grass was long and matted and trailed off into a field. Dead trees peppered it, their gnarled branches shaped like the arms of victims held up in a surrender.

We turned the corner and saw a porch with old wooden furniture. A cat lifted its head from a chair and hissed.

"Back door," Wilson said, tiptoeing up the steps. "Let's try it."

He grabbed the handle and it turned. The door opened with a loud squeak and a wave of hot air hit me.

We froze, listening for any movement in the house.

"Go in," Juan said. "Ladies first."

"You heard him, Tommy," Emma replied.

"Me?" Tommy asked, laughing. He adjusted the baseball bat in his hand. "I'm not going in."

And with that, Juan and Wilson pushed us inside, slamming the door and blocking it shut with their meaty shoulders. Tommy raised the bat and brought it down on the outside handle, shattering it.

I grabbed the knob on our side and it fell off in my hand. The door was stuck.

"Have fun!" Tommy yelled as he ran across the witch's backyard and into the surrounding trees, Juan and Wilson close behind.

"What are we going to do, Duncan?" Emma asked. She was shaking and scared and I wrapped my arm around her shoulder to comfort her.

"We'll be all right," I said. I was scared, too, but I had to be strong for her sake. "Just follow me. I'll keep you safe."

EMMA

Duncan started shaking when he realized we were stuck, and he was ranting like a lunatic.

"You don't understand. She'll kill us. Her eyes. Her teeth. Oh no. Not again. Emma. Oh no."

"We'll be all right," I said. "Just follow me. I'll keep you safe."

Duncan whimpered and nodded.

It took some time for my eyes to adjust. I grabbed Duncan's arm and led him through the kitchen, pressing the button on the side of his wristwatch so the little green light came on.

I followed the light to the nearest wall and ran my hands across it. Wallpaper curled off, old and brittle. There were dust balls in every corner, and cobwebs hung from the ceiling.

We walked slowly, tiptoeing along the floorboards. The house was silent. Could the witch sense us? Smell us?

"Look for a window," I said. "We can escape that way."

At the end of the hall was a door that was cracked open, and I pushed it gently. The hinges groaned.

We stopped and waited, but the rest of the house was silent.

We entered the living room. There were windows on the other side.

"We'll never make it without knocking something over," Duncan said. "She's going to hear us."

I turned a switch and an old lamp clicked on, its small orange glow filling the room. It was large and filled with old furniture, like an abandoned antique store. There were two couches and a fireplace in the center. Stacks of newspapers and magazines filled every corner of the room, and water stains ran down the walls. It was a total stink palace, like someone locked a dozen grandparents in a closet with mothballs.

Duncan pointed to a window with large panes of cracked glass. He moved slowly toward it, watching each step carefully.

"Help me open it," he said.

"No, not that one."

I was afraid the simplest touch might shatter the whole thing. I walked past a warped mirror on the wall, and my reflection looked like a mutated circus creature.

"Whoa, check me out," I whispered, and bumped into a small end table beside the sofa.

A picture in a silver frame wobbled precariously. I grabbed it and held it tight, my heart beating faster than it ever had before.

The picture was of a couple, happy and posing for the camera. The woman was in a skirt, and large shiny jewelry dangled from her wrists. She held a baby in her arms, and a smile lit up her face. Her eyes were fixed on the man next to her. He was tall and wearing a black tuxedo, with a serious expression, his black hair slicked back over his high forehead. His eyes seemed to stare right through me.

Then there was a pop and the light bulb in the lamp went out.

I may have screamed a little.

DUNCAN

Emma screamed and I covered her mouth.

We froze in place.

There was a creaking sound from upstairs.

Movement.

The floorboards groaned, and then there was a loud clumping sound.

We dropped down and crawled along the floor, feeling our way in the darkness.

"What are we going to do?" Emma whispered.

I pointed at a small window across the room.

"When I say go, we run for it."

The clumping continued, getting louder.

We hid behind the couch and I ran my hand along it, the coarse fabric prickling my fingers.

The noise continued, KUH-LUMP KUH-LUMP, down the steps.

Then it stopped.

She was in the room with us, coming toward us.

Everything was quiet.

"GO!" I yelled, grabbing Emma's hand, throwing a smoke bomb, and pulling us as fast as I could toward the window. We didn't make it very far before the room attacked us.

EMMA

The floorboards buckled underneath us like an unsteady diving board. I followed Duncan and hit an ottoman with my shins. It slid across the floor and smashed into the wall, knocking the end table over. A lamp fell and shattered, sending shards of glass everywhere.

The couch jumped across the room and knocked Duncan over like a vicious animal, then reared back and jumped toward me, trying to pin me to the ground.

I rolled, narrowly avoiding a wooden leg smashing through my skull.

I grabbed a metal lamp pole and pulled myself up, but it suddenly coiled in my hand, wiggled down my arm, and hissed loudly at me.

Duncan hid in the corner.

"You again!" the witch screamed, and I looked across the room and saw her moving in the shadows, dark and angular. The room lit up in a brilliant vortex of light and I caught a terrible glimpse of her bubbling green skin and long black hair.

The floorboards continued to crack and snap like the teeth of a hungry monster. I hid behind the grandfather clock and planned my route to the window, but the clock tipped forward and rocked back, slamming into my head.

The witch locked her eyes on me and screamed, "Who are *you*, girl?"

I peeked out and saw her raise her frail arms into the air and wiggle her fingers around like she was playing a large invisible piano.

I ran to the window and the witch pointed at me, following me across the room.

I pulled at the window and it opened just enough for me to slip out onto the yard, where it was safe.

Or so I thought.

DUNCAN

Emma made it out of the house and I heard her scream louder than I'd ever heard before.

The walls of the witch's house erupted in fire and smoke, and the heat pushed me to the center of the room.

"It *is* you!" the witch said. "Who sent you here, little magic boy?"

"Tommy," I croaked. My throat had gone dry and my limbs felt rubbery.

"Tommy?" she asked. "Who is this *Tommy*?"

"A kid at school."

"You lie!" she screamed, thrusting a hand into the air that was holding a twisted wooden wand. A sparkle of green light shot directly at me and I jumped to the side. It hit the couch and turned it into a large wet leech.

The fire in the room disappeared, but the curtains weren't burnt.

The witch screamed louder and she turned the leech back into a couch, giving me enough time to run directly at her, shoving her with my shoulder as I made my way to the hall.

She followed me with her wand, and her next attack missed me again, peeling the wallpaper off the wall in one clean swipe.

I ran down the hall, toward the kitchen. She was behind me now, waving her wand in new patterns. The carpet was moving under my feet, curling up in a roll that grew and grew behind me.

I kept running, but the hallway seemed to stretch longer, the kitchen always out of reach. There was a mirror at the end, and I could see a reflection of the witch floating behind me, her arms raised. The roll of carpet sprang toward me.

Ten more steps.

I ran harder, pushing my legs as far as they could go.

Five steps.

Two.

I was almost at the kitchen.

Just a little bit more.

I spun into the kitchen just as the giant roll of carpet slammed into the mirror and shattered it into large pieces, denting the wall with its massive shape.

The witch growled and the carpet unrolled, settling down on the floor.

I ran to the back door, ready to throw my weight into it and knock it down. Who cares that Tommy broke the doorknob? I'd gnaw through the doorframe if I had to.

Then I saw it.

Hanging on the wall at the far end of the yellow kitchen,

past a table covered with crossword puzzle books and empty microwavable meal containers, was my backpack.

I lunged for it but the witch appeared in the doorway and let out a shrill scream.

"Who *really* sent you?" she yelled, aiming the wand directly at me, her feet hovering off the ground. "Tell me the truth or I'll turn you into a dog."

I pointed at my bag, and my whole arm was shaking.

"I just wanted this back. Please let me have it. My mom doesn't have enough money to replace my books, and I just want to take it and go home. Please. *Please*."

She stopped and returned to the ground, her face softening and a small laugh coming from her mouth.

In a flash she was behind me, unstrapping the bag from the hook and holding it out on one long finger.

"And this is the *only* reason you are here, *magic boy*?"

"Yes, ma'am. I promise."

She leaned in, squinting, one wormy eye staring into mine.

Sores opened and scabbed over on her lumpy face; green splotches spread and disappeared like living creatures beneath her skin.

"Where is he?" she asked.

"Who?"

"You really don't know, do you?"

"Know what?"

She aimed the wand at my face, so close to my nose that my eyes crossed.

I had enough. I jumped backward, threw my final smoke

bomb, and grabbed the backpack strap, pulling it hard from her hand and pushing her over with my shoulder.

"Yeeee!" she screamed, losing her balance and spinning as she fell to the ground.

There was a cracking sound and then an explosion. Everything went white and I was flung through the air, floating up, up, up.

EMMA

As soon as I jumped through the window and landed on the grass, everything burst into flames.

The trees, the field, the street—it was all on fire.

The heat charred my body, a hundred times worse than that time my hand got stuck in Anna's toy oven.

Bunnies ran around the lawn, but they weren't normal ones. They were skeletons that hopped along the ground, eating grass that passed through their mouths and fell back onto the ground. Silhouettes of squirrel skeletons climbed the charred black trees, carrying burnt nuts with them. Birds flew and dove, attacking everything in sight, horrible shadows against the glowing red sky.

Somewhere in the distance, a dog barked and then exploded.

I screamed, louder than I thought possible, and curled on the ground, covering my eyes and rolling, trying to put out the fire in my brain.

"Emma! What happened?"

It was Julianna, one of the girls from the grade above me. I had never spoken to her before, but she was here now, walking through the fire and grabbing my hand, leading me out to the street.

"Make it stop, please make it stop," I said, and when I opened my eyes the fire was gone. A squirrel, covered in flesh and fur, sat on a branch and munched on a nut, as if everything I had seen was just a bad dream.

"Make what stop?" Julianna asked.

I was surrounded by kids from school, all of them staring at me like I was a crazy person.

"The . . . and . . . um . . . nothing . . . I . . ."

I kind of felt stupid, like maybe I had imagined the whole thing, and if I told them what I had seen they'd think I was even more bonkers.

"Where's Duncan?"

"He's still inside," I said, and from the street I could see flashes of light in the windows and loud crashing sounds.

"What about Tommy, Wilson, and Juan?"

"They never went inside. They just locked us in and ran. I don't—"

There was a deafening cracking sound, and a brilliant pillar of white light exploded from the witch's house, shooting into the clouds and popping like fireworks.

The light faded as quickly as it had appeared and there was a scream and a thud as something fell from the sky and hit the ground.

It was Duncan.

THE WAND

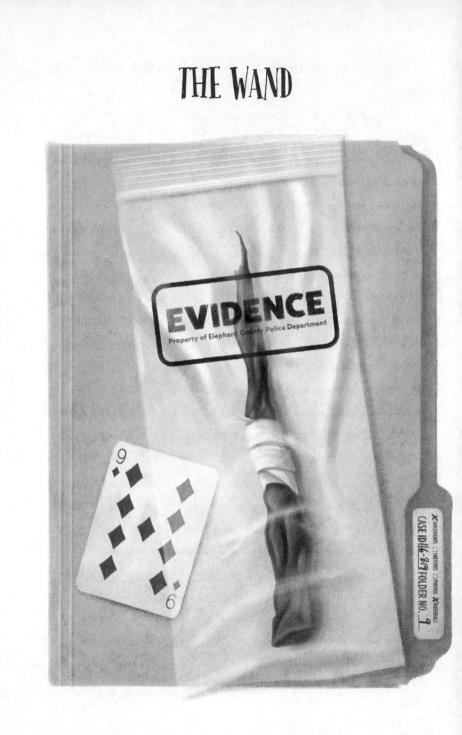

DUNCAN

Emma's face was the first thing I saw, and then other kids appeared, one by one, circling me. I was on my back next to the witch's house, and my head hurt really bad.

"Ta-da," I whimpered.

It took a few seconds for me to realize where I was, and what direction was up or down.

"How are you alive?" Emma asked.

"You sound disappointed."

"What happened?" she asked, and then leaned in to whisper, "I have to tell you what I saw."

There was a loud scream from the witch's house, and the kids from school scattered.

The scream continued, turning into loud sobs of grief.

"What did you do to her?" Emma asked.

"I don't know," I said. "But we need to leave now."

I stood up, despite every muscle begging me not to. I grabbed my backpack and threw it over my shoulder.

Something poked me in the arm and I jumped.

"What is it?"

I examined the bag. Wrapped in the left strap was a small

piece of wood, coarse and twisted. I pulled it off and held it in my hand. It was short, about four inches long, and the top was cracked and splintered and glowed white in my hand.

"What is *that*?" Emma asked.

"It's nothing," I said, shoving it into my pocket. "I don't know."

We hopped on our bikes and rode down the street and turned the corner, staying hidden in the trees.

The piece of wood tingled in my pocket.

I didn't want to tell Emma yet, not until I was sure, but I had a pretty good idea it was half of the witch's wand.

EMMA

The fall made Duncan act kind of weird that night, and he kept shaking his head, drooling like a puppy at a biscuit factory.

"You sure you're okay?" I asked.

He nodded and giggled—not a happy giggle but one of those madman giggles you hear right before someone pulls all their hair out and runs around town in their underwear.

"What's going on? What did you see?"

"Nothing . . . nothing . . . I . . ."

"What did she do to you?" I asked, and slapped him on the face. "Snap out of it."

He snorted and giggled some more.

The clouds above us were moving fast, and weird shapes blocked the moon and made sinister shadows on the ground.

We parted ways at the end of the street. I told Duncan to call me when he got home, but he never did.

DUNCAN

I got home an hour before my mom's shift was over and went to my room. I knew she'd be happy to find out I got my backpack, but I'd have to work out a pretty good story about how I found it.

Turns out it was under my bed the whole time! No, she'd never believe that.

It was just sitting on our front porch. Maybe.

I lay on my bed and spun the piece of wand around in my hand. I pointed it at a stack of books on my shelf and waved it.

"Abracadabra!" I yelled, but nothing disappeared or turned into an animal or anything like that.

I shoved the wand back in my pocket and drifted off to sleep, until I heard the front door open and slam shut.

"Duncan?" Mom asked. "Are you upstairs?"

"Yeah," I said, and I had that horrible feeling in my stomach that some people call butterflies but seemed more like electric eels that night.

My body ached from the explosion and the fall, and I felt like death. I sat up in bed, caught a glimpse of myself in the mirror, and screamed.

"What is it, Duncan? Is everything all right?"

I ran to the door and locked it. I was nowhere close to all right.

The skin on my face had gone lumpy and was covered with green and yellow splotches. My eyes were black and the size of two small raisins, and my teeth were a row of tiny yellow triangles, dripping with saliva. My hair had thinned and grown twelve inches, sweeping down around my shoulders.

I leaned into the mirror and pushed on the sides of a bubbling wart. It exploded, shooting out a hot, slimy liquid that sizzled and smoked as it slid down the mirror.

Mom ran up the stairs and was outside my room, jiggling the doorknob.

"Duncan, the door's locked."

"Give me a second."

"You know you aren't supposed to lock this door."

"I know. I'm changing."

That was an understatement.

"Will you let me in?"

"Yeah, just . . . hold on . . ."

I spun around, saw the backpack on my bed, and wished I had been smart enough to put it somewhere else.

Whoosh.

As soon as I thought it, the backpack flew into the air, spinning around slowly.

"What the—"

"Come on, Duncan, finish changing. I need to tell you something."

I ran toward the backpack and it flew across the room, slamming into my closet door and falling to the floor, emptying books and papers and pencils.

"What was that?" Mom yelled. "Duncan, I'm going to break down the door if you don't open it right now."

"I'm naked!"

"Nothing I haven't seen before."

I doubted that, but since I had no idea how to change myself back, figured I might as well tell her the truth and let her see her monster son. I opened the door, closing my eyes in preparation for her scream.

"Duncan!" she said.

"I know. Look, this might sound weird but—"

"Your backpack!" she yelled, pushing past me. "Where did you get it?"

I opened my eyes and looked in the mirror. I was back to normal.

"Umm . . . would you believe it if I told you it was just sitting on the porch?"

"Ralph must have found it. That's fantastic!"

"I don't know," I said.

She sat on my bed and patted the side.

"Come here, I need to tell you something."

"What?" I couldn't stand the thought of more bad news.

"I was going to wait, because you know how these things go . . . but . . . no, I'm going to tell you, and if something changes, it isn't my fault."

"What is it?"

"Your dad called me this afternoon and told me he was going to try to be at the talent show."

"Really?"

"Look, Duncan, I know he's missed a lot of things, but he has to travel for work and his schedule is tough."

"I know."

"But he's really excited to see you and it sounds like he'll be close to Elephant for the next few weeks. They're putting in a Lots o' Value in Bison County, and they're going to need a bunch of windows. Big windows."

"That's great for him."

"Be nice, Duncan. He tries his best."

I didn't say anything. There was nothing to say. Dad had a habit of not showing up. Work was always more important, and I was sure he'd find some reason to miss the talent show. Anyway, I had bigger things to worry about.

"Good night, sweetheart," Mom said.

She closed the door and now I was alone again. I grabbed the wand and tried to think of how I had made the backpack fly in the air.

I had *thought* about it moving—pictured it clearly in my head—and it did.

How was that possible?

I pointed the wand at the backpack and imagined it floating off the floor, all the way to the ceiling. I concentrated really hard and it wiggled and started to lift off the ground, just an inch at first. It felt weird, like moving something at the bottom of a pool with a thin string, but it got a little bit easier with each attempt.

Then I remembered how the witch had hovered in the hallway. Could I fly, too?

I jumped on my bed and closed my eyes. I imagined myself floating, and when I opened my eyes I was spinning slowly in the air.

"Whoa," I whispered.

I flipped forward and was hanging upside down, my feet upward, so I could walk along the ceiling. For a moment I stopped concentrating and I fell on my bed with a crash.

"Are you okay?" Mom yelled from downstairs.

"I'm fine!" I yelled back. I was better than fine. This was *amazing*.

I pointed at my bed and imagined a giant pile of money appearing out of thin air. Nothing happened.

I tried to think of myself as a monster again, and when I looked at the mirror, I had turned into a creature as grotesque and gnarled as I could imagine.

Emma would never believe this. I put the wand down and I was back to normal, even though I knew I was anything but.

I practiced for hours, floating around my room. By midnight I could lift my dresser a foot into the air before my brain started to feel like it would explode in my skull.

Finally, I hid the wand in my underwear drawer, tucked into a pair of socks. I collapsed into bed, giggling with the awesome power that I had wanted since that first day in Zug's shop.

No such thing as *real* magic? Explain this.

I drifted in and out of sleep, and was right at the point where my dreams blended with reality when I heard a howl and saw a shadow pass by my window.

Then it was morning.

THE FALL TALENT JAMBOREE

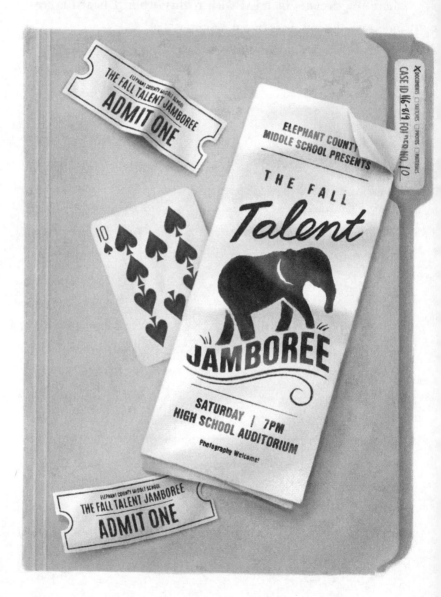

EMMA

According to my lawyer, I need to be very careful about how I describe the events of the Fall Talent Jamboree. Specifically, *what* I knew and *when* I knew it. I want to be very clear that I didn't know squat about Duncan and the wand prior to the show, but I *can* say that he was acting weirder than usual since that night at the witch's house.

We met at Zug's shop early Saturday morning. He had all our props ready, and we did a full run-through of our show in the parking lot. We worked a lot on our patter, which are the stories we tell while we perform each trick.

"Nothing in my hands," Duncan said, showing his empty hands.

"Nothing up my sleeves." He rolled up his sleeves.

"Empty pockets." He pulled out his pockets.

"Sounds like your mom needs to give you an allowance," I said. Zug let out a fake chuckle as Duncan proceeded to pull coins from his nostrils.

Later, Zug filled the Water Torture Chamber with a garden hose and Duncan practiced his escape four times.

"I did a final check for leaks and reoiled the trapdoor,"

Zug said. "Now, look at me, Duncan, if you run into problems, knock on the glass two times and give me a thumbs-down sign. I'll be right up to get you out."

"I'll be fine," Duncan said. "Check out this new trick I've been working on."

He pulled an eight of clubs from a pack of cards and folded it in half, bending back the sides so they looked like wings. He placed it in my hands and passed his hands over it, his face scrunched into a serious scowl just like Quinton Penfold on one of his TV specials.

"Watch closely," Duncan said, and I felt a tingle in my hands as he waved them around. When he stopped, the card was gone and in its place was a beautiful butterfly. On its back was a marking that looked suspiciously like the eight of clubs. The butterfly hopped around, startled, and then flew up and away.

Zug's eyes widened and he clapped his hands.

"Wonderful, Duncan! Wonderful!"

"How did you do that?" I asked, trying my best not to sound *too* desperate. Duncan's tormented me for weeks if he knows there's a trick I can't figure out.

"Magic," he said. "It was real magic."

"You caught a butterfly and stained its wings to look like a card," I said. "Big deal."

"Not even close."

"He palmed the butterfly and switched it out," Zug said. "Oldest trick in the book, but your implementation was superb. I couldn't even spot the switch."

"Right," Duncan said with a wink. "*That's* how I did it."

"Come on, Duncan, you can tell me. Where's the card?"

"It flew away."

"No it didn't," I said, slapping him on the arm. "How did you do it?"

"I already told you. Real magic."

"I'm serious, Duncan. Tell me how you did it. It would be a real shame if the trapdoor on the Water Torture Chamber stopped working, wouldn't it?"

"Look at me closely," he said, and his eyes flashed red and yellow, like there were flames flickering beneath them. "I'm telling you the truth. It was *real* magic."

"I'll glue the hinges and the last thing you'll see before you drown to death is me flapping my arms like a butterfly."

"Very funny," he said.

But there are some things you should never joke about.

DUNCAN

We met my dad in the school parking lot while we were unloading our props. I was surprised he actually came. Last year, something came up last minute and to make up for it he sent me a cheap pack of playing cards from a gas station.

He and Mom usually get along all right. They say a few words and then move on to talking about the weather or something. Sometimes it's weird, and other times it's not. It depends if Ralph is around.

"So you're ready for the show?" he asked.

I nodded at my chest of props, and slung my tuxedo and cape over my shoulder.

"Think you'll win?"

"Oh, definitely," Emma said. "Unless, of course, Evan Sanderson learned a few more chords and how to sing in tune."

Zug grunted in the truck and wheeled the Water Torture Chamber to the front.

"What is *this*?" Dad asked as he helped Zug lower it from the truck. I supervised to make sure nothing got cracked.

"It's the grand finale."

"Looks dangerous. You sure you know what you're doing?"

Emma glared at him and Zug chuckled.

"Don't worry, sir. He's a very talented magician. And I'll be around if he needs any help."

Tommy, Wilson, and Juan came out of the auditorium doors wearing black clothes and tool belts.

"Stagehands coming through," Tommy yelled. "Does anyone need assistance?"

Emma growled. We had managed to avoid them since that night at the witch's house.

"Can we help?" Tommy asked Zug. He was always *so* nice around adults.

"Get out of here, *Tommy*," Emma said.

"I'm surprised to see you here," Tommy whispered, low enough that Dad and Zug couldn't hear. "Thought the witch would have turned you into frogs. That would have been an improvement."

"I decided to be nice and not tell the whole school that you ran away from her house like a sniveling little baby," Emma whispered, her face locked in a smile. "Don't make me change my mind."

"You better watch it," Tommy said.

Zug unloaded a box from the truck and threw it on the sidewalk.

"Let me carry that," Tommy said.

I grabbed the wand in my pocket and imagined Tommy's shoes flying off the ground as he bent to pick up the box. He fell over and landed hard on the sidewalk. Wilson and Juan laughed as Tommy rolled around, his legs flailing.

"Careful, son," Zug said. "Are you all right?"

I thought about snakes in Tommy's shoes, and rats in Wilson's and Juan's underwear.

They danced and squealed until I released the wand.

"Bathroom's that way," Emma said. "Hold it in, boys."

"What are you doing, freak?" Tommy whispered.

I smiled at him, focused my mind, and thought about invisible spiders in his hair.

"Cut it out. *Please*," he said, jumping and running his hands over his head.

"We could use some help getting this thing inside," Zug said, pushing the Water Torture Chamber.

I made the spiders go away and smiled at Tommy.

"It's on wheels," I said. "We don't need them."

"Let the boys do their jobs," Dad said. "Here, help us get it on the curb."

Tommy, Wilson, and Juan looked at me for approval.

"You heard him," I said.

They helped my dad lift it onto the curb and rolled it toward the auditorium's double doors.

Tommy rubbed the hammer on his tool belt and glared at me as he walked away.

EMMA

Two hours into the show and my stomach was beginning to flop around like a fish out of water. Jesse Green was onstage lip-synching and dancing to a song, displaying a talent that I could only assume was *irritating Emma*. It was torture waiting to go out, and having to watch these awful acts from backstage made it worse.

Duncan was quieter than usual, and he practiced a close-up trick in the corner, where he turned raisins into flies, caught them, turned them back into raisins, and then ate them.

"How did you *do* that?" I asked, and he stuck his hand in his pocket and muttered something.

He was still acting really strange.

"I'm sick of waiting," I moaned.

"It's a compliment being put on near the end," Duncan said. He took off his glasses and levitated them in the air. "It means we're one of the best performances."

"Yeah," I said, pointing to the program, "I'm sure that's why we're followed by Tony playing taps on his tuba."

He shrugged and said, "They have to balance it out. Pacing."

Twenty minutes later, Principal Howell walked onto the stage and hit the microphone with the back of her hand, sending large squeals of feedback out of the speakers.

"All right, everybody. We all remember their *astonishing* act from fifth grade, and from what I hear, this year's performance will be twice as good. Please welcome Duncan Reyes, magician extraordinaire, here to mesmerize us with new illusions and astonishing feats of . . ." She flipped the index card over. ". . . escape. Oh, that sounds fun. Also, welcome his assistant, Emma Gilbert."

I glared at him. He shrugged and I pushed him onto the stage, hard enough that he tripped a little as he stepped into the spotlight.

It was *showtime*.

We both smiled as we walked toward the front of the stage, light applause coming from the audience. I could see my parents near the front, and my sisters were seated with their friends a few rows back.

Duncan held his hands out, moving confidently to the middle of the stage.

I nodded at the stagehands, and they wheeled out a chest of props.

Tommy, Juan, and Wilson were waiting on the side, and Tommy held something in his hand that I couldn't see through the spotlight.

"Magic," Duncan began. "The secret art of deception."

He pulled a bunch of flowers from my sleeve.

"But tricks like these are just that. *Tricks*."

He pulled a long row of hankies from his ear.

"You've seen these tricks a thousand times, but what if I told you, tonight, there will be no tricks?"

I held two metal rings up and clanked them together.

"What if I told you everything you saw tonight was real? *Abracadabra!*"

"Gesundheit," I said.

He pointed at me and I hit the rings together. One slipped into the other and I held them proudly above my head.

"Stupid!" someone yelled from the audience.

"We're not doing the good tricks right at the beginning!" I yelled, searching the audience for our heckler.

"Everything you're about to see is real magic, passed down for centuries from magician to magician," Duncan said.

We did the magical top hat (you could pull tons of large stuff out of it), the giant deck of cards (just a normal card trick, but giant), and the color-changing umbrellas (description is in the title).

The best reaction we got was a few claps and light coughing. Zug sat in the first row and gave us a thumbs-up, which made me feel even worse.

"Come on, Duncan," I whispered. "We're dying out here. Do that butterfly trick you showed me."

He ignored me, continuing our routine.

Finally, we got to the Water Torture Chamber, and I was hoping that would get the audience back on our side.

"With *real* magic, nothing can stop us. Even death."

Tommy wheeled the tank out on the stage and whispered, "Escape *this*, magic boy," to Duncan.

"Death. The final adversary," Duncan said as I strapped the straitjacket on him. "To escape its clutches is my final show of strength and power. I ask that you refrain from flash photography. Every second matters as I fight for my life, and every distraction makes this more dangerous. What you see behind me is a water chamber. Used in ancient times as a torture device, tonight it will be a demonstration of *real* magic."

I fastened the final strap of the straitjacket and closed the padlock on the front of his chest. Duncan climbed up the side and sat with his legs dangling into the tank.

"When people had secrets they wouldn't reveal, they were placed in here and told to spill the beans. When they refused, the chamber would be filled with water, drip by drip, inch by inch. It would reach their knees, then their stomach, then their chest. Of course, most people had cracked by the time the water reached their neck, while others took their secrets to a watery grave. It's a shame, really, considering how easy it is to escape by using simple magic. Watch."

The lights dimmed and music began to play.

Duncan jumped in and I slammed the door, locking it closed. I pulled the hose from the side of the stage and screwed it in the top. Water began pouring over Duncan's head.

Tommy laughed from offstage.

I should have figured something was wrong.

DUNCAN

Cold water poured over me, filling the bottom of the tank and covering my feet.

Through the glass I could see the audience watching me as I struggled with the straitjacket, pretending I was stuck. I hit my head against the wall, screamed for help.

The water reached my knees and I thrashed from side to side. I looped my finger into the pull cord that would release the straitjacket and prepared for the exact right moment.

The beat of the music got faster as the water reached my waist. I shivered as it reached my elbows, then my chest. As soon as the water covered my head, Emma would drop the curtain and I would have ten seconds to be on the side of the stage before she lifted it.

The water got higher, covering my cheeks.

I sucked in one last giant gulp of air as the water covered my face.

The hose turned off. The curtain lowered.

It was time.

I pulled the cord, shedding the straitjacket.

I worked my arms above my head and pushed off from the bottom, hitting the trapdoor.

It didn't move.

I hit it again. And again.

Stuck.

Seconds passed.

Emma rose the curtain, right on schedule. The music continued, muffled by the water and drowned out by the blood pounding in my ears.

I knocked twice on the glass and gave a thumbs-down sign.

Emma screamed something but from underwater all I could hear was *Blunnnk gah flobbda.*

Don't panic, I thought. *Don't panic.*

I could see movement in the audience. People were running to the stage.

Zug was there. He unlocked the top and pounded on it, screaming something that sounded a lot like *It's stuck.*

Soon, there were three blurry figures to the side of the stage, and I saw them turn and run.

Dark veins crept in from the sides of my vision, spreading in spidery lines, and my whole body hurt.

I remembered the hammer hanging from Tommy's belt, and how he had whispered, *Escape* this, *magic boy*, as he slid the tank onstage.

In a flash of anger and terror I knew what had happened.

Tommy had nailed the top shut.

EMMA

I ran to the side of the stage and screamed for help.

Zug was already there, standing on a chair and clawing at the trapdoor in the middle of the top panel.

"Someone nailed it shut!" he screamed. "We need help! Quick!"

All of the auditorium lights switched on.

The world went black and white.

People moved in slow motion.

I couldn't focus on anything, could only stand at the corner of the stage, opening and closing my mouth, as people swarmed the chamber and pried at the top.

I saw Tommy, noticed his face was white, and his eyes were wide in terror.

"You," I whispered. "You didn't. You *wouldn't*."

"I just wanted to embarrass him," Tommy said.

He turned and ran and I walked slowly toward the chamber, locking eyes with Duncan.

He was like a corpse, pale and motionless behind the glass.

I got closer, touched the panel.

He reached for my hand and something floated in the

water, a small piece of wood that glowed so bright that I couldn't even look at it.

Duncan glanced at it and gave me a thumbs-up sign.

I didn't understand.

He grabbed the wood, closed his eyes, and made both of us famous.

DUNCAN

Maybe it's true that you see a bright light before you die. I certainly did.

My lungs were burning and spots formed in the dark mist that spread across my vision.

I was one deep breath from being done for. That would be a finale no one would ever forget.

Blobs of people circled me, but they seemed like they were miles away now, and I was so cold.

Emma was there, touching the glass. That's when the light appeared, drifting up until it stopped in front of my face.

It was the wand.

Come on, Duncan, it seemed to say. *I can help you.*

I grabbed it, locked eyes with Emma, and gave her a thumbs-up.

Everything was going to be okay, I thought. I just wanted to escape. I wanted Emma to come with me, and I wanted to be safe and far away from the school.

The wand grew brighter, making the water flash a blinding neon blue.

The chamber shook and the sides cracked.

Zug fell from the top, crawling away as the chamber jumped and pulsed.

Sometimes I wonder what would have happened if I hadn't escaped that night.

Maybe I should have drowned and saved the whole town from all the trouble that was about to come.

I don't know.

I closed my eyes, curled into a ball, and prepared to fly.

What's done is done, and I hope you'll agree that I made the right choice, because what happened next changed everything.

ESCAPE

EMMA

CUH-RACK.

The first crack was the loudest, followed by a web of tiny fractures that ran down the glass walls of the chamber.

Zug was on the floor, and he gasped as the water glowed and popped with tiny explosions.

The audience screamed, running away from the stage.

Duncan closed his eyes and then—

BOOOOOM!

The chamber exploded around him, and a million pieces of glass floated in the air, forming a perfect sphere that hovered on the stage.

The water stayed in place, like a ball of jelly that quivered and shook. The straitjacket floated around in it.

Duncan rose out of the water and spun in a circle. He was flying.

Now, trust me, I know how levitation tricks work. I could draw you a diagram of the web of wires needed for Nevil Maskelyne's famous floating lady trick.

This was *nothing* like that.

He held out his arms to steady himself.

"Come on," he said, waving his hand to me.

I looked at what was left of the audience. They were watching in complete horror and amazement.

Ms. Reyes was crying.

Zug was shaking his head, like this was a dream he wanted to wake up from.

I walked toward Duncan and poked the ball of water. It rippled and a small drip stuck to my finger.

There wasn't a single sound in the auditorium.

"Emma, take my hand," Duncan said.

I did.

Duncan isn't very strong but that day he could somehow pick me up like I was weightless.

"What's happening?" I asked, and I still wasn't sure that this *wasn't* a dream.

He snapped his fingers and the glass and water crashed to the ground in a burst of color and noise.

The stage shook and the floorboards cracked and splintered. The rear curtain ripped and fell to the floor, covered in green flames.

The ceiling of the auditorium split down the middle and peeled back like a milk carton, the metal beams groaning.

There was nothing but black sky above us, peppered with stars, and we flew higher into the night.

All I could manage to ask was, "Where are we going?" He didn't answer.

I felt the cold air on my cheeks and watched in awe as the world below us shrunk.

Then I looked up at him and screamed.

DUNCAN

Emma screamed when she saw me, and I saw that my hands had turned wrinkly and green, covered in scars and black hair.

I had turned into how I felt, which at that moment was pretty angry.

"I'm still me," I said, but my lips were pasted to my fangs and my voice sounded weird and scratchy, like I had swallowed broken glass.

We went higher and higher, escaping into the cold night air. The auditorium was below us, and through the crack in the roof I could see the destroyed stage. People ran around, screaming and fleeing the building.

"Sorry I went off script," I growled. "Thought our show could use a little sizzle."

Emma shook her head.

"I . . . I . . . I don't even—"

It was hard to control our movement through the air. I flew us to the edge of the forest and landed on the soft grass.

"Now I know why witches use brooms," I said, grabbing a tree branch and snapping it off. "Pretty cool, right?"

Emma glared at me.

"Look, I know that was weird, but—"

She pounced on me, tackled me to the ground, and clawed at my face.

"What is going *on*?" she screamed.

"I can't—"

"You better tell me everything! What did the witch do to you?"

"I don't know!"

"Yes, you do! What was that thing in the water?"

"Quiet," I said. There were sirens in the distance. "Do you hear that? We need to go."

I didn't know what they'd do when they caught me. It wasn't my fault. The wand made me do it. And hadn't it been Tommy and his friends that nailed the trapdoor shut?

I looked at my hand, and saw I was back to normal.

"Get on," I said, straddling the tree branch. "And hold tight."

She did.

I pushed off with my legs, wobbled in the air, and balanced us on the stick. It was easier than holding Emma with my hand, but I still had a lot to get used to.

We shot up into the sky, twisting wildly toward the clouds. I tried to steer us, but we flew higher.

"Do you know what you're doing?" she asked.

"Lean left," I yelled, but that didn't work.

I closed my eyes and concentrated on what direction I wanted to go, and the branch obeyed. It was controlled by my mind, and it did anything I thought.

"Slow down!" Emma screamed, but I couldn't.

We did loops and corkscrews, bursting through a layer of clouds. They looked like a field of snow below us, and in the dark sky, the moon shone brighter than I had ever seen before, a giant white ball that looked close enough to touch.

"I'm cold, Duncan," Emma said.

So was I, mainly because I was still wearing my soaking wet tuxedo.

"How high do you think we can go?" I asked her. "Into space?"

"How are you doing this?" Emma asked. She sounded far away, like she was about to fall asleep. Her eyes were glassy and I held her hand.

"I don't really know."

I didn't want to tell her about the wand—not yet. She'd want a turn with it and I'd never get it back.

I flew lower, until I could see the town below us.

We were over busy roads now. Cars looked like they were toys in a sandbox. Police vehicles and fire trucks circled the school. Could they see us? It didn't matter. My secret was already out in a *big* way.

"What's that?" Emma asked.

There was something below us. A shadow blasted from the school and up into the sky, faster than anything I had seen before.

"Just a bird, probably," I said, but it was impossible to mistake the silhouette of the witch. She was out, and she was hunting us.

The sky was open and empty. We shot down so no one would see us, flying over a quiet part of town close enough to the road that we could touch our feet to the tops of cars. We stuck to dark roads and alleys, sometimes landing in the shadows and waiting for a police car to pass.

Finally, we were on my street, and with a flick of my wrist my window opened and we flew into my room.

That's when we were caught.

CAUGHT

EMMA

Hands grabbed us.

Duncan screamed.

Zug wrapped his arms around our shoulders and Officer Ralph hugged Ms. Reyes. Duncan's dad was on his phone, probably searching for *cures for demon-possessed children*.

"We figured you'd come back here," Zug said.

They looked at us like we were freaks, and in a way I guess we were.

I bowed, tried to smile, and asked, "So did we win?"

That got them started. They exploded with questions.

"How did you—"

"What happened when—"

"Where did you—"

"We thought you were dead," Ms. Reyes said. "And then . . . you *weren't* . . . and then . . . you were a monster . . . and you were *flying* . . . and then—"

"She's having a hard time with this," Officer Ralph said. He seemed a lot less surprised than I expected, which I later learned was because he had his own little meeting with the witch earlier.

"This was all part of the act," Duncan's dad said. "Wasn't it?"

"Part of the act?" Zug erupted. "Sir, just how good do you think they are at magic?"

"Well, you said he was talented."

"Not *that* talented."

"Hey!" Duncan said.

"I'm sorry, son. Maybe Quinton Penfold could pull off a trick like that, but not without years of practice and millions of dollars in props and special effects. No, this was not part of the act. I built that water chamber myself and I know what it can do. *That* was not possible."

"Then how did they do it?" Ms. Reyes asked.

"You better start talking," Zug said. "And forget about the Magician's Code."

"Go on," I said, nudging Duncan.

The truth was, I wanted to know for myself.

DUNCAN

I told them everything. Mostly.

What choice did I have?

I started with my incident with Tommy in the cafeteria, how he made me ring the witch's doorbell, and then how he locked me and Emma in her house.

"Emma got out," I said. "But the witch caught me and . . . cursed me."

"Cursed you?" Dad asked. "That witch is just an old legend. I'm pretty sure Danny Weber made the whole thing up in third grade. Right, Elena?"

Mom was too upset to answer.

"She's real," I said. "And now I can do this."

I floated up to the ceiling, flipped over, and hung by my feet. They all gasped.

"Or this."

I landed on the ground and thought of the nastiest creature I could imagine. I felt my skin begin to bubble and morph. They shrieked in terror.

I never mentioned the wand. I clutched it in my pocket, keeping it hidden. I wasn't even allowed to have a phone, so

I knew there was zero chance Mom would let me keep something like this if she knew what it could do.

"That's amazing," Dad said. His face had turned white.

"It's not amazing," Ralph said. "It's a liability. The police station got dozens of calls and they're already on the scene."

Zug held his phone up.

"Not to mention I was filming the show, and I know a bunch of other people were as well. Video is going to get out, and when it does, people are going to start asking questions."

Dad nodded.

"I think we need to come up with a convincing story."

"I think we need a priest," Mom said.

"I'm fine," I said. "I'm sure the curse will wear off, and I promise I won't use my powers anymore."

"There's still a giant hole in the auditorium's roof," Ralph said. "How will we explain that?"

"We can deny it. Blame the roof on . . . umm . . . a surprise tornado," Zug said. "As for the trick, I can tell them I helped him rig up the wires."

"And what about the stage collapsing?"

Zug shrugged.

"Earthquake? Do those ever happen at the same time as tornados?"

"And how do you explain the floating ball of water?" Mom asked.

"Jell-O?"

There were sirens outside, and four police cars parked in front of our house, followed by two news vans.

Mom turned to Ralph.

"So do you believe in the witch now?"

"Recent events have made me reevaluate my position," he said. "I'll take care of the police. You lie low and don't talk to *anyone*, understand?"

I nodded.

Emma snuck out the back door, and I closed the blinds in my room, occasionally peeking out to see reporters setting up lights and cameras on my front yard. This was bad.

Ralph arranged for an officer to stay at the house, which made me feel a bit better.

The next day, I didn't leave my room and practiced magic with the wand. We got so many calls that Mom had to turn off her phone. She said if things got worse we may have to hide out at her grandmother's house in Puerto Rico.

I was finally getting the attention I had always wanted, and it was terrible.

CELEBRITY

KIDS DESTROY AUDITORIUM AND FLY AT TALENT SHOW!!!
13,876,301 views

EMMA

I hid in my room that Sunday and tried to call Duncan, but he didn't answer.

He was on the bus Monday morning, alone in the back row. Kids flinched when I walked by.

"That's right, step aside or we'll turn you into pigs," I said, stomping past them and waving my fingers in the air.

I sat next to Duncan. He didn't talk. He had that awful look on his face like he was about to hurl, and he kept his hands in his pockets the whole way to school.

"So I've been thinking," I whispered, "how long does this curse last?"

He shrugged.

"And why did she only give *you* superpowers? That's not fair. I was in the house as well."

It didn't make sense.

The bus parked in front of the school and as soon as we got out I knew we were in trouble.

Three fire trucks circled the high school auditorium, and there was a news truck parked outside. Libby Blackburn, a reporter from the local evening news, came running over to us in high heels and a bright red pantsuit. Her blond hair looked like half-eaten cotton candy, and her makeup was applied in a similar style to my little sister's finger paintings.

"Duncan! Emma! Hellooo!" she yelled, waving her arms at us and pulling a cameraman behind her. "Can I talk to you? Super quick."

"No comment," I said.

"I just have a few questions about your *remarkable* show."

"It was a tornado, earthquake, and Jell-O," I said. "We didn't do anything special."

"How does it feel to be national celebrities?"

"What do you mean?" Duncan asked.

The camera was rolling.

"You don't know?" Libby turned to the camera, shaking her head. "They have the ability to fly and destroy public property, but they don't have the ability to go online and see what *other* people are saying."

She knelt down beside us, and put her hand on Duncan's shoulder.

"Someone posted a video," she said, "and it's already been viewed *three million times. Everyone* is talking about you."

My face felt hot. I had never been a celebrity before. My sisters would be so jealous!

Libby turned to the camera again and said, "I'm here with Duncan Reyes, and his assistant—"

"Co-magician," I said, leaning in front of Duncan.

"Co-magician . . . ," Libby repeated.

"Emma," I said, waving at the camera. "Emma Gilbert. Hello!"

Libby glared at me.

"Duncan and *Emma* have shot to stardom with their amazing display of magical abilities at the school talent show. Video of their performance has been trending online, so I need to ask the question that's on everyone's mind. How did you do it, Duncan?"

"A magician never tells," Duncan said. "We need to get to class."

"No, no," Libby said, stepping in front of us. "Don't worry about class. This is more important. Since the posting of the original video, several others have popped up, showing the trick from various angles."

"Really?" Duncan asked.

"The tapes have been analyzed by professional magicians and they all agree that there's no way you should have been able to do what you did. Quinton Penfold is on record saying that it is the most amazing trick he's ever seen."

"Quinton . . . *Penfold*?" Duncan asked. He looked like he was about to faint. "He saw my act?"

"Oh, yes, and he wants to talk to you. I don't think you understand. *Everyone's* seen your performance. There were no wires we can see, and you seem to defy the laws of physics. How do you respond?"

"Lots of planning, lots of practice," I said, grabbing Duncan's hand and pulling him to the front door.

"Duncan, how did you do it?" Libby yelled, following us closely. "You're going to have to answer questions. You destroyed the auditorium and the taxpayers have the *right* to know what happened."

"Stop it," I said. "We need to go."

"You're not going anywhere until you talk," Libby said, grabbing Duncan's shoulder. Her eyes narrowed and her white teeth looked like weapons that chomped with each word. "I. Need. This. Story."

"Well, you're not getting it!" Duncan screamed.

Then he turned her into a goat.

DUNCAN

By that evening, the video of our Fall Talent Jamboree performance had been seen five million times. And the one of me turning Libby Blackburn into a goat was already up to eight hundred thousand views.

Mom refreshed the pages on her phone every five minutes.

People started to hang out in front of the house, knocking on the door and asking me to heal their grandmother or fix their ingrown toenails.

Dad sat in my room and made awkward conversation about magic and said stuff like, "You know, Duncan, it's wrong to turn people into animals."

Ralph drove by at seven in his police car and made everyone get off the lawn. It was the first time I was actually glad to have him around.

Emma came a little later. She said it was because her sisters were driving her crazy, but I think it was because she couldn't stand seeing me get all the attention.

"Not a single news van at *my* house," she said. "How do you like that?"

We watched TV, and when our pictures appeared on the

evening news broadcast, Emma squeezed my arm and squealed.

They rehashed the story for the hundredth time, showing footage from the Jamboree and at school.

I wasn't listening.

It didn't feel real. Nothing felt real.

And when Quinton Penfold appeared on the screen, I couldn't even understand what he was saying. His mouth was moving but my brain couldn't make sense of it.

"*Blah blah blah* wonderful *blah blah blah* Duncan Reyes *blah blah* Emma Gilbert."

"Are you hearing this, Duncan?" Emma screamed, jumping on the couch.

I tried to focus, but I felt like I was in a weird dream.

". . . for that reason we have decided . . ."

"Oh my gosh!" Emma shook my shoulders.

". . . relocate this year's Elite Magicians Convention to the small town of Elephant . . ."

"Wheeeeee!" Emma yelled, tilting her head back and pumping her fists in the air.

". . . we extend an invitation . . ."

Quinton raised his eyebrow to the camera, and flashed his dark and mysterious smile.

". . . and we are all so very excited to meet these two remarkable children. In fact, we'd like them to be the opening act."

"This is the best news ever," Emma said, dancing around the room. "It's what we've always wanted!"

She grabbed Mom's hand and twirled around.

I tried to seem happy, but all I wanted now was for life to

go back to normal. This wasn't the way I wanted to get famous.

Later that evening, Dad went home and Emma decided to sleep over on the couch.

For a moment, everything was peaceful.

I never saw the shadows outside. And I never considered that all this attention would make me an easy target for the witch.

THE WITCH APPEARS

EMMA

I stayed over at Duncan's house that night, but I couldn't get to sleep.

The news about Quinton Penfold visiting Elephant was *way* too exciting.

I thought about all our future TV appearances. Magazine spreads. Interviews. Online gossip.

I curled into the couch cushions, listening to the wind through the trees.

A branch shaped like a twisted finger scraped across the window.

A cat howled outside.

There's nothing to be scared about, I thought.

The back door rattled and banged open.

I waited, trying not to make any noise.

The house shook.

Noises came from the kitchen, dull thumping sounds that echoed along the floor.

I ran upstairs to Duncan's room. He was hiding behind the bed, and he whispered, "I think she's here."

He called for his mom, but she didn't answer. Ms. Reyes is a heavy sleeper.

The noises stopped.

A shrill laugh came from the bottom of the stairs.

Duncan had just let the witch know exactly where we were.

DUNCAN

Emma hid behind the bed and I stood guard, wand ready.

If that horrible witch tried anything, I'd zap her out of the house and away from Elephant County for good.

"What is *that?*" Emma asked.

"It's her magic wand."

"You liar! I knew she didn't curse you!"

I called out for my mom, hoping she'd wake up and come to the room, where I could protect her.

The hallway walls shook and picture frames fell to the floor and shattered.

Light bulbs flickered on and off, bright and dim, before popping to darkness.

Smoke billowed from downstairs, and a shadow appeared from the stairwell, along with the sound of the witch's heavy footsteps.

She was coming toward us.

She rose into view, nasty and twisted, her green flesh alive and squirming.

"Ahhh, there you are!" she shouted, her scratchy voice

echoing off the walls. "Duncan Reyes and Emma Gilbert, the greatest fools that ever lived."

I held out my half of the wand and she held out hers in a dramatic standoff.

I tried to think of the worst thing I could do to her, but it was too late. With a flick of her wrist the wand jumped from my hand and she caught it, spit a wad of gum into her palm, and joined the two pieces together.

She giggled and rubbed the wand, pressing it to her cheek.

"There we are, just perfect, perfect."

She walked down the hall, staring at us with her tiny black-and-yellow eyes.

"What trouble you have caused! Any idea? No, no, certainly not. Innocent little kids, remember. So young and dumb."

She laughed, pointed the wand at us, and screamed.

Emma and I floated in the air, spinning as everything in the room hovered around us, weightless.

Mom appeared in the hallway, rubbing her eyes.

"Go back to your room!" I yelled, but it was too late.

"Mother of Duncan, I pray you forgive me. No other choices at this hour, see?"

She pointed the wand at a rug and it sprang to life, wrapping Mom up like a mummy and rolling her back into her room.

"You let her go or else!" I screamed, but it was hard to sound brave when I was floating upside down.

"You're in no position to demand *anything*," the witch said. "Tried to find you before a commotion was made, but too late now. Couldn't have made a bigger spectacle, could you?"

She snapped her fingers and I fell to the bed.

"The flying and the fire and the mess. And then the cops and the news and the goat. Oh, yes, I stole a newspaper or two from neighbors and read all about you. Everyone wants a piece of *Duncan Reyes*, isn't that right?"

"And me," Emma said.

"Sure, you as well. Had to search a bit. Had to wait. No matter. Both *dead* now, I promise you. Walking corpses, you are. Close your eyes and prepare for it."

My body went limp. I was sure this was the end. The witch pointed the wand at me and I closed my eyes, waiting for a zap that would turn everything black, but it never came.

The window opened and cold air blew in the room. She waved the wand at a tall lamp in the corner. It flew over to her, the pole unscrewing from the base. She placed the pole between her legs, kicking off from the ground and grabbing us, one in each hand, pulling us out of the room and into the night sky.

EMMA

We flew above the trees, dipping down before shooting straight up and over the clouds. The witch's hand was tight around my wrist and her black fingernails dug into my skin.

The wind rushed around our faces and I screamed as loud as I could.

"Where are we going?"

She didn't answer.

"Are you going to kill us?"

She looked back at me and smiled in a way that could have meant yes just as easily as it could have meant no.

We went higher, into the dark sky, where all we could see was the moon.

She stopped, and in the stillness of the night she cackled and said, "Hold on tight, my little ones."

There was a pause, and then a drop, like a roller coaster. Faster than my dad's driving. Crazier than Jenna's dancing.

Duncan screamed, and we kept going down, farther and farther, through the clouds, and toward her street.

She pulled up an instant before we would have smashed into the ground and exploded into a million gooey pieces.

I closed my eyes as we flew over rooftops.

Misery Manor was at the end of the road, and we sped toward it.

The twisted house was getting closer and closer, growing in size until I could see the flakes of chipped paint on the shutters.

There was a whooshing sound, and we stopped right over the front lawn.

We hovered above the ground, just a few feet, and the witch let go of us and we fell beside her, moaning. She flipped off the pole, her black boots slapping on the grass.

"Oh, you still be young and bouncy. Get up and never pretend to be hurt when you ain't. Plenty of time for the real thing. Quick, quick."

She stuck the wand in her mouth and grabbed our collars, pulling us toward the front door.

"Please, let us go," Duncan begged.

"I didn't do anything," I said. "It was all him."

"Fault doesn't matter, now, get it? Blame, fine, try all you want, young lady. See where you get. Will be a pity to see you die so soon, but no one can blame *me*, can they? No, I think not. Tried everything I could to avoid it, but you've practically begged for it. Prepare. Bad things happenin' now. Things too wicked for nightmares."

The wand glowed in her mouth. She spit toward the front door and it whipped open. The tattered black strands of her dress fluttered in the wind.

She mumbled and growled and dragged us inside her house.

"Home! Awake!" she yelled, and the lights turned on. "Downstairs we go."

She led us down to a dark, damp cellar with wet walls and a dirt floor.

A pot simmered in the corner, and with a wave of her wand it erupted in green smoke.

I wanted to run but there was nowhere to go.

She waved her wand again and two chairs slid across the floor, hitting us in the back of our legs and knocking us down. A rope slithered around our feet and wrapped around us, so tight that we couldn't move.

The witch pulled a long black tube out of the corner of the room and held it above her head. Her eyes glimmered.

"Prepare," she said, "for *torture*."

THE TREE

CASE ID 116-319 FOLDER NO. 15

DUNCAN

"Absolute *torture!*" she screamed.

Emma started to cry.

"Mercy heavens! I've frightened you, ain't I?" The witch hit herself lightly on the forehead and opened the tube, pulling out a brittle yellow projector screen. She unrolled it and attached it to a stand, then switched on a projector. "They say that looking at other people's pictures is the worst kind of torture is what I meant, you see? Settle, settle."

She smiled, her eyes sparkling in the light. Her skin had gone back to normal and her frayed clothing had changed into a flowing dress patterned with cherubs. She looked like a normal old grandmother, round faced and wrinkled around the eyes, with long gray hair and red cheeks.

A black cat jumped on a ledge and rubbed his head against her.

"Away from here, No Name!" she screamed. "You're getting hair in the drink."

She stirred the steaming cauldron, which I could now see was plugged into the wall behind her.

"Do you like cider, my little ones? I get thirsty for some warmth when flying out in the cold."

She scooped and sipped, belching loudly and scratching her stomach.

"Apologies!" she said, blushing. "Forgot my manners. Not used to company. When one is accustomed to blurping or blarping whenever one wants, why . . ."

She scooped cider into mugs and handed them to us. The heat felt good on my hands, and I took a sip. It was way too late for me to worry about being poisoned.

"Welcome. The name's Edna Bunchwick."

She clicked a button on the projector's remote and an old ink drawing of a tree appeared on the screen.

"Newspapers say you're a magic duo. I assume you know a little history of the craft, but have you ever seen this?" She pointed at the tree on the screen and grunted.

We shook our head.

"Figured as much. Some history is long forgotten. Better never to know it at all."

She frowned at us and shook her head.

"Didn't expect to be telling this story to little neighborhood runts, but what choice do I have now?"

She balanced the wand on the tip of her finger and spun it. The wand illuminated the screen, and the branches of the tree shimmered.

"Your experiences with this wicked twig should tell you it wasn't snapped off a *normal* tree. This here came from a tree of power and magic. Some have said the tree is the oldest one on earth. Some say it grew from an alien seed. Others say it's that nasty tree from the Garden of Eden. Whatever the reason, this tree was possessed by a special kind of magic, and anyone that touched it could do whatever they desired. Oh, you already know a bit of what it can do, don't you? Good or bad, it makes no difference to the tree. Create a tsunami just as easy as a rainbow."

"A magic tree?" Emma asked. "Where is it?"

"Aye, that's the question, ain't it? Only one man has ever laid eyes on it."

She clicked the button again and an ink drawing of a man in a helmet appeared.

"This fellow is Francisco Núñez de Salazar. Spanish explorer. Born 1484, died 1561. Could talk for hours about him, but the important thing is little Franky was sailing to China and got lost on the journey. Where he ended up, no one knows. Some think Africa, others India. Brazil is just as likely as Australia. What's *certain* is he discovered a land of green fields and lush trees, beautiful streams and waterfalls."

Next a drawing of a beautiful forest appeared.

"According to his journal, Salazar fought through the forest, searching for signs of life. He came to a ravine and saw in the center a tree bigger and more beautiful than any he had seen before. He approached it, mesmerized by its glistening bark. He ran his hands over the surface and tapped into a power no human ever felt before. He caused the seas to rise and made gold fall like rain from the sky. He could float through the branches and change himself into any creature he imagined. As long as he touched the tree, the rules of the universe bent around his will, and the feeling was intoxicating. But there was a problem. That stinkin' old tree was large, you see, its roots planted deep into the earth. What good is limitless power without the ability to move around? Which leads us to this."

She spun the wand through her plump fingers.

"The wand," I said.

She laughed. "Ah, what you call a *wand*. Raised on silly stories about witches and wizards. I prefer to call it the wicked twig, because of all the pain it's caused me, but use whatever words you like. Aye, we'll call it a wand for now. Well, the tree is a million times more powerful."

"Wow," Emma said.

"Mr. Salazar couldn't leave the tree without taking a souvenir, so he snapped a little branch off and kept it for himself. The wand only has a fraction of the power, but as you know, it can still pack a punch. Before he left the ravine, he put a spell on the wand to lead him back to the tree whenever he wanted. Provided, of course, whoever held the wand knew the special word he created."

"Special word?" Emma asked.

"A password of sorts," Ms. Bunchwick said.

"Do you know what it is?" I asked.

Her eyes glistened.

"I do," she said.

EMMA

"You know the secret word? What is it?" I asked. I couldn't believe it. My mind was already racing with what I would do with limitless power. I wanted to snatch the wand from her hand and force her to tell it to me.

I'd make myself stand out from my sisters. Longer hair. Taller, maybe. I'd always get to use the bathroom first. I'd get a hundred puppies.

"House on fire, child, don't get ahead of the story," Ms. Bunchwick said. "Like I'd tell you, anyway! *Goodness!* Francisco traveled around the world, returning to the tree whenever he needed more power than the wand could provide. To amuse himself, he performed mischievous miracles every place he went. He pulled rodents out of hats, made women float, and sawed people in half. Put most of them back together, too. He pulled scarves of the finest linen out of his sleeves. He poured expensive spices from his empty hands. He made it really hard to know which cup a ball would be under. Why, he practically invented the magic show, because everywhere he went, people tried to copy his actions. Of course, they used things like sleight of hand, wires, and false pockets, but the effects were the same. And then . . ."

She paused for effect, holding the projector's remote in the air. She clicked it and a drawing of a creepy skull appeared on the screen.

"He died. You must understand, even the wand can't stop death, and Salazar found himself, like many before him, worm food in the cold dark dirt. To keep it from falling into the wrong hands, Salazar made it that if you die with the wand, its power dies with you. Before he croaked he passed it and the secret word to his best friend, a magician called the Conjurer."

Another click, and the picture changed to a pencil drawing of a man with a large mustache.

"Was a good choice, too, because the Conjurer was an honest fellow, and realized the dangerous potential of a magical wand that could lead to a tree with unlimited power. He kept it hidden and safe, only using it on very special occasions. Before he died, he passed it on to another who he deemed was an honest magician, and it's been passed down from generation to generation ever since. A secret society was born, and the wand and the word were kept safe and hidden for centuries."

She cycled through numerous pictures of men and women who had owned the wand.

"Was a time in the seventeenth century when it was *mighty* dangerous for women to have it, 'specially when burning them at the stake was in style. Possessing this thing can be a perilous act, and it ain't wise to keep it too long. It can turn you a bit nutty, as you can see by looking at yours truly. The temptation to use it for ill can be strong at times. If an evil person with nasty intentions ever got ahold of this wand and found the tree, the whole world would be in danger."

Then I felt kind of bad about wanting to steal the wand from her. How long would it take me to use its power in a way that would hurt someone?

"Has an evil person ever gotten hold of it?" Duncan asked.

Ms. Bunchwick laughed, and it echoed on the cold cement walls of her basement.

"Of course they have," she whispered, and her fangs reappeared and her skin darkened. "That's where *I* enter the story."

DUNCAN

Ms. Bunchwick clicked the remote and a new picture appeared—this time a tall man in a tuxedo holding a bouquet of flowers.

"Seamus Kendrick," she said. "Stage name: the Dark Spirit. He was a talented magician, one of the best of his time, but he had some other names that were far worse."

She flipped to a picture of him onstage, a beautiful woman in a ruffled shirt standing beside him.

"My boss."

She clicked the button again.

Seamus stared at the woman as he levitated her in the air.

"And . . . err . . . *husband.*"

"Wait. That's you?" Emma asked.

"Aye. He was looking for a magician's assistant and I was looking for a job. He was older, famous, incredible. His tricks were amazing—like nothing you've ever seen. We performed all across Ireland. We fell in love. He fooled everyone, myself included, into thinking he was a man of good character. The wand and the word were given to us both, but we had different ideas on how to use it. Me? I wanted to hide it away. He wanted to use it for whatever he desired. That's the problem with our little secret society. You never know the true heart of a person until you give them a taste of unlimited power. It's a test many fail, and Seamus was the worst of them."

"How?" I asked.

"It started with hecklers at our shows. With the wand, it was easy to shut them up. *Permanently.* And then anyone that stood in his way disappeared or was turned into a rat or some other creature. Oh, I know, I'm guilty of the occasional transformation myself, but I always turn them back. *Always*, I promise you that."

The skin on her face started to wriggle, turning green and horrible as she talked. Tears formed in the corners of her eyes.

"We had a child together, and for a time, I thought we could be happy without the power of the wand. I begged him to pass it to the next magician but he refused. It was never enough with Seamus. He wanted more. More power, more money, more fame. He wanted to rule the world and everyone in it, but I always stopped him."

The basement lights flickered and the house rumbled. Dust fell from the ceiling and Ms. Bunchwick made a moaning sound more terrible than any I had heard before.

"There was an accident, and my dear little boy was injured badly. The wand may not be powerful enough to stop death, but it can slow it down if you're willing to use some dark magic. *No*, I told him. We can't use dark magic, no matter the reason."

Her body shook in sobs.

"Seamus took the wand, and in his anger he said the secret

word and the wand erupted in light, pointing in the direction of the tree. *See?* he said. *The power of the tree is waiting for us. So much stronger than this little twig. We can control the world. We can fix our child. We never need to hurt again.*"

Emma rubbed her eyes.

"I said no, and our boy passed away. We fought for the wand and I took it and ran. In secret, I whispered the word. I planned on finding the tree and destroying it. Ripping it out from the roots. The world doesn't need real magic, you see."

"Did you do it?"

"I couldn't," Ms. Bunchwick said.

She pointed to the top of the wand, where the bark was ragged and a different color than the rest.

"When I fought with Seamus, a small piece must have broke off. I didn't notice at first, and the spell is such that if you use the word to find the tree without the full wand, it searches your mind for the worst thing you can imagine and makes it come true."

"What happened?" I asked.

"For me, nothing. The worst thing I could imagine had already happened. There was nothing left in my head but sorrow."

There was a long pause, and Ms. Bunchwick stared at the screen, looking at the picture. She spun the wand between her fingers.

"Is Seamus still alive?" I asked.

"In my sweetest dreams he is not, but there's nothing I know for sure. When I took the wand I left Ireland and traveled for years, finally settling in the most boring town I could find. I've been hiding ever since, doing my best to keep the locals away. Change the occasional puppy to a frog and the whole town thinks you're a witch. And every town in the county has a creepy old house that kids are afraid of."

"Told you," I said to Emma.

"Now I admit to playing it up a bit, just enough to keep people from bothering me. But clearly I failed, because here you are."

"Sorry," I said.

"When you showed up at my door and I saw you were a magician, I thought I had finally been caught. Sent by Seamus, for all I knew. The legend of tree and wand is known among certain groups of magicians, but many think it's an old myth. And then you had to go ahead and steal the wand and use it to show the world that real magic exists. Now who knows what will happen? Maybe Seamus is dead, no one will figure out our secret, and things will go back to normal. Or maybe you've made us a target for every dark magician who lusts for power and we're all going to die. It's a fifty-fifty chance, I'd reckon."

"Well," I said, gulping. "Quinton Penfold did just announce that this year's Elite Magicians Convention will be held in Elephant."

Ms. Bunchwick's eyes twitched.

"Do you mean that this whole town will be swarming with magicians?"

"Umm . . . yeah."

"Fabulous," she whispered.

"How can we tell which ones are good or bad?" Emma asked.

"You can't. Not really."

"What do we do if a dark magician comes looking for us?" I asked.

We never got an answer, because there was a loud crashing sound from upstairs.

Someone had kicked down the front door.

ANOTHER ESCAPE

EMMA

I could tell by the footsteps that there were several people in the house.

Duncan jumped from his seat and hid in the corner, and Ms. Bunchwick waved the wand and cast the entire basement into darkness.

"Shhh," she said.

From upstairs, someone said, "Come out and show us your hands, ma'am. We just want the kids. Let them go and this won't get any worse."

It was Officer Ralph.

"I'll go up and talk to him," Duncan said. "He'll listen to me."

"We know you're here," Officer Ralph said, and the footsteps moved through the house.

"Hush yourself," Ms. Bunchwick said. "Ah, so dumb of me to snatch you like that. Of course the constables would be paying me a visit. Needed to warn you, see? Stupid, stupid."

We moved to the bottom of the basement stairs and listened.

"I think they're going upstairs," I said. "You have to escape now."

"We all do," she said. "Weren't you listening to anything I said? For all I know those men upstairs are working for Seamus, and it'll be on my blasted conscience if something happens to you little devils."

"Ralph?" Duncan said. "No way."

"You must never assume, boy. The heart of man is dark, and with tremendous power within its grasp, it's known to—"

She put a finger to her lips and pointed upstairs. The footsteps were softer.

She continued, whispering, "Well, you've seen movies, I'm sure, and you get the idea. Men with unlimited power ain't good, suffice it to say. Stay with me. If things turn nasty, you take the wand from me and run, understand? Keep it hidden and never use it. Trust no one."

The wand ignited in color and she morphed back into the horrible witch, her eyes shrinking to small yellow beads and her clothes transforming to dark tattered robes.

"Apologies for my appearance, but looking dreadful can be an awful powerful weapon against the weak-minded."

"Oh, I'm used to it. I've seen my mom without makeup," I said.

Ms. Bunchwick patted me on the head and turned to Duncan.

"You know that constable fellow upstairs, do you? The one with the high-pitched scream."

"Yeah. He's dating my mom."

"Aye. Seen him hanging around. You like him?"

"No. I mean. He's all right, I guess. It's complicated. Sometimes I just—"

"Should I spare him the worst?"

Duncan nodded.

We climbed the basement stairs and she opened the door slowly, leaning out into the hall. Officer Ralph and the others were upstairs, and by the sounds of it, were almost done kicking in the doors to every room and closet.

"Antique hinges," Ms. Bunchwick moaned, rubbing her forehead. "Do you have any idea the headache I'll have finding those again? Follow me, now. Quickly."

We snuck down the hallway, walking lightly as the floorboards creaked under our feet. We were close to the kitchen when the noises upstairs stopped and a man's voice said, "Do you hear that?"

"Someone's downstairs," another said.

"Duncan? Is that you?" Officer Ralph yelled.

"Keep very quiet," Ms. Bunchwick said. "Slide your little feet as softly as you can."

We turned into the kitchen and almost made it to the back door, when Officer Ralph appeared in the living room, gun drawn, moving toward us.

"Freeze!" he yelled. "Put your hands up! Show me they're empty."

"My, my," Ms. Bunchwick cackled, pushing us behind her. "Come to visit me again, dear constable? What must I do to keep you away for good? Turn you into a walrus and throw you into the sea?"

"I'm not leaving without Duncan. Hand him over."

"What about me?" I asked.

Officer Ralph blinked and looked at me.

"Oh, yeah. Hi, Emma. You too, of course."

Two other police officers came beside him, their guns raised.

"These kids are coming with me," Ms. Bunchwick said, walking toward Officer Ralph.

"Stop right there! I'm warning you!"

"Won't be safe anywhere else," she replied.

"Hand him over, now! His mom is very worried."

"What about me? Aren't my parents worried?" I asked.

"I . . . um . . . well, I haven't had a chance to tell them, yet. Sorry, Emma."

Perfect. My very first hostage situation, and my parents didn't even know about it.

Ms. Bunchwick moved forward, sliding her foot near her umbrella stand. She kicked one into the air and grabbed it, spinning it around and pointing the metal tip at the police officers.

"Don't move!" one of them screamed.

"Boom," she said and the umbrella sprang open.

The guns flew out of their hands and morphed into bats, wings flapping against the ceiling. She spun the wand and sent a wall of crackling static electricity toward them, knocking them over.

"Let's fly," she said.

The police officers shook on the floor from the tiny shocks, and in a quick motion she kicked open the door and placed the umbrella between her knees. We grabbed onto her arms and she jumped off from the ground.

The bats followed us into the night, and we flew through the clouds, hidden in the mist.

"May have underestimated the trouble," Ms. Bunchwick said. She popped the end of the wand in the corner of her mouth and bit it, the glow lighting her face. "So I suppose you need to know how to use this."

MAGIC LESSONS

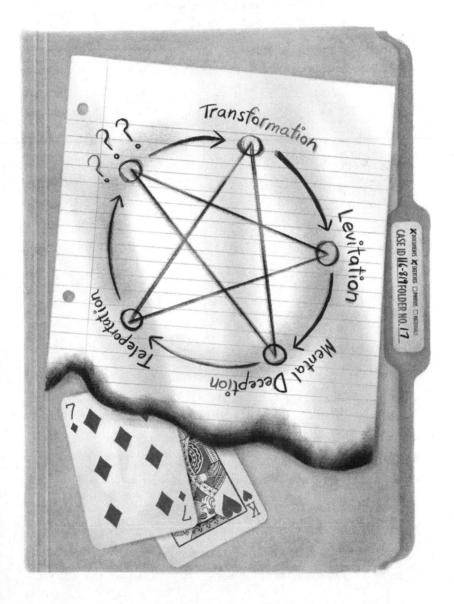

DUNCAN

Ms. Bunchwick screamed into the night and we flew faster, the ground speeding below us until we were at least twenty miles from town.

"Too dangerous for me here," she said. "Really should have taken off and left you two to deal with the problems. But you'd be targets for all kinds of evil, I fear, and I'm too nice for my own good. Teaching is the only option."

There was nothing but woods in every direction, and we landed on a patch of grass on top of a hill. Fog crept from the shadows between the tall trees, and unnatural sounds filled the air.

She grabbed me and Emma by the hands and said, "You must convince your parents and that Ralph fellow that I ain't the devil, you hear? I can live with the rest of the town thinking it, but life will be easier without the constables messing with us every day."

She pulled off the gum from the center of the wand and handed one half to me and the other to Emma.

"You've been using this too haphazardly, getting results here and there with no purpose or reason. You think you have control but it's sloppy and loose. Are you controlling the wand or is it controlling you? Mighty dangerous way to live."

The wand sent a tingle down my arm and made my heart beat faster.

Ms. Bunchwick drew a star on the ground with her toe and circled the five pointed sections.

"I've had years to play around with the wand and have found that it can do magic in five main categories. You must be careful in how you use them. Harm can come to others if you have meanness in your heart, and then you'd be just as bad as Seamus, understand?"

I nodded, but I was thinking about how I had turned Libby Blackburn into a goat and had put snakes in Tommy's shoes, and rats in Wilson's and Juan's underwear and felt kind of bad.

"Lesson one, *transformation*."

Ms. Bunchwick took my hand and pointed it at Emma, then took Emma's hand and pointed it at me.

"Think of a creature and then picture each other changing into it. Go!"

I thought of a mole rat and imagined Emma changing into one.

My vision went blurry and the world grew around me. The wand fell from my hands. My stomach dropped and I felt like I was falling from a high cliff. Ms. Bunchwick towered above me. I tried to walk and fell over, my legs kicking in the air. They were hairy and covered in white fur. Two long ears flopped over my face and a mole rat came beside me and bit me.

I yelled out, but it was a high-pitched squeal instead of my usual manly scream.

Ms. Bunchwick picked up the pieces of wand and changed us back to our normal selves.

Emma hit me on the arm.

"Eww! What kind of animal did you make me?"

"A mole rat."

"Mole rat? I made you a cute little bunny and you made me a *mole rat*?"

"Fight kindly, children. What's done is done. That's what it feels like to be transformed. Not pleasant, is it?"

I sat on the ground, coughing, trying not to throw up.

"No, it's terrible."

"I feel like I ate a pound of sugar," Emma said, holding her stomach.

"Aye, think on that before you change an innocent person into a goat, young Duncan. It feels one way to turn yourself into something, but totally different when someone does it to you when you ain't prepared. And you don't need to change into a real animal. Can just as easily be a creature of your own creation."

She pointed the wand at herself and changed into the witch, with scaly green flesh and thick black robes. She screamed and jumped at me, changing back midair and landing on the ground, laughing as she brushed dirt from her dress.

"Only thing limiting you is your own imagination. Perhaps I should have thought of something scarier than a bog-standard old witch to keep the town away."

She smudged out a section of the star.

"Lesson two, *levitation*."

Her feet left the ground and she lifted up into the air and spun around, hanging upside down, so her long hair cascaded over her face.

"It can be hard to steer yourself in the air, so it's best to sit on something straight and true to point you in the right direction. I won't fib to you, levitation is the funnest type of magic the wicked twig can do, and it's also the most versatile. And levitation ain't just for you—it's for anything *around* you as well."

She waved the wand at a small branch on the ground and flicked it upward, then waved her other hand back and forth like she was directing an orchestra. The branch followed weightless in the air, flying in a delicate pattern of spins and turns. She snatched it in the air and clenched it between her knees, flipping herself upright and throwing half the wand to Emma.

"Duncan's experimented with this one, ain't he? Well, it's your turn now, dear."

Emma grabbed the wand and stared at the glowing tip, the dangerous power reflecting off her face.

"What do I do?" she asked.

"The important thing is to focus your mind. Size and weight don't matter if you don't think on it. It takes a strong mind, and if you ain't intimidated by it, you could move an oil tanker."

Ms. Bunchwick pointed at a rock. It was hardly bigger than

a pebble, and Emma pointed the wand at it and squinted her eyes, sending daggers of concentration through the air.

"You're thinking too hard," Ms. Bunchwick said. "Relax. Let it breathe."

The rock trembled and rolled over. It lifted an inch into the air before returning to the ground.

"It's a start," Ms. Bunchwick said.

"That's nothing," I said. "Watch this."

I guess sometimes I still like to impress Emma, so I took the wand from her and pointed at the largest boulder I could see, flicking my wrist upward. The ground rumbled and the boulder ripped from the ground and lifted into the air. My head buzzed, like a hive of bees had been let loose between my ears, and a warm trickle of blood dripped from my nose.

"Use your other hand, boy! Don't think on its size. It's only a feather."

I flicked the wand up again and waved my other hand in the air. The boulder lifted higher. It was easier now, just a slight tingle in my fingers.

"Good, boy! Higher!"

"Let me try!" Emma yelled. She grabbed the wand from my hand and the boulder crashed back to earth, knocking over a small tree. She pointed the wand and caught the tree before it hit the ground, levitating it so it stood straight in the air.

"Perfect!" Ms. Bunchwick yelled. "Lift it!"

"How?" Emma screamed.

"Picture it going higher! Use your hands!"

Emma raised her hands and the roots of the tree ripped

from the ground. It flew through the air until it was the tallest in the forest. Ms. Bunchwick clapped.

"Now spin it!"

Emma pointed a finger in the air and spun the tree like a dancer, lifting above the others. It flipped upside down and hovered in the air.

"Plant it!"

Emma balled her fists and slammed them down. The tree fell to the ground, the top sticking into the dirt. It wobbled uneasily before settling.

"That'a girl!" Ms. Bunchwick cheered. "You're a natural."

"Should I put it back?" Emma asked.

"Nothing wrong with a little mischief here and there, you see? Keeps people on their toes. On to lesson three."

"Give it back," I said. I wasn't too happy that she had taken the piece of wand from me, and I had this cool idea to pull ten trees out of the ground, roots and all, and have them wrestle in the sky.

"No," Emma said, clutching the wand.

"*Give it!*"

"*No.*"

Ms. Bunchwick landed on the ground.

"As I was saying, lesson three. This is the most powerful thing the wand can do, on account of—"

I reached for the wand and Emma bit my hand.

"Just for a second," I said, but she was being too greedy and kept the wand clutched in her stupid fingers.

"I'm older than you," Emma said.

"By three months."

"So what? Older is older. Every minute counts."

"You stop it now," Ms. Bunchwick said, pointing her half of the wand at us. "That wicked twig is already corrupting you with thoughts of power and magic, and I can't stand to see it. Lesson thr—"

"I *want* it," I said. "I found it, anyway. Why do you get to—"

"Oh, you shut up. I'm sick of you always thinking I'm—"

The ground rumbled.

"You hear that?" Ms. Bunchwick asked.

We stopped arguing and looked behind us. A noise was coming from the distance, but it was getting closer and louder. Trees bent to the side and cracked in half, and a roar swept through them.

"Who is it?" Emma asked.

"*Who* might be the wrong word. *What* is it?"

A giant wave of water appeared, like something from a disaster movie. We weren't anywhere near an ocean, just a few small lakes and rivers, and I screamed as the wave grew in the air and rolled toward us, reflecting dark blue light from the moon before sweeping us away with its unimaginable force.

EMMA

I couldn't breathe. I fought toward the surface, but it seemed far away.

The water pushed us through the trees, and little silver fish swam around us.

We went up and down. Upside down.

I could see Duncan through the water, thrashing his arms, fighting against the current.

I didn't want to die like this, not now. My lungs burned and I felt like going to sleep. The water pushed against me like a dark, heavy blanket. I clutched the wand, but I couldn't get it to do anything.

Poor Duncan, I thought. *Almost drowned at the talent show, and now he'll drown for real.*

Duncan had been a total jerk to me lately, but I still reached for him, grabbing his hand and pulling myself toward him.

I stared into his eyes, and saw that same sad, blinking look I had seen the first day of kindergarten. So much had changed, but in a way, nothing had. I wanted to tell him I was sorry. I felt really bad for all the times I had been mean to him.

He opened his mouth and a stream of bubbles came out.

We continued through the forest, moving faster, narrowly avoiding big tree trunks and branches.

We hugged each other tight, unable to do anything but move with the flow of the water.

I wondered what my family would think when they found I'd drowned in the forest. Anna and Jenna would probably laugh and say, "Only *she* could drown in a place with no water."

And where did the water come from, anyway? It didn't make any sense.

There was a light in the distance and I pulled Duncan toward it.

It was moving, up and down, left and right.

Then I saw a hand attached to the light and as I pulled Duncan closer I saw Ms. Bunchwick's face, floating in front of us.

She smiled and snapped her fingers and the water evaporated into thin air.

Just like that, we were on the ground, and our clothes were completely dry.

We were back where we started.

"What? *What?*" Duncan sputtered.

"As I was saying," Ms. Bunchwick said, clearing her throat. "Lesson three, *mental deception*. One of the most powerful kinds of magic. For the first ten years I had the wand, I didn't understand how to use it. Now that I do . . . well, it's quite astonishing."

"Where did the water go?" Duncan asked.

"Not a drop around us. It was only in your mind."

She looked at me.

"You remember the fire?"

She held the wand up straight between her eyes, and squinted, a small smile cracking on her face, and the whole forest erupted in flames. The heat baked my cheeks, and flames rose higher into the air. The skeletons of birds flew in the sky, their charred feathers drifting to the ground. Smoke surrounded us and I could hardly see.

With a snap, the fire disappeared.

Duncan spun in circles, touching tree leaves to see if they were still hot.

"I can make you think just about anything if I want. Use it too long and cracks begin to appear in the illusion. The person is likely to figure out the trick. But in small doses it can be quite powerful. Just be careful where you use this. Someone's likely to run off a building if you ain't careful, and if no one's around to catch them"—she clapped her hands loudly—"splat!"

She repositioned the wand in my hand, balancing it between my thumb and finger, and pointed it at Duncan.

"You try," she said.

"How do I do it?"

"Think whatever you want. Imagine the thought leaving your mind, soaring through the air, and squeezing in through his ears. Go ahead."

I imagined the tallest mountain I could, covered in snow and ice, and thought of the picture I had in my mind entering Duncan's mind.

"Wow!" he yelled. "Look at the view!"

Duncan moved to a rock and jumped on top of it, using his hand to shield his eyes as he stared into the side of a tree.

"I can see forever, and the sun is so bright. I must be a million miles high."

He looked really goofy standing on the rock and I looked at Ms. Bunchwick and laughed.

"Even the air smells different."

He spun around and I imagined a giant eagle soaring through the air, swooping down to attack him.

Duncan screamed and ran, and the witch snatched the wand from my fingers and waved it at him.

"Quite enough of that, young lady. Except for occasional mischief, we only use magic for good. Evil starts small. Before you know it you're the bad guy in a story."

Ms. Bunchwick paced the ground of the forest, her legs stirring the mist.

"On to lesson four, *teleportation*."

She bent down and picked up a small frog, holding it in the palm of her hand. She pointed the wand at it, and it was gone.

"It disappeared!" I yelled, clapping my hands and making a mental list of all the things I'd make vanish as soon as I had some precious alone time with the wand.

"Laws of the universe state that nothing can ever *really* disappear," Ms. Bunchwick said. "It may be gone from where it *were*, but now it exists where it *weren't*, if you catch my meaning."

She opened her other hand and the frog leapt out, ribbiting as it ran away.

"Mighty valuable skill, being able to make something move

from here to there. The distance you can manage is dependent on how much you practice, and I'd advise you to spend some time building the muscles."

She pointed at the boulder Duncan had lifted and it vanished. "Farthest I've managed to move something is a few hundred feet. Handy way to move yourself around if you're in a pinch."

She disappeared and appeared on the far side of the forest, and then disappeared again and appeared in front of us.

She gave us each a piece of the wand, and said, "Imagine each other someplace else, in as much detail as you can manage. Vague images won't work. You need to *see* where you're sending something, otherwise it's likely to reappear smack in the middle of a tree, and that can make a bloody mess, I tell you. Show the wand exactly where you want something to be if you want it to abide."

I stared behind Duncan and memorized every branch of the woods around us and closed my eyes, picturing it as clearly as I could. When I opened them he was there. I teleported to the other side of the forest and then next to Duncan.

"That's *awesome!*" Duncan yelled.

"Aye, and it's the end of our lessons for tonight."

She snatched the pieces of wand from us.

"I'll keep these for now. We'll practice more tomorrow."

"Wait a minute," Duncan said, pointing at the star in the circle. "You forgot one. You said the wand can do five things. Lesson one, *transformation.* Lesson two, *levitation.* Lesson three, *mental deception.* Lesson four, *teleportation.*"

"You managed to count that high without the use of your fingers?" Ms. Bunchwick asked. "Aye, I did say there was five, didn't I? It ain't that I forgot one, young man, but there's nothing more for me to teach tonight."

She spit out her gum and wrapped it tightly around the pieces of the wand and waved it at her umbrella. It flew over to us and she grabbed it by the top and squeezed it between her knees, extending the handle, and motioning for us to join her.

We sat down behind her and she jumped from the ground, flying through the air, out of the woods, and back toward town.

She leaned back and talked loudly, the wind whipping her hair in our faces.

"The fifth thing the wand can do is dark magic, and it's a lesson I won't ever teach you. Curses, death, pain, turmoil—all span from dark magic. But the allure of dark magic ain't just the nasty evil things you can do; it's the things you can do that *seem* right at first glance. Sometimes, you think you are doing something for good, even though your methods might be evil. Had Seamus cured our boy with his dark curses, it would have turned out wrong, I promise you. Dark magic is powerful bad, and it ain't worth it, children, because the evil will seep out in unexpected ways. That's why the wand is so dangerous, and why it must not fall into the fingers of an evil-hearted magician."

"Ms. Bunchwick," I asked. "Why don't we just destroy the wand? We could throw it into a volcano or grind it to dust."

"Ah, a volcano! You've been reading too many books, young lady. If you throw this wicked twig into a volcano, it's likely to make the whole thing erupt for years in protest. And as we know, snapping this thing in half gives each piece half of the power, so I reckon if you grind it into dust you'll have magical dust. What do you do with it then? Throw it in the ocean? You're likely to cause the water to revolt. I've thought a lot about this, you see, and protecting it is the best way."

"I'll do whatever I can to help," I said, and I really meant it, even though it was taking all of my self-control not to snatch the wand from her and keep it for myself.

"Me too," Duncan said.

She laughed and patted our heads.

"I know you will. You're good kids."

"What can we do?" I asked.

"First things first, we need to get you home. And you both need to convince your parents that I'm not as terrible as they think. Will be a real hindrance if they do. If things get as bad as I think they will, we're going to need everyone we can fighting for us."

DARK MAGICIANS

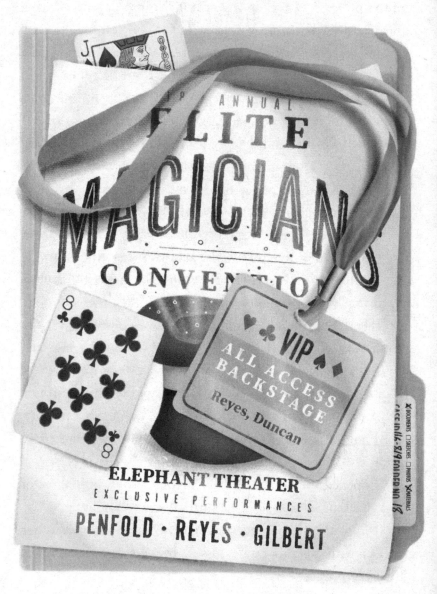

DUNCAN

From the sky, my street looked like a Christmas tree blinking in the darkness, the lights of a half dozen police cars surrounding it.

You know, just another normal night at the Reyes house.

Zug's van was there, and Emma's parents' minivan was parked out front, which I could tell made her pretty happy.

Ms. Bunchwick dropped us across the street and Emma and I ran to the front door.

The house was full of cops, and I could see through the window that Dad was pacing in the living room talking to Zug, and Emma's parents were making phone calls in the kitchen. Mom was sitting on the couch with a blanket wrapped around her shoulders, and Ralph was next to her, holding her hand.

Pretty dramatic, if you ask me. We were gone, what, three hours?

I opened the door and they surrounded us, pulling us in and checking us over to make sure we were all right.

"Stop it!" Emma yelled as Mrs. Gilbert smothered her cheeks with wet, motherly kisses, but I knew she kind of liked it.

"Hang on," Ralph said. "How do we know this is really them?"

"Of course it's them," Mom said.

Still, he asked us a bunch of questions, like our birthdays and middle names, the names of our first pets, and who our favorite magician was.

"Zug," we both said in unison.

Ralph told the other cops they could leave.

"Just checking," Ralph whispered as the last one closed the front door. "For all we knew, you could have been some trick by the witch."

"How did you get away?" Dad asked. "Ralph and all his police buddies couldn't manage it."

Ralph glared.

"We . . . I . . . well . . . ," Emma said.

"We should lock the doors," Mr. Gilbert said. "She could have followed them."

"Locks don't matter to the witch," Ralph said. "I'm not even sure a maximum security prison would hold her."

"Where did she take you?" Mrs. Gilbert asked.

There was really no way to answer any of those questions without spilling the whole story, so once again I found myself in the position of recounting everything to a room full of adults, who I was sure would do anything in their power to stop me from having any fun with the wand.

"Remember that curse I told you about?" I began. "Well, it wasn't exactly true."

I told them the real story of what happened in the witch's

house—how I broke her wand in half, how the piece I took could do real magic, and how evil people might be looking for us now. I explained how she taught us to use the wand to protect ourselves and that she was (just as I always suspected) a misunderstood weirdo that we never should have been afraid of.

"So yeah," I said. "That's about everything. If she's right, a bunch of dark magicians should be coming to town any day now. We have to help her and protect the wand; otherwise an evil person could use it to gain unlimited power and potentially destroy the world. Any questions? Because it's getting late, and I'd kind of like to go to bed."

The adults stared at me.

I admit, it was a lot to take in all at once.

"They must have Stockholm syndrome," Ralph said. "That's the only answer."

"We have what?" I asked.

Emma touched her forehead and said, "I have been feeling a bit warm."

"After three hours? Seriously, Ralph?" Mom asked.

"Listen to them. They sympathize with their kidnapper."

Mom glared, and finally turned to us and asked, "What do you want us to do?"

"Well, there is *something*," I said. "But don't freak out."

"What?" the adults asked in unison.

"It's just . . . well . . ."

"Duncan, what is it?" Mom asked.

I opened the front door and yelled, "You can come in now!"

Ms. Bunchwick teleported across the road and stepped inside, scanning the room with suspicious eyes.

"Mercy," she said, staring at the floor and rubbing her toe in the carpet. "Ain't been around this many adults since . . . well, I can't even recall. Weird, isn't it? Yes, a bit. Good evening. Pleasure to meet all of you, even if it is in such an odd manner. The name is Edna Bunchwick, and I want to apologize front and center for ruining your lives."

Mom screamed and hid behind the couch.

Emma's parents made the sign of the cross.

Ralph fainted.

EMMA

So that's how the adults met Ms. Bunchwick.

After Officer Ralph regained consciousness, she showed them the wand, did a few transformations to prove she was the real deal, and they agreed to help her. Good thing, too. I don't even want to think about what would have happened without them.

With the news of the Elite Magicians Convention coming to town, the next week at school we had gone from the scary kids that everyone wanted to avoid to the famous kids that everyone wanted to be around.

We'd walk through the halls, flanked by our entourage, kids swooning and laughing at our every word. It was everything I always dreamed of.

By now, our videos had been viewed over thirteen million times.

We were a pretty big deal.

Tommy, Wilson, and Juan still avoided us, probably because they knew they could have killed Duncan at the talent show and were really scared about what we could do to them.

Please. They were small potatoes, and we had bigger issues

on our hands, mainly the upcoming convention and the threat of dark magicians.

Buses and trucks came to town that weekend and started setting up stuff at the theater in the center of town. Elephant was smaller than they were used to, so additional stands and stages were set up outside and in local stores. Our parents were really worried about us, and Officer Ralph followed us around all the time for protection.

"Doubt anyone's dumb enough to grab you in plain daylight," Ms. Bunchwick told us. "They'll come in the dark or when you're least expecting it."

That made me feel *so* much better.

The entire town had gone magic crazy, and Zug's shop was pounded with visitors, half of them looking to buy tricks, the other half asking for our autographs.

We were superstars, but we still helped him out after school, answering questions and ringing up about a million cup-and-ball magic sets every day.

"Maybe we should come up with our own magic sets, slap our faces on them, and sell them for three times the price," I said, but Duncan wasn't interested. He was too worried about the swarm of magicians coming to the town, and trying to tell which ones were good and which ones were bad.

That was hard, but at least it was easy to tell who was a magician. Adult magicians all kind of look like the dorky kid in class who grew up and is now trying really hard to look cool. Like, they seem to always wear bright suits or expensive tuxedos, and often have facial hair that's cut in funny shapes and angles. Oh, and their hair is almost *always* slicked back in gross greasy strands. I told Duncan it's like looking into his future.

He didn't like that at all, let me tell you.

Things slipped into a nice routine. We'd go to school in the day, Zug's shop in the afternoon, home for dinner in the evening, then the woods at night where Ms. Bunchwick would be waiting for us. She was a great teacher, and taught us lots of cool ways to use the wand. It didn't take long for me to get the hang of it, and even though Duncan had had a ton more time with it in the beginning, I was soon levitating bigger rocks and trees than he could even dream of.

Ms. Bunchwick sat with No Name curled on her lap and whittled sticks around a campfire, watching us out of the corner of her eye and barking instructions.

"Faster! More with the wrist! Keep your arm straight! No kicking!"

Duncan and I ran around the woods, teleporting around the forest and flying through the trees.

"Ms. Bunchwick, why is your cat named No Name?" I asked one night, spinning around and transforming Duncan into a mangy-looking dog.

No Name hissed and leapt at him.

"Because I never gave him no name," Ms. Bunchwick said, shaking her head like it was the stupidest question she had ever heard.

We'd talk for hours. She told us crazy stories about her days touring with Seamus, and all the famous magicians she had met.

It was pretty nice, and I would have been happy if things stayed that way.

But that weekend was the Elite Magicians Conference. Duncan and I were the opening act. If anyone out there knew about the wand and thought we had it, we had to show them otherwise. Our plan was to do some simple tricks for the audience, the kind that everyone had seen a bunch of times. After that, no one would think we had real magic powers, and this would all blow over, just as quickly as it had started. Our reputations would be ruined, but at least we'd be alive.

Then Duncan went and screwed everything up.

If he just would have stuck with our plan, things might have been different.

But he couldn't help himself, could he?

I shouldn't be too hard on him. I don't know what I would have done if I met my hero. I probably would have done anything they asked, too.

In case you haven't guessed, this is where Quinton Penfold entered our lives.

QUINTON PENFOLD

DUNCAN

For an early October afternoon, it was unusually warm, and I felt like I was crawling out of my skin all day. Fridays were always like that, but on this particular one I just wanted to get out of school and for this whole Elite Magicians Convention to be over with.

Zug drove us through town and I watched the crowds gathering on the streets. It was weird seeing so many people in Elephant, and buses were coming in every hour, filling the Lobster Hut and strip mall parking lots. All the hotels were booked, and a bunch of families rented out their houses and left for the weekend. They were the smart ones.

"We'll start our show with the cut-and-restore shoelace," Emma said. "That's the biggest snoozer we have."

"Right. Then we'll go to the Mentalist's Pocket Watch. It didn't even fool my mom the first time I did it."

"It's the *worst*," Emma moaned, and laughed in her seat.

Basically, you could have an audience member set the time on a watch, put it in a bag, and then you'd guess the time. Whoopee. The watch was so obviously gimmicked that you'd have to be half asleep to be fooled.

Zug shook his head. "I used to open my show with that."

"Then on to our grand finale," I said. "The teleporting fruit box."

"Terrible!" Emma yelled.

We were going to be the worst magic act ever. If we were lucky, the other magicians would boo us off the stage and we'd never be heard from again.

Career suicide, but it was our only choice.

Maybe someday I'd change my name, wear a mask, and try to rebuild my career. For now, I just wanted to stay alive.

When we got to Zug's shop, there was already a line forming outside. The crowd cheered when we stepped out of the car, and camera flashes went off. We shuffled toward the front door, hiding our faces like famous people and felons do.

Emma stopped and did a twirl and a bow as Zug unlocked the door and changed the sign from Closed to Open.

There was a relentless stream of people into the store that afternoon, and even though they clearly weren't from Elephant, they still asked the same old questions and bought the same old tricks.

Svengali deck. Magic sets. Bite-out quarter. Disappearing hanky. And, of course, the pen through dollar bill (which I warned younger kids wasn't worth the trouble).

Most of them wanted to get their picture taken with us, and the rest looked over all the tricks and display cases. Like magic, time seemed to disappear. The hours seemed to slip by, and every second brought me closer to the big day.

I don't remember exactly when *he* came in, but I do

remember how the crowd went completely silent and then parted down the middle. People pressed their backs against the walls and let him enter. They stood on their tiptoes to get a peek at him and whispered his name.

There he was.

In Zug's store.

A million times cooler in person than he had ever looked on TV.

Quinton. *Freaking*. Penfold.

He was taller than I expected, his long hair pouring down to his shoulders, and half a dozen scarves around his neck. His eyes, surrounded by dark makeup, scanned the shop and made him seem even more mysterious than he was in his TV specials. He was wearing all black except for a brightly colored vest, and a dozen necklaces dangled over it, with all kinds of charms and symbols. He had beaded bracelets on both wrists, and he waved in my direction, a friendly smile cracking on his usual, serious face.

"Duncan!" he yelled, like we were old friends. "There he is, the magical young boy."

I felt like I had been punched in the stomach, and managed to squeak out a few sounds.

He came closer, stopped and snapped his fingers. Flames burst from his fingertips and a bird appeared in the smoke, wings flapping as it lifted from his hand and perched on top of Zug's cash register.

The crowd went nuts.

"I asked around town," Quinton said, his deep voice

masking a hint of a faraway, mysterious accent. "Everyone told me I'd find you here. And where else should I look for the magical *Duncan Reyes* than a magic store?"

"Mr. Penfold, it's a real honor to have you here," Zug said, extending his hand for a shake. "The name's Zug. I used to perform as the Amazing Zuggarino."

"Pleasure to meet you, Zug," Quinton said. "What a cute shop."

Zug smiled.

"So what can we help you with?"

"I see that you're busy, so I will be quick. I have come to extend an invitation for young Duncan to assist me in a trick during my presentation at the Elite Magicians Convention tomorrow." He turned to the crowd and winked. "I am the headlining act. Tomorrow. Five o'clock. Be there."

"No, thanks," Emma said. "We're already performing."

"And who is this?" Quinton asked, extending a hand to Emma.

"I'm Duncan's co-magician," Emma said.

"Ah, she's your *assistant*, no?" Quinton asked.

"No," Emma said. "Co-magician."

"Yes," I said.

"Duncan, I only ask for your help tomorrow in the same manner you might use your assistant. Simply follow some instructions, and together, we will create a breathtaking illusion. No practice is required, but it would be ever so helpful if we could get some video of the two of us onstage together. Your popularity is rising, young boy, and my publicist would be forever in your debt if you would allow me to share the stage with you."

Share the stage with *me*? I couldn't think. Of course I'd help him. I said yes before I even considered our plan and how important it was for us to do a horrible job at the show the next day.

And how many times in life do you get to do a trick with *Quinton Penfold*?

"Excellent," Quinton said, and in a flash of sparkles and smoke, he vanished completely.

EMMA

Seeing a celebrity up close is kind of a disappointment. In person, Quinton Penfold looked like a pirate who had survived an explosion in a teen fashion store.

You don't realize how silly a full-grown man looks wearing thickly caked black eye makeup and a bunch of scarves until they're standing right in front of you. Quinton jingled when he walked. He had more jewelry around his neck and wrists than my sisters own (combined), and his greasy hair was practically screaming, "Hey, buddy! Shampoo me!"

He smelled like baked beans.

I wasn't impressed.

Quinton snapped his fingers and his hand erupted in flames. A dove appeared and flew around the store, resting on the counter next to Zug.

Duncan's reaction to Quinton was a little different than mine. He went all weak in the knees, and blubbered and shook. Everyone in the store felt embarrassed for him, and I moved closer in case he passed out.

"What can we help you with, Mr. Penfold?" Zug asked. "It's an honor to have you in my store."

"The honor is all mine! Elephant is such a remarkably quaint town. Sometimes the biggest talents come from the humblest beginnings, so I've come to extend an invitation for young Duncan and Emma to assist me in a trick during my presentation at the convention tomorrow."

"Forget it," I said. "We're already performing."

"I'll do it," Duncan said.

"*Duncan,*" I whispered.

"It would be an . . . um . . . honor, sir . . . um . . . just to be in your . . . um . . . presence."

"Well, you can count me out." I stomped my foot. Duncan was totally *not* sticking to our plan.

"But I can't do it without you, Emma," Quinton said. "You're a co-magician, every bit as important as Duncan."

"Nope. Not happening."

"Please?" he begged. He held out a hand, his fingers covered in rings, each more tacky than the last. You won't believe this, but he even had *two* on his pinkie. Yuck.

"I need both of your assistance with a trick. You don't need to practice. Simply follow some instructions and everything will work out fine for everyone. You children are the reason we're here, after all, and my publicist would be eternally grateful if I could get some video of myself performing onstage with you."

"Sorry," I said.

Quinton clutched his heart, stumbling backward.

"Your resistance has wounded me, young lady. I seek only

to help *all* of our careers. Very well. I will see *you*, master Duncan, at the show tomorrow."

He clapped his hands and in an explosion of smoke, ran awkwardly out of the store, tripping a bit on the floor mat and setting off the little bell above the door, his dove watching from the counter like a forgotten child in a grocery store.

Before the end of our shift, that stupid bird pooped six times on the carpet.

THE WICKED TWIG

DUNCAN

In the woods that night, the dark red moon hung over the tops of the trees, and creatures moved restlessly in the cold fall air.

Ms. Bunchwick had made a fire in the center of the clearing, and we watched as the embers twirled in the smoke, rising through the branches and into the sky.

No Name licked his paw and purred on top of a tree stump and Ms. Bunchwick gathered a pile of sticks. She pulled out a knife and began to whittle, sliding the blade smoothly over the bark.

"What are you doing?" I asked.

"Just keeping myself occupied."

"Can we turn these rocks into marshmallows?" Emma asked. "I want to cook s'mores."

"No time for that," she said. "You need to practice."

Emma and I each took half of the wand. We flew above the trees, turned into horrible creatures, teleported, and moved the biggest rocks we could find. I tried even harder to beat her that night because I was still mad at how rude she was to Quinton Penfold.

"You're going to get us killed," Emma said. "We had a plan and the first time you caught sight of Quinton's silly scarves you blew the whole thing."

"I did not," I said. "If I had said no, that would have raised more suspicion. Besides, we still don't know who's *good* and who's *bad*, do we?"

Emma slapped me.

"Stop it, you two," Ms. Bunchwick said.

"I bet Quinton's bad, and then you'll feel like the biggest fool in the world," she yelled.

"Quinton can't be bad; he's on TV. Besides, I'll just be onstage with him for a minute and everyone will be watching. Seriously, what could happen that—"

"STOP IT!" Ms. Bunchwick screamed. "I can't have you two bickering on a night like this."

She grabbed us by the hands and we lifted up, going higher and higher until we were over the tops of the trees and could see the town in the distance, flashing with lights and excitement.

"If anyone ought to be yelling, it's me," she said, pointing. "There it is. My greatest fear, realized completely, and sitting smack in front of me. Hundreds of magicians in Elephant, mere miles from my front door. Since I heard they were coming, my stomach feels like it's full of acorns, all rattling around. Still, you don't see me treating you like you're treating each other, do you?"

"No," Emma said.

"I'm really sorry," I said.

"Don't be sorry. Truth is, I'm not as scared for me as I once was, you understand? It's the two of you that I'm fretting for. Been so long since I cared for anyone that the feelings took me by surprise, if I ain't lying. Made me feel all sick and gooey inside."

We floated back down to the ground, and sat beside the fire. Emma leaned her head against Ms. Bunchwick.

"Are we going to be okay?" Emma asked.

"I don't know," Ms. Bunchwick said. "Must be careful and assume everyone out there wants what we have."

"Ralph will be at the show," I said. "And a bunch of his police friends. They won't let anything happen to us."

"Oh, I do hope you're right," she said, then grabbed our shoulders and pulled us tight, staring deeply into the flames.

"There was a time not long ago I had every intention of hanging on to this wicked twig and letting myself slip into the darkness with it clenched in my fingers, taking its power out of the world with me. But what would that do? The tree would still be out there, and who's to say someone couldn't stumble upon it by accident?"

"Well, it's been hundreds of years and no one has," Emma said.

"Aye, but the world is smaller than it once was. People are expanding, and what once was well hidden may not be anymore. Once this is over, the tree must be destroyed."

She held the two pieces of the wand in the air.

"If Seamus is still alive, he'll find my house and look for it there, so it ain't smart that I should hang on to this. Better for you to have it for now. Duncan, I'd recommend you keep yours with you, just in case. Emma, hide yours somewhere no one will suspect. Must keep it safe. Use it only if you have to."

Emma twirled her half in her hand.

"We'll protect it," she said.

I nodded. "You can trust us, Ms. Bunchwick."

"Oh, I know I can trust you. That ain't my fear."

We leaned in closer, watching the fire until it went out, then returned back to town, ready for whatever would happen the next day at the Elite Magicians Convention.

✦ EMMA ✦

So anyway, the next day was the Elite Magicians Convention and everything that went with it. Once again, my lawyer has advised me to be very careful with what I say.

THE ELEPHANT THEATER

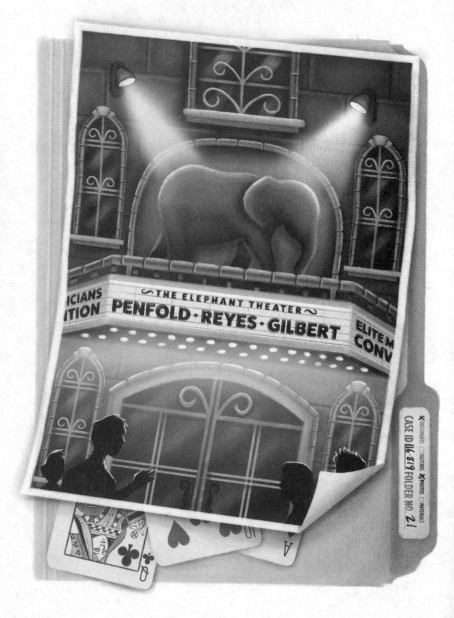

DUNCAN

Saturday morning the streets of Elephant were packed with people. Police barricades were set up, diverting traffic from the center of town, and loud music pumped from speakers surrounding the Elephant Rock.

There were giant posters advertising Quinton Penfold's appearance slapped on the front of buildings, as well as a dozen other signs announcing mystical and mysterious acts that would perform throughout the weekend.

Food vendors pushed around carts, and I couldn't help but wonder if someone out there was buying a hot dog and simultaneously plotting my demise. Ralph followed behind us in plainclothes and dark sunglasses, keeping an eye out for anyone that seemed suspicious.

Mom and I walked toward the Elephant Theater, stopping briefly under a thirty-foot-high poster made from a screenshot from the video of Emma's and my talent show performance.

TODAY ONLY! DUNCAN REYES AND EMMA GILBERT! PERFORMING LIVE @ 11 A.M.!

It didn't take long for the crowd to spot me, and people held up their phones and took pictures, screaming my name. I waved and tried not to look.

"Are you ready?" Mom asked.

"Yeah," I said, but we both knew it was a lie. No one could be ready for something like this.

We passed one of Ralph's friends guarding the alleyway beside the theater, and he stepped aside and waved us through.

Mr. Gilbert's Mercedes was parked in the private lot that was reserved for performers.

The Elephant Theater was a historic building, with an outline of the rock carved into its tall stone front. My name was on the marquee, right next to Quinton's.

A dream come true.

Now I had to sabotage it.

Inside, the carpet on the lobby floor was bloodred. Gold-flecked columns went the whole way to the high ceiling, which was painted with scenes of cherubs and rolling countrysides.

The Elephant Theater was the kind of place Mom and I would normally never go to. It was meant for different types of people than us, and Mom spun and gawked at how beautiful it was.

I spotted Anna and Jenna playing with Molly near the souvenir counter, and Mr. and Mrs. Gilbert waved at us.

"Isn't this place amazing?" Mom asked.

"It is," Mrs. Gilbert said. "Anna was in a performance of *Peter Pan* here last year. She played Wendy. Did you see it?"

"No, we didn't get a chance to," Mom said. If I survived this, I decided, I was going to take her to more places like this. Without Ralph.

"Where's Emma?" I asked.

"Already in your dressing room," Mr. Gilbert said. He walked us backstage, while stagehands and other performers paced the halls, making phone calls and practicing sleight of hand.

It felt like all of them were watching me.

"Ah! There you are!" a woman yelled from a doorway. She was about my mom's age, with black hair tied in a tight pony-tail. She wore glasses with dark frames and a headset with a microphone attached to the side. "Young Duncan, yes? That is you? A bit late."

"Sorry," Mom said.

"I am Willow Jacoby, and I work for Quinton Pen—" The woman touched the side of her headset and yelled, "Yes, Quinton, I know, love! Relax, the little one is here now. Never you worry."

She leaned down and patted my head and said, "Apologies for my client, he does get rambunctious before a show, as I'm sure you can understand. Life is quite difficult for a performer, especially when there is always someone *better* and *younger* waiting in the wings, ready to swoop in at any moment and steal the attention."

She smiled a slightly unfriendly smile at me and pointed to a door.

"As I was saying, I work for Quinton Penfold, so if there's anything *you* need, let me know immediately and I will make it a reality. Your girlfriend is already here, prompt and ready. Quinton is ironing out a few last-minute details for a new trick, and then he will find you for a run-through."

"She's not my girlfriend," I said, but Willow was already halfway down the hall, screaming into her headset.

"Is there anything more I can do?" Mom asked.

"No."

"I'll be in the lobby until the show starts."

"Yeah."

"Ralph is setting up guards at all the entrances. If you think you're in danger, just—"

"I *know*, Mom."

I knocked on the door and Emma let me in. Our dressing room was small, with a little leather couch in the corner and hand-drawn posters on the walls of old shows that had been performed at the Elephant Theater. There was a large mirror surrounded by lights, and a table piled with little plastic containers of makeup.

Emma was already in her tuxedo, and she punched me on the arm when I stepped in.

"You're so late!" she yelled. "I thought you were going to bail on me."

I hung my tuxedo on the back of the door and opened the suitcase of props. The tricks looked pretty pitiful compared to the ones I had seen in the hallway.

"Do you want to practice the routine?" I asked.

"What's the point?" Emma said. "The worse we are, the better." She picked up the Mentalist's Pocket Watch. "Everyone's going to laugh at us. This is the end of our magic careers. Are you sure you're okay with that?"

"No, but there isn't another choice." I touched the half of the wand in my back pocket and felt a bit better. As long as it was there and safe, everything was all right.

"Where'd you hide your half?" I asked.

"Like I'd tell *you*. Ms. Bunchwick told me to keep it a secret. If someone captured you, I think you'd break under five minutes of torture."

"And what if something happens to *you*?"

"Oh, come on. You just want the whole wand to yourself, isn't that it?"

"No, I just . . . I—"

"We *both* need to protect it. Speaking of which, did you see the guy out there with the rabbit?" Emma asked. "He looked at me funny when I was walking down the hall. And that lady with all the costumes? She was whispering in her phone when she saw me. There's something really weird about her, too. Oh, and the guy with coins kind of grimaced when he saw me, and—"

"Not *everyone* can be dark magicians," I said. "Turn around, I want to get dressed."

Emma faced the door and cupped her hands around her eyes. I opened a container of black makeup and smeared a bit around my eyes. I posed for the mirror, trying to look a bit like Quinton Penfold, then took off my pants and threw them on the couch. I was just about to put on my tuxedo when Emma turned.

"Hey! What are you—"

"Duncan, come here," she whispered. She pressed her ear against the door and I leaned in.

"What is it?"

"Listen."

There was mumbling outside, and I could only make out a few words, but it was enough to know something bad was going on.

". . . kids are in . . ."

". . . did you see if they . . ."

". . . whatever it takes, we have to . . ."

". . . kill them . . ."

EMMA

"Duncan, we have to get out of here," I said, pushing him away from the door.

He held the wand in front of him like a sword, and it glowed in the room, reflecting off his eyes.

"Wait. Are you wearing makeup?" I asked.

"No. A little. Shut up," he said. "Follow me."

"Listen buddy, your ace of spades boxers are pretty cool, but you should probably put some pants on if we're going to run for our lives."

"Right."

He grabbed his tuxedo pants and pulled them on, then wrapped his arm around me.

"What are you doing?" I asked.

"Teleporting," he said, closing his eyes. "I scouted out the rooms before I came in."

We teleported to an empty room across the hall and peeked out. Two men in black suits and purple ties stood next to our dressing room door, whispering to each other. Officer Ralph was down the hall, talking to another cop. He didn't notice them, and they turned and walked the opposite direction, blending in with the other performers and stagehands.

"Who are they?" I asked.

Duncan shrugged. He cracked the door open and waved at me to follow him.

"Come on," he said, stuffing the wand up his sleeve. "Let's try to get a better look."

We ran past a group of people, down the hall and toward the lobby. I glanced back and saw one of them had noticed us and pointed.

"Hey! It's the magic kids! Duncan! Emma!"

The men in the purple ties turned and looked.

"Keep moving," I said.

We ducked into a room full of tables stacked with lunch meat and crackers, and kept moving until we made it to a stairwell that led up to the second floor of the theater.

At the top were large wooden doors that led to the balcony, and a small door that said *Private—Employees Only*.

We checked that no one was around and wiggled the knob.

Locked. Of course.

There were footsteps coming from the stairs.

"Hang on," Duncan said, and in a flash we teleported to the other side, in a blue cement hallway with cracked fluorescent lights that flickered above us.

"You could have killed us," I hissed. "You teleported without seeing where you were going."

Duncan shrugged.

"Don't do that again."

Down the hall, there was a door that led to a sound booth with a large window overlooking the balcony. In front of the theater, stagehands slid props into place, and from this height we could see the large rolled curtain and spotlights dangling from metal catwalks on the ceiling.

"Can you see them?" Duncan asked.

I shook my head.

We ran out of the sound booth and back into the hallway, following it to the front of the theater. At the end was a ladder that led up to the ceiling.

"I think this goes to the catwalks," I said, and we started to climb.

The catwalks were narrow and hung directly over the stage, and the floor was a metal grid that you could see right through, all the way down to the ground. Lights and wires hung from the sides and bottoms, and we tiptoed across until we were over the stage, able to see everything in the theater.

"There they are," Duncan whispered.

The two men in purple ties were on the balcony, stopping at each row to look under the seats.

"I told you she was headed toward the bathroom," one said.

"No, she wasn't. I saw her coming toward the balcony."

Stagehands moved under us, assembling props and sliding them into position. More people were coming into the theater, and I grabbed Duncan's wrist and checked his watch.

One hour till showtime.

"We need to get out of here," I said. "It's not safe."

Duncan nodded. He held up the wand and pointed it at the men.

"I can handle them."

"Are you crazy?" I said, and pushed his hand down. "Not yet. Someone might see us."

We kept moving, crossing over to the other side. We climbed down the ladder and came to stairs that led right down to the stage.

Duncan leaned out.

The two men walked toward the balcony exit, heading back in the direction of the lobby.

"I got a good look. Let's go back to our dressing room. I'll turn anyone that bothers us into a rat."

I nodded.

We snuck down the little stairs by the side of the stage and crouched in front of the first row of seats, slinking toward the other side of the theater.

"There they are!" a voice yelled from the balcony. "Up front!"

We moved faster, pushing through the side doors and running toward the entrance to the backstage hallway. We could hear the heavy footsteps of the men in the stairwell, and we rushed toward our dressing room.

That's when he grabbed us.

DUNCAN

"There he is, the magical young boy!"

An arm wrapped around my shoulders. It was a man I had never seen before, and I tried to push him away. He was tall and skinny, with hair pulled into a loose ponytail. He wore jeans and a T-shirt, and a ratty old pair of flip-flops.

"Where are you going in such a hurry? I've been looking everywhere for you. Willow told me you were in your dressing room, but, *POOF*, you seemed to have vanished on me."

The way he said *poof* seemed familiar to me, and I squinted at him.

"Mr. Penfold?" I asked.

"Yes," he said. "And call me Quinton."

Without his makeup and scarves and jewelry, Quinton looked like a completely different person.

"Doors are opening in thirty minutes, and we have very little time to practice. I've been looking everywhere. Come."

I followed him, and Emma came with me.

"I must say, this is not very professional of you," Quinton said. "There is nothing more serious in life than the performance, and you must treat your preparations and rehearsals with respect."

"I'm sorry, sir, it's just that we were being ch—"

Emma kicked me.

Quinton stopped.

"Being what?"

"Nothing," I said. "We were looking for a vending machine."

He laughed and continued walking.

"I need to show you the trick you will be helping me with and explain how it works. The mechanics are old and a little clunky, but it's nothing too complicated. You just need to smile when I tell you to and stand in exactly the right spot."

He stopped at the door to the stage and waved a finger at Emma.

"Uh-uh, you must stop here, young lady. You didn't agree to perform with me, so there's no reason for me to reveal the secret to you. I believe you will find it much more enjoyable to experience along with the rest of the audience."

Emma glared at Quinton, and turned and ran to our dressing room.

We entered the stage behind the curtain and he led me to a black wooden box the size of a closet. There were angels and demons painted on it, and large straps and locks dangling from the sides.

"The Box of Judgment," he said, extending his hand and waving it across the front. "Those who enter are judged for their deeds, and sent either to heaven or hell."

"Wow," I said.

"Either way, you disappear."

He opened the front of the box, revealing a small space to stand.

"I will tell the story to the audience and place you inside. See the tape on the floor? That's where you stand. Once the straps are fastened and the locks engaged, I will continue my story, and when I say the words *final judgment*, you stand in the corner and pull this handle."

He pulled a handle and the wall of the box slid out, revealing an angled mirror that reflected the other side of the box. It was pretty much the exact same trick I had used to fool my mom years ago, and I was a little disappointed at how simple it was. Frankly, I expected more from Quinton.

"Cool," I said. "And then what? Do you stick swords through the box? Do you light the box on fire? Do I reappear on the other side of the theater?"

"Err . . . no," Quinton said. "You must understand, Duncan, this is an old theater, devoid of any usable trapdoors and pulley systems. This forces me to be a bit more . . . how should I say it . . . *conservative* in my illusions."

"Oh," I said.

"After that, I will move on to my next trick and one of my assistants will wheel you offstage to watch the remainder of the performance from the side. If all goes to plan, you can join me for a bow at the end. I can tell you are less than enamored with this one, but I assure you, in the context of the show, it will be quite effective."

"Awesome," I said. "I can't wait to see it."

I peeked around the curtain and scanned the theater, looking for the men in purple ties. They were gone.

"Is everything all right?" Quinton asked. "Preperformance jitters? You look half sick, my boy."

"Yeah, I guess."

"You'll grow accustomed to it with time."

There was a sound from the lobby, a low hum that grew and grew into a deafening roar.

"Doors are open," Quinton said. "The crowds are coming, so I must get into my attire. I look forward to seeing your performance, young man. You open the show, and I close it. I quite like the sound of that. Perhaps this is a glimpse into our futures."

"Yeah," I said.

He winked at me.

"By the way, Duncan, I really like your eye makeup. Very mysterious. Wherever did you get the idea?"

THE ELITE MAGICIANS CONVENTION

EMMA

"As you can see," Duncan said from the center of the stage, "this shoelace was once cut in two, and is now"—he pulled it tight between both hands—"one solid piece."

Silence from the audience.

Maybe a few coughs.

The theater was packed, and a bunch of performers were watching us from the side.

"Okay, so yeah," Duncan said, fidgeting with his bow tie. "That's . . . uh . . . the cut-and-restore shoelace."

It was hard to see the audience through the spotlight, but people in the front row were covering their faces. Zug smiled and gave us a thumbs-down.

"For our next trick, I need a volunteer," Duncan said, holding up a pocket watch. He waved his hand toward the audience and a half piece of shoelace fell from his sleeve. At least that got a laugh.

I picked out an old man named Gary and led him to a chair in the middle of the stage and asked him to set the watch to whatever time he wanted. Then Duncan wrote a prediction on a piece of paper and put it in an envelope.

"Now, based on my psychic powers and stuff, um . . . I am able to . . . you know . . . tell what time he set it to," Duncan said.

We hadn't worked on our patter at all, and even though we were *supposed* to do bad, this was still really embarrassing.

"All right, Gary," Duncan said, handing him the envelope. "Show the audience the watch and then open the envelope and tell them my prediction."

Gary held up the watch and said, "I set the watch to eleven fifty-three."

He opened Duncan's envelope and said, "And you wrote eleven fifty-*five*."

"Most people round up," Duncan growled, and then turned to the audience, saying, "Close enough. Let's give a round of applause for Gary."

About seven people applauded.

Someone from the back yelled, "BOOOO!"

Whatever.

Next was our grand finale, and we set up two boxes on opposite ends of the stage and teleported fruit back and forth.

"It's over here," Duncan said, placing an orange into the box and waving his hands over it, then pulling a lever that hid the orange in a secret compartment.

"And now it's over here," I said, pulling a lever and opening my box. Except I had forgotten the order of fruit we were supposed to do, so when I opened my box, there was a bright red apple sitting there.

"Ta-da," I said. "Oh, and it's also changed into an apple."

We did this a few more times until our time was up, and when we finally finished, we got a good amount of applause, mainly from people that felt bad for us or were glad to see us leave.

If anyone still thought we were really magical after that, they were seriously delusional.

Quinton was waiting offstage when we left, and he smiled weakly at Duncan and said, "That was *interesting*. Good . . . uh . . . effort. I think you really fooled some people with the pocket watch. But I must ask, why did you skip the water chamber escape? That was quite the trick, and I would have loved to see it in person."

"It's an old theater," Duncan said. "You know. Like you said, it's harder to do the really big tricks without trapdoors and stuff."

"Yes, of course," Quinton said, smiling.

Willow whispered something into her headset and glared at us.

We had reserved seats near the front, and crept through the side door to join our parents and Officer Ralph and Zug for the rest of the show.

The pressure was off.

We tanked hard.

No one would be after us anymore and everything could go back to normal.

This was the end, right?

Wrong.

DUNCAN

There was *way* too much magic that day, which means some-thing coming from me.

Acts were scheduled throughout the day in twenty-minute intervals until Quinton's hour-long performance at 5:00. Some of the performers did pretty cool tricks that I had never seen before. Every once in a while someone did a presen-tation about magic history and theory. Still, after a few hours of that I started to feel like I was in school and my butt hurt from the old theater chairs.

I scanned the crowd for any sign of the men in purple ties, but couldn't find them.

Fifteen minutes before Quinton's performance, Willow came into the crowd and tapped my shoulder.

"It's time," she said.

I followed her out and went backstage.

Quinton was waiting there for me, in his full outfit, look-ing like a totally different person than he had earlier in the day.

"You ready, my boy?" he asked with a wink.

Soon the theater went dark and smoke machines belched

fog onto the stage while mysterious violin music warbled over the sound system.

Quinton stepped out from the curtains to thunderous applause.

Showtime.

He moved across the stage with a confidence and speed I could never match. His patter was fast and polished. His tricks were flawless, large, amazing, and even from the side of the stage I couldn't tell how they were done. They almost looked like *real* magic, and he always had the audience right where he wanted them. With a turn of phrase he could scare them or have them erupt into laughter.

The music fit the mood of the show, slowing down to deep bass notes and then accelerating into a high, frenzied scream at moments of peril.

He spun, disappeared, survived knives and fire, flew, and amazed.

It was perfection. He was even better in person than on TV.

"*That's* how an act is done," Willow said, smiling at me and twirling a strand of her black hair with a finger.

"Yeah," I whispered, and before I knew it, his show was nearly over and he was pointing at me to join him.

"The Box of Judgment," he said, extending a hand and waving me on. "For this trick I will need the help of a special young boy who put this small town of Elephant on the map. Please welcome the incomparable Duncan Reyes. Let's hear it for him!"

Only a few people clapped. The audience hadn't forgiven me for my terrible performance.

I walked into the spotlight.

"Angels and demons, heaven and hell, this box will decide your fate, Duncan. Will you live or will you die?"

I turned to answer but he was already moving, spinning the box and showing all four sides.

The music got louder and a throbbing bass note shook the floor.

"No matter what happens, know that whatever this box does is final. Your decisions were your own, and you must live with your choices. Do you understand?"

I nodded, and he opened the box.

"Step inside."

He knelt down, the charms of his necklaces clanking against his chest.

"Are you ready?"

I nodded.

The audience was silent.

He closed the door, strapped the straps, and bolted the locks. I was in total darkness, and the music was deafening.

"Now, young Duncan, let us begin your *final judgment.*"

Those were the words I was waiting for. I stepped into the corner and pulled the handle.

Quinton screamed, "Judgment has begun!"

Then the world exploded.

EMMA

I hate to admit it, but Quinton's act wasn't bad, and halfway through I started to wish that I had agreed to help him, too.

I mean, what would it have hurt?

"The Box of Judgment," Quinton yelled, pulling out a large black box with scary paintings on the sides.

He waved Duncan onstage and had a whole silly routine about how whoever went inside would be sent to heaven or hell or something.

"There is no going back," Quinton said. "Are you ready?"

Duncan nodded.

I looked for any trapdoors or secret exits but couldn't see any.

I stood up a bit, and a person in the row behind me kicked my seat.

Duncan stepped inside the box and Quinton locked it down tight.

"And now, young Duncan, let us begin your *final judgment*."

The music ripped through the speakers, so loud that they shook on their hinges, and more fog spread on the stage in gray wisps.

Quinton adjusted his necklaces and threw his hands up in the air, strobe lights temporarily blinding the front rows, and screamed, "Judgment has begun!"

There was the sound of ropes snapping and a giant boulder was released from above the stage, dropping down on the box, shattering it into a million splinters.

The crowd gasped.

I looked over at Zug, who nodded his head and gave me a thumbs-up.

The crowd exploded into hysterical applause.

That trick was *too* good.

From the time Duncan got into the box until it was locked and smashed to smithereens had been no more than ten seconds, a really short time to make a proper escape.

Amazing.

I had to know how it was done.

Quinton moved right on to his next trick, levitating, and the giant rock still sat on the stage, the pieces of the box spread all around it.

"When are they going to make him reappear?" I whispered to Zug.

He shrugged.

The show continued, but something about this whole thing didn't make sense.

I mean, anyone could put a person in a box and drop a rock on them, right?

That's not really magic. That's just cruel.

I looked around the theater, at the box seats, the mezzanine, the balcony. Any minute, Duncan had to come out from some-where.

"Sit *down*," the person in the row behind me whispered.

There was something happening at the back of the audito-rium, but with the loud music and bright lights I couldn't quite see what it was. It looked like someone had pushed their way through the doors and was running past the ushers.

The music got even louder.

Duncan?

I turned around and Quinton was on the stage, fire com-ing from his hands, and he looked right at me and smiled.

The person was running to the front of the theater, the ushers close behind.

I squinted through the spotlights as the figure got closer and closer to me, grabbed my hand, and pulled me out of my seat and into the aisle.

DUNCAN

There was a deafening crash above my head and the sound of a box being shattered. Then there was darkness.

An Exit sign glowed a dull red in the corner, and my eyes adjusted to the room.

Coils of ropes hung from the ceiling, and racks of old costumes lined the walls, faded and musty. There were boxes of wigs and jewelry spread around the floor, and rolled-up posters crammed in boxes.

I was still in the theater, under the stage, but how had I got there?

There were no trapdoors above me, and the only way into the room was the one door in the corner.

I felt my back pocket. The wand was still there.

Had I teleported here?

Had the wand done it on its own?

No, it couldn't have been.

The door opened and a blinding light poured into the room.

Silhouettes of two men appeared, and I transformed into

the most horrible creature I could imagine, with a mouth full of fangs and fingers full of claws.

I snapped, snarled, growled, waved my hands at them.

"There he is. Delivered just as promised," a man said through a thick accent. "Wrapped like a present. Enough with the little games, boy. We ain't afraid of nasty creatures."

"Least now we know he has it," another man said.

"True."

The men got closer, and I could see they were the same ones that had chased me and Emma earlier.

Up close, I could see tattoos crawling out of their sleeves and collars.

"We've been real busy searching for this. Tore your bedroom apart. Would have saved us a lot of trouble if you had let us talk to you. Had to go running, eh?"

I gripped the wand and cast a mental deception, igniting the walls into flames.

One of the men screamed and dropped to the ground, covering his head with his hands.

"Vince, you fool, it ain't real. You know that."

"But it's so much stronger than I'm used to, Ronan," Vince said, clawing at his eyes.

I couldn't risk trying to teleport out of the room, so I flew to the ceiling, but one of them grabbed my ankle and pulled me down, pinning me against the wall.

"Gotcha," Ronan said.

"What you have there doesn't belong to you," Vince said.

"No," Ronan said, pointing at the door. "It belongs to *him.*"

The door creaked open, and the men ripped the wand from my hand.

EMMA

"Where's the boy?" Ms. Bunchwick said, hauling me down the aisle.

"I . . . I don't—"

She looked at the stage, squinted at Quinton, and watched as white doves flew from the long flames that shot out of his hands.

The ushers closed in, grabbing Ms. Bunchwick by the shoulders.

"All right, you caught me, I'm leaving," Ms. Bunchwick said, raising her hands in surrender. She turned to me. "We have to move. Quick."

Quinton bowed.

The crowd stood and cheered.

She pulled me, hard, and we ran up the aisle of the theater, out to the lobby. I searched for any sign of the men in purple ties, but there was no one around.

"Where's your wand?" she asked, crouching down and sticking her face in mine.

"At home. In my room."

"How well was it hidden, child?"

"Trust me, I know how to hide things."

Tears streamed down her cheeks and she took my hand.

"What's wrong?"

"What happened to the boy, dear? Please tell me you know."

"He helped Quinton Penfold with a magic trick and then he . . . he . . ."

"He what?"

"He disappeared."

"Had the wand on him, did he?"

"Yes. He's probably just backstage," I said, but I was really starting to doubt it.

"Can't risk it. No time," she said, and kicked open the theater doors.

The sun was setting, and the whole town was bathed in a gold and red glow. Black clouds rolled in from the far side of town, and thunder rumbled in the distance. Street magicians performed on the corners, and people streamed in and out of storefronts and buildings to see magic-themed exhibits and pop-up shops.

"What's going on?"

"This way," Ms. Bunchwick said. "Hurry."

Next to the theater was a small black motorcycle with a sidecar and the words *Cruisin' Time* written across the side in pink paint.

"This is yours?" I asked.

"Belonged to my older sister. When I went on the run, she followed me to keep watch. We used to go for rides back in the day." She sat on and turned the key. It roared to life. "Still take it out for groceries sometimes."

She pointed to the sidecar.

"Hop in."

"Where are we going?"

"Your house," she said. "And you better pray the wand is still there."

DUNCAN

"Does he have it?" the man asked.

The first thing I noticed about him was the horrible sounds—deep, painful gasps and a wet rattle that made every breath seem painful.

He was old, and seated in a wheelchair, an oxygen tank attached to the side. His legs were covered in a thick blanket and his hands looked like bones.

"Right here," Ronan said, proudly handing it over.

"Ah, thank you, Ronan," the man said, grasping it in his long fingers and rubbing it under his nose. "Still smells as sweet as I remember, like the ocean breeze on a spring morning. But"—he examined it closely—"where is the rest?"

I didn't answer.

"Where is it?" the old man screamed.

"Is it enough?" Ronan said.

"Not for me," the old man said. "Tie him down."

Ronan pulled a rope from the ceiling and Vince slid a chair across the room. They tied me up tight, then turned on a lamp and pointed it at my face. It felt like hot needles were being stabbed into my eyes.

"Where is the rest of the wand?" the old man asked.

"I don't know what you mean. This is all I have."

"You lie," Ronan said.

"Where is *she*?" the old man asked.

"Who?"

"You know exactly who I'm talking about!" he screamed, breaking into a fit of coughs. "Edna Bunchwick."

"The horrible woman that stole the wand from this poor fellow," Vince said, adjusting his tie.

"She didn't steal it. You forced her to—"

"So you *do* know of whom I speak," the old man said, moving closer. "Then I suppose you know who *I* am."

"You're Seamus. The Dark Spirit."

He laughed.

"I see she's told you part of the story, but as is so often the case with lover's quarrels, there is another side. This wand was never intended to be used for such small and meaningless purposes. Silly mental tricks. Flying around, transforming, and teleporting things. It's pathetic. If real magic can be replicated with a bit of string or sleight of hand, what's the point of having it at all? Magic tricks are a game for children, and nothing more. This small twig has so much more to offer, and it should never be held back by the fears of simpleminded people."

Above, the crowd cheered for Quinton's show, and the footsteps on the floor sounded like an earthquake.

"I had learned of the dark magic it was capable of, and had

experimented for years, awaking an astounding range of powers. And right when I began to master its secrets, she wanted me to pass it on."

Seamus gripped the wand in his fingers. He whispered things in a different language that sounded like deep growls.

"All these years have been wasted."

A bright white vapor came from the tip, circling Seamus like a silk blanket that radiated light.

"She's selfish, Duncan," Seamus said. "Even faced with losing our son, she wouldn't listen. *That's not what magic is for*, she said, but the truth is she didn't trust me with the power."

I could only see a shadow of Seamus through the bright light that circled him. He stood from his wheelchair and extended his arms.

"Who would have thought that she'd steal the wand and waste it by hiding for decades in some sorry little town. She never gave me a chance to explain. I could never tell her the truth."

The light faded, and Seamus stood in the room, as young as he was in the picture Ms. Bunchwick had shown us that day in her basement.

He adjusted his suit jacket.

"Much better. And this is just a taste of what I can do," Seamus said, tucking the wand into his breast pocket. He checked his watch and turned to Ronan and Vince. "Any doubts you may have had on my ability to repay you should be gone. We're almost done, boys. Earlier than planned. Find the other half and we can be on our way."

"Where do you think it is?" Ronan asked.

"Difficult to say, but if I know Edna, she'll lead us right to it."

THE DARK SPIRIT

EMMA

Ms. Bunchwick swerved around incoming traffic, scraping the mirror of her motorcycle down a row of parked cars. She didn't bother to brake when she turned the corner into an alley, and the wheels of the sidecar left the ground and thumped hard on the pavement. I held on as tight as I could.

"Too much traffic!" she yelled. "We're taking the back way."

"Do you know how to drive this thing?"

"More accustomed to flying, but this thing handles like a dream. Practically steers itself."

We hit a bump and went airborne, jumping onto a sidewalk and speeding in the direction of my house. It started to rain, and the wet ground made her crazy driving even more terrifying.

"What's happening?"

"They found you, child, and they know where you live. Your bad routine didn't throw 'em off the scent. I was keeping watch and saw two men break into your house. Tore each room apart."

I didn't like the thought of anyone going through my stuff, but that was a small problem now.

Behind us, thunder roared, and a spinning tornado of black clouds formed above the town, right where the theater was located. Orange light came from the center and shot down like a lightning bolt. It was so bright I could hardly look at it, and I buried my face in my hands as the rain fell harder.

"Guessing that means they got Duncan's half," Ms. Bunchwick said, hunching down and revving the engine. "We need to get yours, pronto."

She drove through yards, took shortcuts through alleyways, and even ran a few stop signs and red lights. Cars honked at us and Ms. Bunchwick stuck her tongue out at them.

"Did they search your house, too?" I asked.

"No, which I'm praying means they ain't discovered me yet."

"How are we going to get Duncan's half back?"

"Never mind that. First order of business is keeping *your* half safe. As long as we have it, Seamus can't get to the tree."

We turned on my street and sped up the hill toward my house, the wind and rain whipping against our faces.

The front door and windows were open, and trash blew across the yard.

"Oh no," I said.

"Aye. Real bad."

She parked the motorcycle on the side of the house, behind a tall row of shrubs, and we ran inside.

DUNCAN

Ronan pulled me through a series of dark hallways under the theater. We came to an exit that led to the parking lot. Mr. Gilbert's car was still there, and through the alley I could see a stream of people exiting.

The sky spun with black clouds, popping and glowing with bright lightning.

"Where does Edna live?" Seamus whispered. His fingers curled around my neck and the pupils of his eyes glowed a dark red, like some evil flames were shining beneath them.

"W-West End Avenue, s-sir," I said. "At the end of the street. You can't miss it."

Okay, Emma was right. Even without torture, I cracked like an egg. But in my defense, he was really scary.

"Want me to go?" Vince asked.

"No. If the boy had half the wand, I assume the girl would have the other half. And if I know Edna, she would tell them to keep one part with them, and one part hidden. The boy had *his* half which leads me to believe—"

I looked at my feet.

"Yes, that's correct," Seamus said, smiling. He turned to Ronan and Vince. "You fools missed it. The other half is still at the girl's house."

EMMA

My house was a mess.

A total crime scene.

Every bookshelf and table had been flipped over, and papers and boxes were scattered across the floor. In the kitchen, they had pulled out every drawer and dumped it, along with all the pots and pans.

Upstairs, my sisters' rooms were thoroughly trashed. The mattresses were ripped off their beds and all their clothes had been pulled from their closets, like some natural catastrophe had just passed through.

"Anna and Jenna are going to freak," I said. They hate it when anyone so much as *breathes* in the direction of their rooms.

The paintings in Molly's nursery had been torn from the walls, and her crib had been taken apart. Even the trash can full of used diapers had been sorted through.

Gross.

"There sure are a lot of you Gilbert girls, aren't there?" Ms. Bunchwick, examining our family portrait. "Hard to believe your parents would want another baby after you three."

"Yeah. Molly's the only one I like."

"That ain't true. You might not realize it, but sisters are the greatest gift you could ever hope for. Remember that."

"No. Anna and Jenna pretty much hate me. They have a ton of friends and think I'm an embarrassment."

"When times are tough, they'll always be there for you. I miss my sister terribly."

Another flash of lightning lit up the sky and the power cut out.

"Perfect," she said.

We continued in the darkness. My door was propped open, and it looked like someone had taken a sledgehammer to my dresser. The grating on the air conditioning vents had been pulled from the walls, and my closet had been completely emptied and half my clothes were cut to pieces. I felt rage boil throughout my body. Whoever did this was going to pay.

"Is the wand still here?" Ms. Bunchwick asked, and I could tell by the way she was looking at the room that she doubted it.

"I told you I was good at hiding things."

Ms. Bunchwick noticed a framed picture on the floor and bent down to pick it up. It was of me and Duncan after the talent show last year, both in our tuxedos, arms wrapped around each other and smiling. Simpler times.

"You really love him, don't you?"

"What? No. I mean . . . no."

"Love has many forms, child."

"Maybe."

I opened my window, stood on the ledge, and popped out

the screen. I reached as high as I could, and felt around the front of the rain gutter.

On the street, a black car pulled up in front of my house, and a man who I hadn't seen before stepped out. He pulled Duncan out by the collar and threw him to the ground.

"Ms. Bunchwick, who's that?" I asked, and she came to the window, her knees buckling a bit.

"Mercy heavens, it can't be."

"Who?"

One of the men from the theater stepped out of the car and pointed at me, screaming, "There she is!"

My hands were shaking and I rubbed them back and forth along the rain gutter, searching for the piece of duct tape I had used to secure the wand in place.

"Hurry, child, where is it?"

"Just a second," I said, grabbing a corner of tape and ripping it free.

Ms. Bunchwick snatched it from my hands.

"Come," she said, and she led me down the stairs, navigating over broken pieces of furniture, the wand held in an attack position.

"That way," I said, pointing to the sliding glass doors at the back of the house.

I heard yelling from the front and I held on to Ms. Bunchwick's dress.

"Was that Seamus?"

"Aye," she said. "A younger version, indeed, but just as he lives in my memory. I'll distract him out back. You grab

Duncan and I'll circle around for you. We're all leaving here together."

"Then what?"

"Probably die in a gruesome way, but at least you can say we tried."

She patted me on the head, and we ran to the sliding door.

Lightning rattled the house, lighting up the backyard in a sickly green glow.

Ms. Bunchwick opened the door, and in a flash, Seamus appeared, the wand held an inch from her nose.

DUNCAN

"Do you remember the death spell?" Seamus asked, pointing the wand at Ms. Bunchwick's face. Emma shook behind her, kneeling, her face hidden in her dress. "I learned it right before you left me."

Ronan had dragged me to the back of the house, his big arm wrapped around my neck.

"No, Seamus, you know I never was one to concern myself with the dark magic," Ms. Bunchwick said.

Seamus twisted his body and pointed the wand right at me.

"Let's see if I can remember how it works."

"Don't!" she screamed, falling to her knees. She pointed the wand at Seamus, and her hand trembled so much I was afraid it might fall out on its own.

"Hand it to me, Edna."

"Not likely. Not with the evil you'll do."

"Do you really think that poorly of me? After all we've done together?"

"You went mad," Ms. Bunchwick said. "And now you're threatening to kill that sweet boy, so aye, I *do* think that poorly of you."

"You never let me *explain*," Seamus said. "You didn't understand. You're blinded by the darkness, and you can't see the good I can do with it."

"Let the children go. We'll talk, dear."

"First give me the wand. I don't want to hurt you."

"You already have. Deeper than you could ever imagine."

Ms. Bunchwick tried to move and Seamus shot a bolt of red lightning an inch from her head and pointed the wand at me again.

"We can be a family again if you listen to me. I can make you young. I can make you perfect. We can find the tree and live together, forever."

"You . . . you'd do that for me?"

"I would. I've never stopped thinking about you, darling. What you were, anyway. Not . . ." He waved a hand at her wrinkled face. ". . . this."

She laughed.

"*This*, Seamus, is reality. *This* is truth. Magic isn't meant to bring darkness into the world. It's not meant to make you more powerful at the expense of others. It's meant to bring *joy* to others. And I don't want to spend another second with your evil black heart."

He shot a bolt at her feet and she screamed in pain, toppling over and rolling into the backyard.

"You don't understand," Seamus said.

"Kill her!" Ronan screamed.

"No, you fool! If she dies holding the wand, the power goes with her," he said, walking toward her crumpled body.

"It's much easier to just take it."

Emma used the distraction to run away, through the house and to the front door. I can't say I blamed her.

Seamus bent down and pulled the half of the wand from Ms. Bunchwick's fingers, caressing it across his cheek.

"Finally," he said. "Back where it belongs. And, Edna, I now must confess that I feel *nothing* for you. With the wand in my possession, I never need to think of you again."

He held both halves to the sky and the black clouds rolled in circles above him.

"IT'S MINE!" he screamed, head tilted back and arms held up in a super-evil pose.

A powerful bolt shot from Ms. Bunchwick's hand and Seamus fell to the ground, rolling in the grass. She stood and brushed off her dress.

"Always was better than you at sleight of hand," she said, still holding her half of the wand. She kicked pebbles into the air and transformed them into blue bolts of light, shooting them around him as he crawled backward through the yard. "You let go of the boy now or I'll zap you till you beg for mercy."

"NO!" he screamed, firing blood red bolts back at her. He turned to Ronan, yelling, "Get Vincent! Now!"

There was a rumbling sound from the side of the house, coming toward us, and I saw Emma riding an old black motor-cycle with a sidecar. She was hunched over, gritting her teeth and aiming for Seamus. He screamed and jumped, rolling on the ground. He shot a bolt at her, barely missing the back tire, and chanted ancient curses under his breath.

Emma hit the brakes, skidding to a stop in front of us.

"Hop on," she said. "We're all leaving here together."

EMMA

"That's my girl!" Ms. Bunchwick yelled.

I slid back on the seat to let her drive, grabbing the sides of her dress. She turned the throttle and started across the yard. Duncan jumped in the sidecar and we were off, careening through my neighborhood as Seamus shot red bolts behind us, sending chunks of smoldering asphalt into the air.

"We'll stick to the roads for now. I don't have the strength to fly the three of us *and* play defense," she said. "Seamus was always faster. He'd catch me quick, all things being equal, and we need to put the wand to better use."

"How'd you do it?" Duncan asked.

"Do what?"

"Trick him into thinking he had the wand."

"Can't tell you my secret, but I'll give you a hint."

Ms. Bunchwick lifted up a fold of her dress and pulled out a handful of twigs, each meticulously carved to look like half of the wand.

"You think I was whittling in the woods for the joy of it?" She winked at me. "Never know when duplicates might be handy."

It was dark, and the occasional explosion of lightning lit up the sky as we worked our way onto the main street. She switched on the headlights and swerved into the traffic.

"Wish I had helmets for you children. Suppose your heads are still soft and bouncy at this age."

Ms. Bunchwick never worried about which side of the road she was meant to stay on. She went wherever there was an opening. If we *were* going to die, I would have bet it was just as likely to be because of her.

"Keep an eye on the skies, children. He'll be coming."

Duncan turned backward in the sidecar, crouching down so only the top of his head was sticking out.

"Here, boy," she said, throwing the real half of the wand at Duncan. "Reckon you'll need to protect us."

It glowed in his hands, lighting up his face. I could see the terror in his eyes, and for the first time I got a really sick feeling that something bad might happen to him.

"There!" he yelled, pointing.

There was a speck in the sky, no bigger than a bird, and I could tell by the way it moved that it was something different. It dove and spun, did flips and twists, getting bigger every second.

Seamus.

DUNCAN

"He's going to catch us!" I yelled.

The wind and rain stung my face and I ducked low in the sidecar, watching as Seamus swooped through the sky.

Ms. Bunchwick twisted the throttle and the bike shimmied and squealed, sounding like at any moment it might collapse into a big pile of metal pieces.

Seamus was close enough now that I could see the outline of his body against the clouds. He was riding on a fireplace poker, probably snatched from Emma's living room. It was smaller than anything I would ever try, but he handled it with skill, going faster than I thought possible and spinning upside down and sideways.

I aimed the wand at him and tried to move him with my mind. If I could just get a hold of him for a second I could send him crashing to the ground, but it wasn't possible. By the time I aimed at him he was already long gone, getting closer and closer to us.

"What should I do?" I screamed. "This isn't working!"

Ms. Bunchwick craned her neck back and laughed, then

turned a sharp corner onto a side street, narrowly missing a group of men that were standing on the corner. They turned to watch us, their mouths open in confusion.

"It's time you learned to combine the types of magic. You know those lightning bolts I shot at him?"

"Yeah. How did you do that?"

"Levitation mixed with a bit of transformation. Do you got anything you can throw at him?"

I felt my tuxedo pockets.

"All I have is a deck of cards."

"Perfect. Pull out a card."

I opened the pack of cards and pulled out the Joker.

"Now what?"

"Toss it, boy! Make it levitate," she said.

I threw the card and made it float a few inches from the tip of the wand.

"Transform it into a ball of pure energy."

I closed my eyes, imagining the card transforming into one of the bolts Ms. Bunchwick had shot. The air began to smell funny, sort of like chlorine in a swimming pool. A small spark of static appeared and then the entire card transformed into a brilliant ball of green light.

"That's good! Now fly it toward him!" Ms. Bunchwick yelled.

I whipped the wand and sent the bolt of crackling light into the sky toward Seamus. He ducked and rolled in the air, and the light hit a tree on a neatly manicured front lawn and burst into flames.

"Might want to be careful with that, boy. Can do real damage."

We turned another corner, our rear tire skidding on the ground and leaving a long black trail behind it.

In the sky, Seamus screamed and a bolt of red lightning hit the pavement in front of us. Rocks and asphalt flew into the air, creating a large crater in the ground that Ms. Bunchwick barely managed to swerve around.

I threw another card, transformed it into lightning, aimed, and missed. This time it went into the air above his head and evaporated in the sky.

"Don't shoot where he is—shoot where he's *going* to be!" Ms. Bunchwick yelled as we turned into a yard, cutting through an alley in the direction of the highway entrance.

"I don't want to kill him!"

"You think Seamus is that fragile? It'll stun him. Burn him a bit. Maybe knock him out of the air if we're lucky." She shook her head. "He's protected by dark magic."

I watched how he was flying and aimed again, narrowly missing him. The lightning bolt grazed his hand and he yelled out as the tree beside him exploded into flames.

"Need some help here!" Ms. Bunchwick yelled.

There was a chain-link fence separating the backyard from the small road that led onto the highway, and I pointed the wand at it and ripped it from the ground, launching it into the sky.

Seamus ducked to avoid the flying fence and hit the

ground, rolling to a stop as the fireplace poker spun in the air and lodged itself into the dirt.

"Wa-hoo!" Ms. Bunchwick screamed. "Good work, boy!"

We turned onto the road, and I looked behind us and saw a black car entering the highway.

"Ms. Bunchwick! Those are Seamus's men!"

"It don't let up!"

She leaned in, and we veered onto the highway. There weren't many cars out and the road was wet from the heavy rain. The tires of the motorcycle spun and squealed, sending up tidal waves of water as we sped toward the events that would be forever known in Elephant County as "the Highway Incident."

THE HIGHWAY INCIDENT

The Law Offices of
Barker & Haldeman
161 Tusk Avenue | Elephant County

Dear Sir or Madam

It has come to our attention that you wish to question our client, Emma Gilbert, regarding the situation that occurred earlier this week. We must insist that you do not discuss the events, hereby referred to as "The Highway Incident". Since the matter in question concerns damage to private property and eyewitness accounts that are, frankly, preposterous to anyone with a sound mind, we request that you preserve any and all inquiries until more facts are uncovered.

In truth, Emma Gilbert was neither d...
magic paraphernalia, which ...
way, shape, or form. We reque...
Gilbert, and limit all communi...

I hearby demand that anyone re...
statements regarding Emma Gilb...
relevant facts, and nothing herein i...

Yours truly,

Larry Barker, Attorney at Law

i plead the fifth

CASE ID 116-819 FOLDER NO. 24

EMMA

The Highway Incident?
I don't know what you're talking about.
I plead the Fifth.
Fifth, Fifth, Fifth.

DUNCAN

The black car was gaining on us, flashing its headlights and forcing other cars off the road.

"What's the plan?" Emma asked.

"We lose them and keep driving," Ms. Bunchwick said. "My sister's old house is in the next county. It's still empty. They'll never think to look there. We'll hide out there and regroup, try to figure out a plan to get the wand back."

"How are we going to lose them?"

"Don't worry," she said. "This old bike is quicker than any car. We have a bigger problem now. Look!"

Seamus was back, far in the distance, but moving fast.

We crossed into the other lane and a car honked at us. Ms. Bunchwick grabbed the cards and wand from my hands and turned around.

She threw a card and shot a bolt that sizzled into the sky. Seamus ducked. The light passed over his shoulder and exploded.

"Can't focus!" she yelled, screaming into the sky as her flesh morphed to a wart-covered green and her hair thinned to a stringy black. "You drive, girl!"

"What? I can't drive on the highway."

"It practically steers itself, remember? You managed just fine back at the house. This ain't much different. Duncan, keep a watch out for Seamus."

She slung her leg over the side of the motorcycle and grabbed Emma, throwing her to the front. The handlebars of the motorcycle shook and Emma clutched them tight, twisting the throttle as hard as she could.

We kept moving, and Ms. Bunchwick shot light at Seamus and he ducked and rolled at an amazing speed.

"He's getting closer!" I yelled.

Up ahead were dots of red lights. Cars were stopped, backed up for miles.

"Ms. Bunchwick, I think there's an accident ahead."

"Mercy heavens, the bad luck never stops!"

My heart was pounding and I couldn't breathe. I was soaked, cold, and tired. The rain came down heavier and it was hard to see.

Ms. Bunchwick sent out a gigantic bolt into the sky, lighting up the highway in a brilliant shimmering blue. Seamus leaned to the left but wasn't fast enough. The bolt hit him in the chest and he spun and landed on the highway, bouncing and rolling hundreds of feet back on the road.

"You got him!"

"Aye, but don't celebrate yet," she said.

We approached the stopped traffic. Emma tried to stay in the middle of the lanes, but the space was really tight and the motorcycle's mirror rubbed against a row of cars and SUVs.

There was a lot of honking and screaming behind us.

"Pick us up, Ms. Bunchwick, what are you waiting for?" Emma asked.

"You want me to fight him or fly us? I can't do both."

She scanned the sky, searching for Seamus.

"Don't see him. Fine, we'll fly for a bit."

She flicked her wrist and the front wheel left the ground, tipping us back at an extreme angle.

We launched up and wobbled in the air, the tires of the motorcycle and sidecar just a few inches above the cars below.

"There," Ms. Bunchwick said, pointing into the distance at the long bridge that crossed the river. There must have been an accident halfway across, because I could see the flashing lights of police cars and fire trucks, and cars passed it at a slow drip. The other side of the bridge was nearly empty, and we could go as fast as we wanted once we reached it.

"When we get across the bridge, I'll take over again. Seamus's men'll be stuck"—she scanned the sky—"and he's nowhere to be seen."

"We did it!" Emma yelled, pumping her fists.

"Careful," Ms. Bunchwick said. "No celebrating till we're clear. Bad luck, you see?"

Bad luck indeed.

EMMA

Look, I'm sorry about the bridge and all, but I was really just along for the ride.

DUNCAN

The highway sloped downward as we approached the bridge, and as we got closer to the accident I saw a bunch of orange cones surrounding a twisted mess of cars. Ms. Bunchwick waved the wand up, trying to keep us higher than the traffic while still watching the sky behind us. It was darker than I'd ever seen before, lit up from time to time with cracks of bright lightning.

"We'll land when we get over the worst of it," Ms. Bunchwick said, squinting her eyes to see the scene ahead of us. "Won't be long now."

"Look!" I yelled. "There he is!"

Ms. Bunchwick twisted around, throwing cards and waving the wand in a circle, firing blindly behind us. The motorcycle dipped and our wheels bounced over the top of an eighteen-wheeler. Emma tried to steer us straight along the narrow top, and the driver yelled and honked his horn.

Seamus was in the air behind us, getting closer and closer.

"Emma, look!" I yelled, pulling at her shirt.

Police cars were driving down the shoulder of the road, and other cars moved as much as they could to let them through.

Behind them, Seamus's men followed closely, headlights off, blending in with the road.

"Ms. Bunchwick!" I screamed.

"I see 'em, I see 'em."

Seamus was getting close enough that I could see his face and flapping black suit coat. He aimed his wand at us and shot a bolt, skimming the side of the motorcycle and leaving a crooked black gash. It burned the hem of my tuxedo pants and flew on, hitting the concrete barrier of the highway and blowing it into chunks of smoking rubble.

"Are you *sure* these bolts won't kill us?" Emma asked. Her face was white and she looked sick.

"Oh, no, child, I never said that. Believe I said *ours* won't kill *him*. He's using dark magic, remember? His will most definitely kill us."

Emma leaned over and threw up onto a car beneath us.

Ms. Bunchwick patted her back.

"Don't worry, dear. One direct hit of that and you won't even know it. Six times hotter than the surface of the sun. You'll be a pile of ash before you can blink. Won't feel a thing, I promise you."

Emma threw up again.

Seamus shot another bolt and hit the road in front of us. A pillar of smoke rose from the smoldering tar and we closed our eyes to fly through it.

"Enough of this nonsense," Ms. Bunchwick said. She grabbed a handful of cards and threw them, shooting a wave of bolts at him. Seamus swerved and twisted in the air to avoid them and lost his balance, landing on top of a car and rolling down the hood.

"You got him!"

"You ain't learned nothing about luck, have you?"

The cop cars were closer now and the officers were leaning out of their windows, gesturing wildly and yelling at us through their megaphones. The sirens and lights made it hard to concentrate and Seamus's men were right behind them.

"Ignore them," Ms. Bunchwick said, pointing. "Focus on the bigger problem."

Seamus was back in the air when we crossed onto the bridge. Below us, the river ran fast, and large rocks poked from the surface, like a herd of elephants crossing over to the next town.

The accident was close, and cars passed it one by one, each driving slowly so they could investigate the scene.

"Thank goodness for nosy drivers! We'll have a straight shot over!" Ms. Bunchwick yelled as we flew over the cones and ambulances. She lowered her hand on the other side and the motorcycle settled onto the bridge, tires bouncing and groaning on the road.

"Half mile and we're on the other side. It's cruisin' time!"

Emma leaned in and we sped off. The cops were having a hard time getting around the accident, which bought us some time and meant that Seamus's men were still behind them.

In the distance, a little dot twisted in the air, flying to the side of the bridge and over the river.

"There he is!" I yelled, but he was far enough away that I didn't think he was too big of a threat.

But then his wand began to glow, like a match held in a dark room, and then the light grew and grew until it was the size of a beach ball and then a small car, as bright as the sun.

"What's he doing?" Emma asked.

Ms. Bunchwick looked back, squinting her eyes at the impossibly large ball of light.

"Oh no."

"What?"

"No, no, no, no, no! Faster, Emma! Just a bit farther!"

The rain beat against our face like pellets, and the wind shook the bike.

She threw the rest of my cards, waving the wand and shooting bolt after bolt into the sky, desperately trying to hit him.

Seamus tilted the wand back and flicked it at us. The large ball of light shot through the sky, arcing upward a hundred feet in front of us.

"He's a bad shot," Emma said.

"Wasn't aiming for us," Ms. Bunchwick said, leaning in lower. "Close your eyes, children. I'm taking over."

She lifted us off the ground, and above, I could see the light coming down like a missile toward the bridge.

It made impact, and then everything exploded in blinding light, like a supernova had erupted in front of us. We flew backward, the motorcycle breaking into little pieces.

Time seemed to pause. We hovered in the air, Ms. Bunchwick beside me, wand gripped tightly in her hand.

She looked over at me and nodded, seemed to mouth

words, but I couldn't understand them. She waved the wand at me and Emma.

We hit the ground and rolled along the asphalt. My tuxedo was burned, and large holes were torn in the pants and jacket. Fire and smoke lit up the sky, and twisted pieces of concrete and metal flew through the air and landed around us.

A high-pitched sound rang in my ears, and my whole body hurt.

I opened my eyes. Everything was hazy, blinking in and out of focus.

The world spun around me.

Ahead, I could see a large hole in the bridge. A huge section was gone, and pieces along the edge crumbled and fell into the rushing river below.

Behind me, Emma lay on the road, unmoving. I called out to her, but she didn't answer.

Ms. Bunchwick was on her stomach, the wand several feet in front of her. She groaned, pushed herself up, and crawled toward it, each inch a painful endeavor.

Blurry lights blinked in the distance. The cops were getting closer, which meant Seamus's men were close as well.

Ms. Bunchwick reached the wand, grabbing it with a shaky hand and sitting up. She crawled toward Emma and shook her, pushing her hair out of her forehead.

"Oh, dearie. Oh, dearie," she mumbled.

The police cars stopped in front of us, forming a barricade. Doors opened, sirens stopped, and guns were drawn.

"FREEZE!"

"Ms. Bunchwick, what do we do?" I asked.

"Never you mind them," she said, leaning in and whispering things into Emma's ear.

"Put your hands in the air and walk toward us!" a cop yelled. "No sudden movements."

"Ms. Bunchwick?"

She continued to whisper, and Emma moved a bit and coughed.

Seamus circled above us, and the black car parked behind the police cruisers.

"We don't mean no harm," Ms. Bunchwick shouted, her frail arms shaking as she raised them to the sky. "It weren't us that did any of this."

"What's in your hand?"

She looked at the wand.

"This? Oh, just a stick. Nothing special. Makes me feel better to hang on to it."

I scanned the police officers for Ralph. I never wanted to see him more than I did at that moment, but he wasn't there.

"Drop the stick, ma'am."

"Afraid I can't do that."

"Did you kidnap those kids?"

"No!" I yelled, and Emma shook her head, rubbing her eyes with the back of her hand.

"Walk toward us, ma'am. Hands up."

"Oh, you can stop calling me ma'am, Officer." She turned to us and said, "Stay here. He's coming, and we best be ready."

"One step at a time," a police officer said. "No sudden movements."

"Any second now," she said.

"Drop the stick. I won't ask you again."

She took another step forward, and a circle of fire erupted around us. Flames shot dozens of feet in the air, roaring with heat, and Ms. Bunchwick fell on her back, sliding back toward us.

"Mental deception!" Ms. Bunchwick screamed. "It ain't real . . . I think."

It didn't matter if it was real or not—it was the hottest I had ever been in my life, and I fell to the ground, covered in sweat, unable to stand.

Seamus landed on the road and walked through the fire, unburnt, his eyes glowing.

"Oh, my dear Edna. When will you learn that there's no point running from me? I will always catch you, and other people will get hurt."

He pointed his wand at me and Emma.

"Must I go through this whole speech again?" He faked a disinterested yawn and held out his palm. "Give me the wand or I'll blast these little weasels into the river."

"No," Ms. Bunchwick cried.

"You have such a predictable soft spot for children. It's a weakness, my dear. You must work on it."

"It's not a weakness, Seamus. You loved our little boy, too, and don't pretend otherwise."

"Yes. I would never deny it."

"Magic ain't meant to raise the dead. It ain't meant for any nasty thing you can think of."

"Magic is *meant* for whatever I say it is. That's where you've always been confused. You should have listened to me. Our boy wasn't dead yet. He could still be saved. There was still time. But even with our dear child's life at risk you wouldn't join me. I do wish you hadn't run away so fast, because I never got to explain. I never got to tell you the truth of what happened that night. I never got to tell you how I faked it all."

A rattle started deep inside Ms. Bunchwick, radiating out until her whole body shook.

"What are you saying Seamus?" she asked.

"I mastered mental deception long before you understood it, and created the accident to tip you onto my side. Who would have guessed it would push you so forcefully to the other? I thought saving our boy was the only way you would let me find the tree."

"Is he—is he still alive?" Ms. Bunchwick said, her hands clasped in a prayer. "Is he all right? Please tell me. Please."

"I'm grateful in our struggle I broke off a small piece of the wand; otherwise you may have found the tree on your own. Who can imagine what you would have done to it."

"Where is he? Tell me."

"He's here."

In the distance, a small speck appeared, flying toward us. It landed, and from the other side of the flames, a voice said, "So *this* is my dear mother?"

EMMA

Duncan didn't say anything about the Highway Incident, either, did he?

He better not have.

We promised each other.

I mean, not that anything happened.

But still.

Okay, he was driving.

Now I plead the Fifth again.

Do I have to say that every time?

Is it hot in here?

DUNCAN

Quinton Penfold walked through the fire, removing a necklace from underneath his scarf. Attached to the black cord was a small, half-inch piece of twisted twig. He handed it to Seamus.

"Yes, boy, this is your mother, in the flesh."

"She's shorter than I imagined."

"Quite," Seamus said. He turned to Ms. Bunchwick. "I've told him all about you, Edna. How you ran away with the wand, abandoned him, and left him to die."

Seamus removed the piece from Quinton's necklace and held it to his half of the wand.

"It was a small piece that broke off. Not enough to do anything spectacular. Just enough to do smaller magic, the kind that might fool the average numpty in front of a television set. Couple that with my catalog of old tricks and I could turn anyone I wanted into the most famous magician in the world."

"Quinton Penfold's my stage name," he said, sliding over to Ms. Bunchwick. "Sounded good when I thought it up as a teenager, but I have to admit it has a cheesy ring to it these days."

Ms. Bunchwick sobbed, falling to the ground, her knuckles white from gripping the wand.

From the other side of the fire, the police officers yelled, looking for a way to get through.

"I figured you might have passed it on ages ago, considering how much you loved following rules," Seamus said. "But I knew you didn't destroy it. The fact that my small piece still worked told me it was still around. I've been traveling the world on Quinton's tours, watching for magicians that displayed, what you would call, *unnatural* abilities."

"Then we saw the video of these two *children*, and it was like . . . BOOM, there it is," Quinton said. He grabbed Ms. Bunchwick by the shoulders and pulled her up. "Hand it over, Mum."

"Never," she whispered, rubbing her hand across Quinton's cheek. "Don't do this, love. Please. You don't have to listen to him."

Quinton laughed and pushed her hand away.

"Ronan, Vince, get in here."

They walked through the fire, unharmed, and surrounded us.

Past the roaring flames I could still hear the sirens of the police cars and the distant thumping of a helicopter.

"Don't do it," Ms. Bunchwick said.

"What right do you have to tell me anything? You left me to die and missed my whole life."

"I didn't know, boy. I thought you were already gone, and . . ."

"I don't want to hurt you, Edna," Seamus said, extending a hand. "I am not a monster. I only want what is mine. If you fly, I'll catch you. We're too far from land to teleport, and the river is fast and cold. You've reached the limits of your good magic. It's over. Give it to me."

"Never," she said. She turned and ran through the flames, toward the hole in the highway bridge, Seamus, Quinton, Ronan, and Vince close behind her.

"She's flying away!" Ronan screamed, but he was wrong.

Ms. Bunchwick leapt in the air, paused for a moment, and then dropped like a stone into the rocky water below, making a distant splash.

"NO!" Seamus screamed.

"She'll die down there," Vince said with a smirk.

"She still has the wand, you idiot. Form a chain. Follow me," Seamus said, grabbing their hands and flying off, leaving Emma and me alone on the bridge.

The wall of flames disappeared into smoke, and there we sat, facing the police, in front of several million dollars worth of property damage.

Sorry. I know that probably looked bad.

ARRESTED

EMMA

So that was the first time I got arrested.

I didn't put up much of a fight. I'd been knocked around hard that night, and my head felt like a rock tumbler. It's hard to keep handcuffs on wrists as thin as mine, and they kept slipping off every two minutes. I'd hold up my hands in the back of the police car, and say things like, "Hey, guys, look, I'm free again," or "Wowee, I really *am* magic."

They didn't think that was very funny, but I didn't care. I was half delirious, and was in no mood to make their lives easier.

Finally, they used zip ties on my wrists and ankles and buckled me in tight.

They put Duncan in another car, probably because they thought we were possessed or something and would be dangerous together.

We were taken to the police station and questioned separately for a couple hours to see if they could figure out exactly what happened. As you know by now, I lied about everything until my parents' lawyer, Mr. Barker, showed up. He told me I shouldn't say anything and that we were being charged with multiple counts of arson, damage to public property, fleeing the police, and a whole list of other stuff that was *technically* true but only half of the story.

They told me they'd go easier on me if I cracked first and told them where Ms. Bunchwick or Seamus (who they called That Weird Man in the Sky) went, but I didn't know anything.

The only thing Ms. Bunchwick had told me (when I was still lying practically unconscious on the road) was, "I learned something special about you today. Never suspected it. Seamus won't, either."

I grunted back to her and she pushed the hair out of my face and leaned closer.

"Keep it hidden," she said, slipping half of the wand into my back pocket. "Use it when things are at their worst. Show the old fool some *real* magic. Let him have it."

And that was the end. She jumped into the river and left us there, all alone.

I just want you to remember that when things got serious, *I* was the one she picked to fix things. Does that sound like an assistant?

I don't think so.

The bad news was, I had no idea what she was talking about.

DUNCAN

I was taken to the police station that night, and they took my picture and fingerprints. My burnt tuxedo was thrown in a box, and they promised I'd get it back eventually. Not like I'd ever be able to wear it again.

Ralph brought some clothes for me to change into, and then the other cops questioned me for hours. They told me I was in big trouble and would be lucky to get out before my eighteenth birthday if I didn't start talking.

I'm really sorry, but I lied. *A lot.*

What was I supposed to do? Tell the truth? No one would believe it, and Ralph didn't want to back up my story because he was afraid of looking crazy and getting fired.

I bet half the people reading this think I'm crazy, too, and I don't blame them, but now I'm telling everything that happened as honestly as I remember it.

My parents decided the safest place for me was at the police station, so Ralph kept me in the holding cell that night for my protection. I sat in the corner, wasting away while Seamus and his men were still out there searching for Ms. Bunchwick and the wand. Maybe they'd caught her. Maybe they were torturing her. Maybe she was already dead. Maybe they had the whole wand and were already on their way to finding the tree.

The worst punishment was not knowing.

I felt rotten, and all I wanted to do was talk to Emma. What did Ms. Bunchwick say to her on that bridge?

Would we ever see her again?

If I were her, I probably would go on the run and find another small town to hide in. And if some stupid kid came ringing my doorbell, I'd turn him into an ant and squash him with my foot. The end. That's what she should have done to me.

I sat in my cell that night, head pressed against the cold concrete wall. Each minute dripped by, slower than the last, the clock in the hallway making a torturous CLICK CLACK CLICK as who-knows-what happened outside in the world.

I marked down the passing of hours on the wall like I've seen in the movies, scratching the paint from the cinder blocks with my fingernails.

I got the whole way to six before he returned.

EMMA

After my interrogation, the police released me to my parents' custody and Officer Ralph sent one of his friends to guard my house.

I think I would have rather stayed in jail with Duncan.

My house was much worse. Anna kept asking me if I was some dangerous magical witch-girl, and Jenna taped up her gymnastic mats on my walls in case I went totally bonkers. I'm just glad they didn't try to burn me at the stake.

I sat on my bed that night and thought hard about what Ms. Bunchwick had said to me. She said she had learned something special about me, but that didn't help much. Anna was good at acting and always got the lead role in every production she auditioned for, and Jenna could do thirty backflips in a row. Other than knowing a few magic tricks, there wasn't much special about me.

Maybe the explosion had rattled Ms. Bunchwick's brain loose.

The officers had taken everything from me when they signed me in to the station, including the half of the wand that Ms. Bunchwick had given me.

That was a fake, too, just one of the decoys she had made to fool Seamus. I tried to use it in the police car, but it didn't do anything.

I hoped she knew she still had the real wand. If she did, why would she plummet all the way off the bridge into the icy water?

I started to cry. I had been holding it back for a long time, but I finally let it all out. My body shook, and when I was done I felt like an empty eggshell.

I missed her.

I missed Duncan, too, but don't you dare tell him that.

I curled into a ball and rubbed my arms and legs to make myself warmer. It was colder than usual that night, and I could see my breath in the air.

I felt really bad for myself.

Maybe I wouldn't have if I had known what was happening to Duncan at the police station.

DUNCAN

I lay on the hard cell mattress, staring at the ceiling, and thinking about Houdini. I wondered what he would do if he was locked up with me. He would have escaped hours ago, I bet. What was my problem?

I counted the tiles on the ceiling (thirty-six), and then started counting the spots of chipped paint on the walls. I got to five hundred and twenty-two before I heard a soft banging sound in the distance and the whistling of wind through the halls.

I sat up and looked out the window.

There was nothing in the parking lot—just a few old cars that belonged to the officers.

I grabbed the bars and tried to push my head through to see the front desk.

"Ralph?" I yelled. "Are you there?"

No answer. Where did he go?

Everything was dark, except for the bright red Exit sign at the end that reflected light off the linoleum floor.

I listened closely.

BOOM.

Another sound, louder than before, and distant screams and the sound of metal scraping against concrete.

Someone was coming.

Sirens sounded in the building, and a blinking blue light pulsed on the ceiling.

There were muffled calls for help, then motion in the shadows.

A silhouette moved at the far end of the hall, head and chest visible through the half-windowed door, moving in a staccato rhythm through the light of the alarm.

I leaned in closer and watched as the door at the end of the hallway slammed open, cracking at the hinges and falling to the floor. A figure stepped in, pointing something directly at me.

"Ralph?"

I squinted. It wasn't Ralph, but something about his hair and the way he walked was familiar to me. He slid across the floor, like he was onstage performing.

Quinton.

"Sorry, boy, it's only me. Your little cop friend put up an admirable fight, but it wasn't enough."

There was a ball of light and the cell door flew through the air and slammed to the ground, the banging sound drowned out by the alarms.

Quinton raised his hands and the sirens ripped from the walls, making a final dying squeal.

"There's nowhere you can go that we won't find you, Duncan."

"I don't have the wand," I yelled, sliding back into my cell.

"It doesn't matter. Someone who cares about you does, and that's all we need."

With another flick of his wrist he sent me backward, and I landed hard on the floor.

"This is only going to end one way," Quinton said, using the wand to lift me up and slam me into the ceiling, breaking three of the thirty-six tiles.

"It's over, Duncan. Don't feel bad, it never really started. You were always outmatched."

"She's your mother," I said. "She loves you."

Quinton didn't respond.

He grabbed me, tied me up, blindfolded me, and pulled me through the halls until we were outside.

It was really cold, and he dragged me across the gravel parking lot, then lifted me up and held a cloth that smelled like bitter chemicals against my face.

The trunk slammed shut and everything went black for a while.

EMMA

The sounds started after midnight. There was a lot of weird movement and noise outside.

A car door slammed.

There was thumping. Arguing. Grunts.

This is it, I thought. *They're back, and this time, they're going to finish the job.*

I heard my dad yell, "What's going on?" and then there were footsteps in the hallway and my door creaked open.

I stayed in the corner, curled up, peeking through my eyelashes as a man limped into my room and came closer. He was breathing heavy and clutching his side.

"Come on, Emma," he said. "We have to go."

I recognized the voice.

It was Officer Ralph.

"Where?" I asked, but he didn't answer. He grabbed my hand and pulled me up. We ran down the hall. Anna and Jenna peered out of their rooms and Molly began to cry.

"Ralph?" Mom asked. "What's happening?"

"You have to leave," he groaned. "Go somewhere safe. They're coming."

Dad grabbed Molly and said, "That's it, we're taking the girls to Aunt Carol's house."

"Good idea," Officer Ralph said. "Drop them off and meet us at Zug's shop."

We went outside and I jumped into the back seat of Officer Ralph's car and he started to drive before I could even close the door.

"They took Duncan," he whispered. His voice shook. He drove his car through the streets with the headlights off. "I tried to protect him, but I couldn't. Quinton was too strong."

"Are you hurt?" I asked.

"Just bruised. Figured it wouldn't be long before they came for you. Looks like I made it right in time."

I turned and watched as a black car sped in the direction of my house.

I didn't know where we were going. We were taking the long way, snaking through alleys, driving through grass, going faster than we should have.

I shivered in my pajamas.

"Here," he said, throwing a box on my seat.

Inside were the clothes I was wearing when I was arrested, and the half of the wand Ms. Bunchwick had given me. I pulled it out and held it up, spinning it in my hand.

Officer Ralph's eyes widened in the rearview mirror.

"Emma, where did you get that?"

"She gave it to me. But don't get excited, it's not real."

I waved it in the air and imagined Officer Ralph turning into a zebra. Nothing happened.

"Why would she give you half of a fake wand?"

"She told me there was something special about me, and I could use it to beat Seamus."

"What do you mean?"

"I don't know. She said I didn't think anything of it, but that Seamus would never see it coming."

We turned onto a familiar street and Officer Ralph parked in front of Zug's shop. It was still dark out, and frost caked around the windows.

A light switched on and Zug opened the door and peeked out.

Officer Ralph started to giggle, and turned around and smiled at me.

"What?" I asked.

"Emma, I think I know what's special about you."

DUNCAN

I was alone, in the middle of a field full of brown grass where dry, dead stalks of corn lay on their sides. The sky was a dark green and the clouds rolled fast, curling over themselves and dancing across the hazy sun.

Everything was swimming around me, like my eyes were full of water. I tried to walk but I wasn't strong enough.

I heard her voice, far away.

"You're in trouble, boy," she said. "You must be smart now."

Ms. Bunchwick floated in the distance, transformed into the worst witch I could imagine. She wore a black robe that squirmed like snakes, and her yellow eyes glowed at me. I wanted to run toward her and hug her, but I couldn't move.

"Where are we?"

She laughed.

"In your mind. A scary, dark place at the moment, it seems."

"Am I dreaming?"

"Aye."

"What should I do?"

She shrugged.

"No use running. I tried, and look what good that did.

Only thing left to do is defeat him."

"What will he do if we don't?"

She laughed again, this time so loud that it made the sky rumble and the earth shake.

"He'll destroy you. And then he'll destroy the town and everything you love. Now wake up, Duncan. Wake up."

REAL MAGIC

CASE ID116-819 FOLDER NO. 26

EMMA

Officer Ralph moved his car to the alley behind Zug's shop so no one would see it.

Zug let us in and paced the floor of his shop, staring at the posters of old magicians on the walls. There was Howard Thurston holding a skull with angels and demons flowing from the eye sockets, Harry Kellar levitating a woman in a red dress, and Charles Carter staring into a crystal ball.

It was still dark out, and only a single dim bulb lit the room, barely bright enough to see anything.

My parents arrived after dropping Anna, Jenna, and Molly at my Aunt Carol's house, and Officer Ralph watched at the front window for Ms. Reyes and Duncan's dad.

"We'll have to keep moving," Officer Ralph said. "They know where we live and they know about this store. It's not safe to stay anywhere for too long."

"I suppose it isn't," Zug said. He rubbed his hand on a poster from the late 1800s advertising the "Original Pepper's Ghost" and straightened the frame on the wall. "But how long can we run? Days? Weeks?"

"As long as we have to," Officer Ralph said. "They'll give up eventually."

"I don't believe that," Zug said. He turned to me and knelt down. "You say she gave you a fake half of the wand?"

"Yeah, she slipped this in my pocket, then jumped into the water. But I think she meant to give me the real thing."

I handed the half to Zug and he spun it in his hands, making it disappear and reappear.

Ms. Reyes arrived, and Duncan's dad led her to the door. She was crying, and I gave her a big hug as soon as she entered the store, but I don't think it helped much.

Zug nodded to them and went back to pacing.

"Did she say anything else after she gave this to you?" Zug asked.

"Not really. Just that I should show Seamus some real magic and then let him have it."

"Let him have it?"

I shrugged.

"I think she just meant that I should be tough on him." I threw a few punches in the air. "You know, like, really let him have it? Ms. Bunchwick has a lot of weird expressions."

"No," Zug said, snapping his fingers. "I don't think that's what she meant at all. I think she *knew* the wand was fake and wanted you to give it to him. Didn't Duncan say if he uses the spell to find the tree using a fake wand, the worst thing he can imagine will happen to him?"

"That won't work," I said. "He'll know right away that it isn't real."

"Will he?" Zug asked with a smile. "What if he sees it doing *real magic* with his own eyes?"

DUNCAN

I woke up in darkness. I didn't know how long I had been out, but I knew that we were moving. I was tied up, tighter than I ever had been before, but this time there were no pull cords to release the knots.

My head hurt and the smell of bitter chemicals was still strong in my nose.

Soon, the car stopped and a door slammed.

We sat for a few minutes and then I heard muffled voices.

I shimmied over in the trunk and pressed my ear against the side, trying to hear anything.

"She ain't around," Vince said. "Don't know why we're even looking. She died in that water, sure as I'm standing here."

"She may be dead, but the wand is still working. That means *someone* has it," Ronan said.

"Then we have to find the girl."

EMMA

"What kind of magic can the wand do?" Zug asked, pulling every magic book he owned off the shelves.

"Well, there are four main things," I said. "Ignoring dark magic, of course."

"Of course," my mom said.

I grabbed a piece of paper and drew a copy of the star Ms. Bunchwick had drawn in the ground during our lessons in the woods.

"First there's transformation. We can change into animals or monsters. That's how Duncan turned the reporter into a goat. And that's how Ms. Bunchwick turns into a scary-looking witch. You can pretty much turn anything into anything."

"All right," Zug said, clapping his hands and pointing to a poster of Nevil Maskelyne. "Metamorphosis has us covered on that one. Staging it out in the open will be a challenge, but we'll do it with a small animal, which will make it easier. And we'll have to lead them where we want them. What's next?"

"Levitation," I said.

Zug rubbed his hands through his beard and murmured to himself.

"Maskelyne's technique might be too cumbersome for that one, especially if we're outside. The setup is too long, and we'd need too many wires. We need to simplify. Maybe Copperfield? Detaching Emma would be the hard part. But we could divert their attention long enough that they won't see it. Yes, that's it. Fine."

He scribbled notes on the piece of paper and turned to me.

"What's next, Emma?"

"You're not going to like this one," I said. "Mental deception."

"Mental *deception*?" he asked.

"Yeah, like, you can make people think terrible things. It's really freaky. One time I saw a whole wall of fire, and all the animals in the trees turned into walking skeletons. Oh, and another time we saw a giant wave of water that swept us up and—"

Zug tapped the poster advertising Pepper's Ghost and said, "Got it. Mr. John Henry Pepper has us covered here, but we'll need some help on that one."

"Pepper?" Ms. Reyes asked.

"It's an old technique. You've probably seen it in haunted houses. Simply speaking, it involves using a large piece of glass standing up and tilted at a forty-five-degree angle. At the right angle, your viewers can look right through it, but it will reflect whatever is beneath it in a transparent, ghostlike way. But I don't know where we'll find a big enough piece of glass."

Duncan's dad whispered something.

"What was that?"

"Umm . . . it's nothing . . . just . . . you know I sell windows, right?"

"I don't think a window will be big enough," Zug said.

"My guys are installing one this week at the new Lots o' Value. Would sixty feet wide and fifteen feet high be enough?"

Zug's eye bulged.

"You could get that?"

"I'll have to bend a few rules. And you have to promise to be careful with it. It's really expensive, and if it breaks, or gets even the smallest scratch, I'm—"

"This is for Duncan," Officer Ralph said, and his voice cracked a little.

Duncan's dad nodded. "I know. I'll get a truck and bring it over."

"What's next?" Zug asked.

"Teleportation."

Lights lit up the store for a moment, and a black car drove past.

"That's them," Officer Ralph said.

We ducked behind the counter and waited.

"Did they see us?" Ms. Reyes asked.

There was a loud noise and the front door shattered. The alarm sounded, and the lights switched off.

"We know you're inside," one of the men said.

"Come out," the other said.

"Follow me," Officer Ralph whispered. He took my hand and pulled me through the store and out to the back alley.

We all squeezed into his car (which was a magic trick

itself), locking the doors just as the two men from the theater burst into the alley and pulled at the door handles.

"Go!" Zug screamed.

We sped down the alleyway, hitting a trash can as we turned onto the road, then zipping through side streets to lose them.

I looked back in horror and saw smoke and fire coming from Zug's Magic Shop.

DUNCAN

The car sped around town, stopping just long enough for me to hear broken glass and a squealing alarm. Then we were moving again, like we were chasing someone, never able to catch up.

I was thrown around the trunk and slammed into the sides, so hard that my head throbbed and my arms tingled with a numb pain.

Finally, we stopped and the trunk opened.

The morning sun blazed high in the sky, and I was pulled out and dragged through familiar hallways, back to the small room in the basement of the Elephant Theater.

Seamus paced the floor, swimming in the blurry haze of my vision.

"Bad luck, Duncan," he said. "We couldn't find what we were looking for, which means we will have to get it by *alternate* means."

I moaned.

"Whoever has the wand cares about you. And sometimes, that's all that matters."

PREPARATIONS

EMMA

Luckily, Seamus and his men didn't know about Zug's storage space.

Officer Ralph drove through large rows of cement buildings with metal doors until we found his unit.

Zug ran to the door, unlocked it, and waved us in. For someone who had just seen their store set on fire, he was handling it pretty well. The whole ride over he had been sketching out tricks on a notepad and talking to himself.

"Do you need help?" Officer Ralph asked.

"We'll be fine," Zug said, sorting through big boxes of chains and dusty props. "You know, we just need to put on the most convincing magic show of all time by the end of the day. Simple as that."

My dad and Duncan's dad stayed in the car with Officer Ralph to go get the window from the Lots o' Value construction site. As they were pulling away, Officer Ralph opened his window and yelled out, "Emma, don't forget—you're special!"

I growled at him.

"What's he talking about?" Ms. Reyes asked.

Ugh. I had hoped to avoid that.

I told them all about what Ms. Bunchwick had said to me on the bridge, and what Officer Ralph *thought* she meant.

Zug laughed.

"It's perfect," he said. "Why didn't we ever use it before?"

"Because," I said. "It's just that . . . well . . . you wouldn't understand. . . ."

"Maybe it's a bad idea," Mom said. "It sounds extra dangerous."

"I'll be the one in danger," I said. "Not like it'll work, anyway. Vanishing the Statue of Liberty would be easier."

"You're so dramatic." Mom said.

"You seriously have *no idea*."

We went inside the storage unit, and I helped Zug push everything we'd need toward the front.

"It's an awful lot of stuff," Mom said.

"Big illusions to create," Zug said, sliding boxes around with his foot and sorting through props. I'd never seen him this intense in my life. He turned to me. "I think we're going to need even more help. Can you get some of your friends here?"

"Friends?" I asked. "What friends? Do you think Duncan and I eat lunch by ourselves for the fun of it?"

"Well, we need some people to help with the mental deception. The scarier looking the better."

I thought for a bit and then grabbed an old bike of his and jumped on.

I knew just the person to ask, and he owed me one. I just hoped he wouldn't try to kill me, too.

DUNCAN

Quinton pointed at a map of the town. My house was circled in red, along with Emma's house, Ms. Bunchwick's house, and Zug's shop.

"We've torn through the houses, yeah, and nothing's there," Quinton said.

Ronan and Vince sat on folding metal chairs and nodded.

"So what do we do? How do we draw them out?"

Seamus was in the far corner of the small room, facing the wall, hands clasped behind his back.

"We don't even know if the wand is close," Ronan said. "Your old lady could be hiding out in the Antarctic by now. Face it, Seamus—we're finished. It don't matter how much damage and destruction we do here, that selfish old hag ain't going to be coming back any time soon."

"Be careful how you speak about my mother," Quinton said with a smile.

"Apologies," Ronan said, holding up his hands in mock surrender.

"We saw with our own eyes how slick she was with sleight

of hand," Vince said. "I'd swear on my life that I saw her give something to that girl."

"Why would she do that?" Quinton asked. "And why wouldn't Emma use it if she had it? There's been no magic since last night."

"Of course there ain't. They're smarter than they used to be. They've been keeping it hidden, boss. That's the only thing that makes sense."

"Maybe we should call it quits here. Move on," Ronan said. "If she's gone, torturing these people won't do anything. Much as I hate to say it, it may be time to start over."

"Start over?" Vince said.

"Yeah."

"No," Seamus said. He spun to face them, holding the half of the wand in the air. "When things get bad, it's time for us to get worse. I'm not leaving without the wand, even if I have to kill the boy and destroy everything in this miserable town."

EMMA

I pulled up in front of a small house. There were long strands of weeds and grass surrounding the mailbox and light pole, and a rusted-out shell of an old sports car sitting beside the garage.

I had never been to Tommy's house before, but for some reason I expected it to be bigger and more expensive than mine, especially considering how much he loved to make fun of how poor Duncan was.

I walked halfway up the front lawn when I heard, "I ain't looking to buy anything."

A tall man with a potbelly covered in a stained T-shirt stood at the door.

"I'm looking for Tommy," I said.

"What do you want with him?"

"We need to talk. It's important."

"Tommy don't play with little kids. Think you got the wrong house."

There was movement inside.

"Hey, aren't you one of those Gilbert girls?" the man

asked. "The one from the news that's been causing all that trouble?"

The door opened and Tommy stepped outside.

"What do you want, Emma?" he asked.

"I'm sure you've heard that Duncan and I are in a lot of trouble."

"Yeah. So what?"

"We need your help. All of this is kind of your fault."

"What are you talking about? I didn't do anything."

"Really? You don't remember locking us in the witch's house? Or how you nailed the top of the water chamber shut? Everything that's happened has been because of *you*."

"Was not."

"Was too!"

"You better go," the man said. "He ain't interested in whatever it is you're doing."

I turned to leave and then stopped. Tommy wasn't getting off that easy. If I was ever going to say what I really thought about him, it was now.

"You're a bully," I said. "You never think about anyone else. You just walk around and make fun of everyone to make yourself feel better. I don't get it. People would like you if you were just nicer. And now Duncan's in real danger, and if anything happens to him, I'm blaming *you*."

Tommy laughed.

"I'm the bully? You guys always sit at your little table and act so special and superior to everyone else. I asked Duncan to teach me a trick and he stuck a card to my face and made the whole school laugh at me. And we only locked you in the house because you told everyone we were chickens. You're the bullies."

Excuse me? *We* were the bullies? Yeah, Duncan embarrassed him in the cafeteria, but he didn't really want to learn how to do a magic trick, did he? We were the good kids and he was the bad kid. We were never mean to anyone. Okay, yeah, we spread that rumor last year about him being part reptile, but he started it by saying Duncan and I were dating. And we spilled disappearing ink all over his pants, but that was because he pushed Duncan in the hall. He deserved all of it, didn't he?

I started to feel bad.

"I'm sorry," I said, and I really meant it. "We didn't want to hurt you. I guess we just never thought you had feelings. If we survive this, I promise we'll teach you how to do a trick. And maybe we could both try to be nicer to each other?"

Tommy didn't move.

I walked back toward the bike.

Tommy sighed and walked out of the house.

"Wait," he said. He opened the garage and pulled out his bike.

"I'll get Wilson and Juan. Where should we meet you?"

DUNCAN

Seamus whispered something to Quinton, and then there was another damp rag pressed against my face and a strong smell of chemicals. My vision went brown, and pulsing veins and sparkling dots of light appeared in the corners. Then everything slipped away, like a dark curtain had been lowered.

EMMA

We didn't stay in any one place for too long. The preparation took all day and the hours raced by. Soon, it was getting dark, and the chilly wind blew in strong gusts down the road.

I wished more than anything that Ms. Bunchwick would appear, like magic, and tell me what to do, but I was seriously starting to doubt that would happen.

She was gone, and it was all up to me now.

Zug prepared all the magic gear and brought it to my aunt's house. He sat out front as a lookout and talked to Duncan's dad on the phone about where to put the giant panel of glass and how to set it up.

"Behind the fence will be perfect," Zug said. "The rock wall is high enough that they can lay underneath it. . . . Forty-five-degree angle . . . I don't know, you'll have to measure it. . . . Yes, the brightest lights you can find. I'm sure the church has electric outlets in the lobby. . . . Door is never locked. . . . No, don't call and ask permission, they're going to wonder what you're doing in the . . . All right, yes . . . I understand . . . Good idea."

I sat in a corner with a notebook and sketched out a plan for my grand finale. It was the biggest, most dangerous trick of my life, and after it was done, nothing would ever be the same.

One way or the other.

DUNCAN

When I awoke, I could see the town around me, like I was at the center of a bicycle wheel, the roads of the town branching out in every direction like spokes. The sun descended through the sky, and the fading light cast long shadows on the ground.

It was getting darker earlier, I thought, but wasn't it just morning? How long had I been out?

I tried to move but was tied tight. A cloth had been shoved in my mouth and taped down.

I was *really* high up.

I have never seen the town from this angle.

I looked around. It was empty. The storefronts were closed and trash blew across the streets. I saw the Elephant Theater to my left, and the giant poster that advertised Emma's and my performance had been torn in half and hung in shreds.

To the right, I could see the top of my house in the distance, and I wondered where my mom was. I hoped she was all right.

I looked down, wiggled my arms, and saw that I was sitting on something hard and gray. It was cold and bumpy, and slanted downward on every side. Toward the front, two giant pieces of rock stuck out from the sides like ears, and a thin piece jutted out from the front.

Then I realized: I was *on* the Elephant Rock.

Hands touched my shoulders and I looked back to see Seamus standing behind me, whispering strange things to the wand.

He held it in the air, and dark clouds swirled in the sky, a cyclone of black. A bolt of light shot down and covered him in a strange green glow. He quivered and shook, standing with his face pointed to the clouds, arms raised to the sky.

The fire in his eyes burned brighter than before and he pushed his long black hair off of his forehead.

"Do you think they'll notice that?" Seamus whispered. "Impossible to miss."

He jumped into the air and floated to the ground, landing next to Quinton.

"We've set the bait," Seamus said. "Now we just need to wait."

EMMA

Clouds spun in the sky, right above the center of the town. It was that same tornado of black that appeared the day before at the Elite Magicians Convention, with bright bolts of electricity crackling in the center.

My dad, Duncan's dad, and Officer Ralph met us at my aunt's house.

"They're at the Elephant Rock," Officer Ralph said. "My guess is they have Duncan and want us to go there, so now's our chance."

"I'll be close to you the whole time," Zug said. "If anything bad happens, just keep moving forward with the plan."

I glanced over a map one more time and then gave my mom a hug before stepping out into the dusk.

The entire town was my stage, and the bad guys were my audience.

It was showtime.

SHOWTIME

DUNCAN

A cat walked down the middle of the street, hissing at Ronan and Vince before slithering between Quinton's legs.

I was too far away to see much, but I noticed a few clumps of mangy black hair sticking out from behind his ears.

No Name.

"Look at that," Vince said. "Stupid thing's gonna get smushed."

"Come here, kitty," Ronan said. The cat arched his back and took a swipe with a fanged paw and continued on. "When do you think they'll show up?"

Seamus wasn't listening. He paced the sidewalk in front of the Elephant Rock, waiting.

The streets were nearly empty, and the few people that did notice me just shook their heads and walked away.

I couldn't blame them. They probably thought it was just another one of my magic tricks about to go terribly wrong.

But what was No Name doing here?

He slinked onto the sidewalk, rubbing his side against a lamp post before hopping onto a blue mailbox. He paused, turned and hissed, then leapt into the air. In a puff of smoke, he morphed into Emma.

"It's the girl!" Ronan screamed, running down the middle of the road. "Did you see that? She transformed from a cat!"

"She's got the wand!" Vince yelled.

"Then get her," Seamus growled.

Emma ran and turned the corner, disappearing onto my street, Ronan and Vince close behind.

EMMA

Metamorphosis.

It's Magic 101.

Commonly used onstage, with a magician locked inside a big trunk, a trapdoor, and an assistant. A curtain goes up, and in an instant the assistant and magician switch places, making it look like they morphed into each other.

That day, we needed to improvise.

Duncan's dad drove his truck onto the main street and I ran behind it, ducking onto the sidewalk and hiding under a mailbox. I had a small angled mirror that Zug had cut to the perfect length, and I wedged it at an angle. Now if anyone looked at the mailbox from a distance, they wouldn't see me crouched behind it.

At the other side of the Elephant rock, Duncan's dad let No Name out of the truck.

I opened a can of tuna and waved my hand over the top to spread the fumes into the air, then waited, hoping No Name would smell it and come, just as we had practiced.

Soon, I could hear the soft pattering of his feet against

the pavement. He meowed and rubbed his ribs on a light pole, then leapt to the top of the mailbox.

It's always risky putting an animal into your act, especially one as crazy as No Name, but we had to make a memorable first impression.

"Pssst, *No Name*," I whispered. "Pssst."

He looked down and hissed at me.

I held the tuna up and whispered, "Jump, No Name, jump."

He tilted his head at me and began to lick his paw.

"Bad kitty, *jump*," I said again, but he wasn't listening.

There wasn't time to waste. I held the can up as high as I could and waved it in a circle, gripping the smoke bomb in my other hand.

He meowed again, and I pulled out the biggest, greasiest piece of tuna I could find and threw it in the air.

No Name jumped, paws spread out, his mouth open. I dropped the smoke bomb and leapt into the air, catching him in my coat and pausing to make sure Seamus, Quinton, and their thugs had seen me.

I caught a quick glance of the Elephant Rock and saw something small strapped to the top.

Duncan.

Dark clouds rolled above his head.

There was a scream, and someone pointed at me and yelled.

Transformation was a *success*.

I ran as fast as I could down the street, taking a shortcut through an alley and cutting through the backyards, leaping over small fences and avoiding coiled garden hoses.

Dogs barked, kids stared, and an old man raking leaves howled in surprise.

I kept moving, never stopping to apologize.

Soon, I was at Duncan's house. His mom, Officer Ralph, and Zug were waiting for me with a leather harness.

"How'd it go?" Ms. Reyes asked.

"I think they bought it," I said. "But they're on their way."

"Good," Officer Ralph said. "Then it's time to fly."

DUNCAN

Ronan was already half way to the mailbox and Vince followed behind.

"What do you think?" Seamus said.

"Hard to say from a distance," Quinton said.

"You think it's a trick?"

"I think they're trying to lure us somewhere."

"But why?" Seamus asked, pulling his half of the wand from his shirt pocket.

Quinton shrugged.

"Consider me intrigued," Seamus said. "You wait here. Watch the boy."

He walked calmly down the sidewalk, his long fingers tip-toeing up the side of the blue mailbox. He grasped a light pole with an extended arm and spun himself around the corner, walking quickly toward my house.

Quinton stood in the distance, waiting, watching, making sure I didn't move.

That's when I saw movement in the corner of my vision, a figure hunched along the street, covered in a shawl.

From within the shadowed hood, eyes glowed, and a finger waved at me, pressed to the lips, telling me to be quiet.

It was Ms. Bunchwick.

EMMA

I grabbed a broom and jumped out of Duncan's window, onto the large limb of the tree out front, climbing up, higher than the rooftops, toward the thickest branch that would support me.

There were a dozen thin cables attached to each side of the harness, and Zug and Officer Ralph fed them out, making sure they didn't tangle.

I crouched on a branch, watching, waiting.

The men were close, and in the distance, I saw Seamus walking down the street, wand held high.

The clouds and darkness followed him, and the wind blew trash and leaves in a cyclone down the street.

"I'm going," I said, wedging the broom between my knees and kicking off from the tree.

The cables whirred as they rubbed against the bark, and I held the fake wand up, making sure everyone could see it.

"There she is!" Ronan yelled.

"Sh-sh-she has the wand!" Vince stammered.

I slowly lowered down, passing the rooftops.

Seamus pointed his wand and shot bolts at the tree, hitting

limbs, wood exploding into splinters. The tree shook and my harness groaned and squeaked.

I was still at break-your-neck-if-you-fall height, and I really didn't want to see what would happen if he hit the branch that was supporting me.

"Hurry up!" I shouted to Zug and Officer Ralph.

I lowered faster and Seamus shot again. He hit some wires on my left side, and they whooshed as they spun in the air, like the strings of a guitar that had violently snapped during an intense solo. I wobbled and leaned, trying to keep myself upright. I dropped the broom.

"Faster! Faster!"

I was at shattered-ankles height now, and he fired again, hitting a giant branch that cracked and fell, smashing onto the ground below.

That was it. I was done with this.

By now I was at minor-cuts-and-bruises height, so I grabbed the side of the harness and pulled the release pins, dropping to the ground and landing on my feet.

Ta-da.

No applause.

There was a ripping sound behind me. The tree shook and lifted out of the ground, roots and all, tearing the grass from Duncan's small front yard like that time my uncle's toupee got caught on the coat hook.

A shadow passed over me, and I looked up to see the tree flying above me, spinning in position. The long cables whipped the air as they twisted around.

"Give me the wand, girl!" Seamus yelled.

But it wasn't time for that yet.

I ran beside Duncan's house, crouching on the narrow cement path.

Bolts of red light hit the sidewalk, sending rocks into the air.

Things were not going as well I had hoped they would. Seamus was more dangerous and psychotic than before. One wrong decision and I'd be deader than Houdini.

I leaned around the corner of the house to see him. He was fifty feet away now, and a bolt passed by my head so close that I could smell burning hair.

I pressed my hands against the brick wall of Duncan's home, waiting until he was even closer. Waiting until he could see where I was going and follow me. I was sticking with the plan, even though things were going horribly wrong.

The house began to shake. Dust and dirt rose in a cloud, and the walls moaned and creaked. It ripped from the ground, raising up, hunks of concrete still attached to the bottom. A large crack formed on the side of the house, running all the way down from the roof.

There were screams from inside, and through the window I watched Zug and Officer Ralph run downstairs, grab Ms. Reyes, and pull her to the kitchen. They jumped out the back door just before the whole house rocketed up, leaving only a small patch of dirt on the ground.

The house went higher, spinning until it was smaller than

a dollhouse. Books and pans and chairs and papers fell around us, out of the shattered windows and opened doors.

Seamus conducted it in patterns, rotating it and shaking it. I watched, unable to move, mesmerized.

"What are you doing?" Zug shouted to me.

I didn't answer. I couldn't.

"I'll destroy everything, you know," Seamus said. "There will be nothing left of Elephant but a burn mark."

Seamus laughed and dropped his arms. The house paused in the air and then began to fall.

"Emma, *go!*" Zug shouted.

I ran down the sidewalk.

Behind me, Seamus shouted curses and shot bolts around my head.

The concrete slabs of the sidewalk began to tremble and rip from the ground, hovering in the air, wobbling under my feet. I hopped from one to the other and jumped back to the road, forcing myself to move faster. Faster.

BOOM.

There was a crashing sound behind me, so loud and violent that it made my ribs feel like they would shake out of my chest.

I turned to see a pile of bricks and wood in the center of the road, surrounded by a cloud of dust.

People leaned out of their front doors to see what had happened, and in the distance, I heard police sirens.

I turned down a side street and ran toward the center of town, two streets over from where Duncan was strapped to the

326

Elephant Rock. Bolts hit around me, getting closer and closer, the smell of burning blacktop around me.

I had to keep moving, because whether or not I was successful, I was headed to the same place: the Elephant County Cemetery.

DUNCAN

Ms. Bunchwick had finally returned, but why now?

I only looked in quick glances so Quinton wouldn't see. She was hunched by a building, trying to blend in with a pile of trash bags on the curb.

If she was still able to change into the witch, that meant that she still had the wand. So why didn't she untie me? Why didn't she help us?

Based on Emma's sloppy execution of metamorphosis, she could use *a lot* of help.

I looked toward my house.

Something was moving. Something big.

A tree seemed to grow in an instant, raising higher than the rooftops.

But it wasn't growing, it was *flying*.

It spun in the air, its roots dangling below like the crusty arms of an octopus.

Ms. Bunchwick removed her hood and smiled at me, and I wanted to scream to her, beg her to help us.

I don't care how good Emma was, stage magic could never beat real magic. She had to know that.

I looked back. Something else was happening now, something worse than I could ever imagine.

My whole house shot into the sky, and twisted in circles.

Bricks and roof shingles fell to the ground, surrounded by everything I had ever owned.

My brain couldn't process what my eyes were seeing. There was no way this was real.

Ms. Bunchwick nodded her head and teleported across the street.

I twisted and pulled, trying to see where she had gone.

"Settle down up there," Quinton yelled from the road.

My street glowed from the bolts of light shooting from Seamus's wand, each burst powerful enough to kill.

I groaned and wiggled more, but the ropes were too tight.

Police sirens sounded in the distance.

Quinton grasped the little piece of wand on his necklace and levitated, landing on the head of the Elephant Rock.

"There's nothing left to do but enjoy the show."

And then my house was falling, in one perfect piece, down to the ground, shattering into a cloud of dust and wood.

EMMA

The cemetery gates were made of old and rusted bars of iron that arched up toward the center. A three-foot-high wall ran all the way to the old church, with a fence of metal spears sticking from the top.

There was a small window next to the church's side door, and Duncan's dad waved at me, holding up the end of an extension cord.

He gave me a thumbs-up signal and I shook my head.

Not yet.

The street was empty. The only sounds were the police sirens in the distance, and judging by the direction they were coming from, they had finally made it to Duncan's house. They wouldn't find anything there but rubble.

Black clouds rolled overhead, belching thunder.

I stood on the short stone wall and waited, my heart pounding so hard that I thought Seamus might find me just from the sound of it.

I spun the fake wand in my hand and waited.

Then I saw him in the sky. Seamus landed at the end of

the street in a crouched position and stood, walking down the center of the road, his wand pointed at my face.

"I must admit, I rather enjoy the chase," he said. "Yes, you *could* just hand me the wand, but then I would have little reason to destroy this wretched town. Thank you for this opportunity."

He waved his wand and the road buckled under his feet and cracked down the middle, curling up at the sides likes ocean waves. He sent out a blast of sound and every window on the street burst.

He laughed and clapped his hands. A high-pitched buzz rang in my ears.

Ronan and Vince appeared from an alleyway behind him.

"And you . . . *you* I can't figure. What should I do with you? I see great potential here. Such a cunning little girl. So quick and smart. I can see why she liked you. Give me the wand and come with me. I'll teach you everything I've learned about dark magic."

Seamus held out his hand and smiled, his eyes twinkling with an evil light.

"I need someone like you," Seamus said. "I'll forget everything else you've done. Be my assistant."

"Really?" I asked. "You'd let me?"

"Of course, child. Just give it to me."

He nodded and stepped forward, waving his hand at me.

"Thanks, but no thanks. I'm not really assistant material," I said. I looked at Duncan's dad and nodded. I raised the wand.

There was another puff of smoke and a groaning sound came from the cemetery. Behind me, the ghosts of the dead appeared in tattered clothes, arms held out, eyes white and glazed.

A large piece of glass, invisible to the naked eye, stretched the length of the cemetery at a forty-five-degree angle. Tommy, Wilson, and Juan were on the ground, dressed in old clothes my mom had cut apart from my dad's closet. Work lights lit them, making them bright enough to reflect off the panel of glass and look like pale, transparent zombies. It was the perfect Pepper's Ghost. They screamed and moaned, making threatening hissing sounds and snapping their teeth.

"Stand back," I said.

Ronan and Vince backed away.

Seamus watched. His eyes open wide in amazement.

Then he began to laugh.

THE ELEPHANT ROCK

DUNCAN

Quinton sat on the curb and bit his fingernails as the last sliver of sun sank beneath the horizon, and the town faded into shadows.

I couldn't see anything—no flying objects, no bolts or screams.

Light rain smacked the roads.

I rubbed my hands on the side of the rock, feeling its cold, smooth surface.

If Ms. Bunchwick wasn't going to help us, maybe it was time I helped myself.

The rope was tied tightly around my arms, and my legs were tied to the elephant's head, wrapped around the neck a bunch of times.

I leaned over and looked at more of the rock, planning my escape. The first step was getting my arms free. Once I did that, I could work on my legs and then run down the elephant's back and slide down the stumpy piece of rock that looked like a tail.

It was still a high place to fall from, and I'd be lucky if I didn't hurt myself. If I could get out before Quinton noticed, I could run and help Emma. But what would I do then? How much help would I be against Seamus?

I didn't know, but I had to try.

I squirmed and moved my shoulders back and forth, loosening the rope, all while watching Quinton in the corner of my vision.

A finger poked through, just enough that I could free my hand. I pushed it out and separated the rope, sliding it off my arms.

Blood tingled through my chest and I swiveled around and stretched.

Now I could see Ms. Bunchwick on the road behind me, blocked from Quinton's view by the large legs of the rock.

She watched me with a smile and held up her hands, making whipping motions with her arms.

I shrugged my shoulders and she shook her head, placing a broken tree limb between her legs and flying to the top of the elephant.

She ripped the tape from my mouth.

"Where have you been?" I whispered.

"I've been watching. Waiting for the right time." She made a whistling noise and waved at Quinton.

"Hey!" he screamed. He jumped to his feet, but he was too late.

Ms. Bunchwick pointed her wand at the Elephant Rock, then flew down the street, screaming, "Follow me, boy!"

"How?" I yelled back.

The ground began to roll and buckle, so violently that I thought the rock might shatter into pieces.

But it wasn't breaking—it was alive.

The hard rocky surface had turned into lumpy gray flesh that buckled underneath me. The large legs of the elephant pushed the creature forward, careful at first, then gaining confidence, each step denting the road and shaking everything around us.

Ms. Bunchwick turned around and winked, yelling, "Biggest transformation I ever did. Takes a lot of energy, so we can't keep it for long. Best get moving."

My legs were still tied to the head, and the giant elephant raised his trunk and blew a trumpet noise into the night.

Then it began to run, straight down the main street, its large ears flapping in the breeze. Ms. Bunchwick did a corkscrew in the air and turned down my street.

Suddenly, the whipping motions made sense. She wanted me to *steer* the elephant.

I grabbed the ropes that were tied around me and pulled them to the side. The elephant's head turned and it rounded the corner, running down my street, past the rubble pile that used to be my house.

Ms. Bunchwick flew higher, searching the town for Emma and the others, and yelled out, "This way!"

We turned again, moving through the tight streets. The elephant's sides scraped road signs and lights, bending them in half. I tried to keep it from stepping on cars, but some of them were unavoidable.

"Where are they?" I yelled.

"That way!"

I knew we were getting closer. The rain was falling heavier and the clouds were black and spinning in the sky.

Ms. Bunchwick flew down, landing on top of the elephant's head.

"You ready for this?" she asked.

I nodded.

"They're down that road, at the cemetery," she said. She pulled a deck of cards from her dress. "Emma's holding them off, but it ain't gonna work for much longer. Time for us to use everything we have."

EMMA

Seamus was laughing so hard that he had to bend over and put his hands on his knees.

"Stupid, stupid girl," he said. "I can't pretend anymore. This game is too tiring. What did you think would happen tonight? Did you think that you could fool me with your silly little magic show?"

Tommy, Wilson, and Juan continued their act, pretending to feast on each other's brains.

"You thought *this* would convince me you had the real wand? And then what? I would use it to summon the location of the tree, being cursed with the worst thing imaginable?"

He grabbed Ronan and Vince.

"There's nothing to be afraid of, you idiots," he said, dragging them closer to me. "These weak tricks may deceive them, but you forget that *I* was once was a magician. I noticed the angled mirror under the mailbox. And your flying was very good. Whoever set up the wires was quite skilled. As for your mental deception, why, you did your best under the circumstances, but Pepper's Ghost is hardly new territory."

He shot a bolt directly at Tommy, hitting his reflection, and the glass shattered into a million pieces and fell to the ground.

Inside the church, Duncan's dad screamed.

"Fake magic can never top real magic," Seamus said. "That's something *she* never understood."

He stepped closer. There was nowhere for me to go.

He waved his hand, and the fake wand shot from my fingers and into his. He held it under his nose, sniffing it.

"A convincing copy," he said. "Nearly perfect."

He snapped it in half and threw it behind him, then aimed his wand at my forehead.

"Where are they?"

"I don't know."

The end of the wand glowed red, and sparkled with energy.

"This won't hurt a bit," he said, pulling back his arm, ready to strike.

I closed my eyes, waiting for the bolt to hit my brain.

He muttered ancient curses, terrible things that sounded like burping and growling.

A trumpet sounded.

I opened my eyes.

The road that ran from the church sloped upward, and at the top, a giant elephant stood and stomped its feet like a kid having a temper tantrum. It was massive, as big as the rock at the center of town. Its head was twice as tall as Duncan.

Duncan!

He poked his head from behind the ears and the elephant stood on its hind legs, made another insanely loud blast, then charged at us.

DUNCAN

"Let's go!" Ms. Bunchwick screamed.

She flew above me, throwing cards and firing bolts, hitting the ground, closer and closer to Seamus and his men.

I whipped the ropes around the elephant's head, and it snorted and kicked its rear legs, then thumped down the road, smashing more cars, and ripping fire hydrants from the sidewalks.

Seamus's wand was pointed at Emma's face, and behind her, Tommy, Wilson, and Juan stood from behind the cemetery wall and brushed pieces of glass from their clothes.

What were they doing here? I wondered.

Ms. Bunchwick flipped and landed, shooting another bolt at Seamus. It hit his leg and he screamed and fell, rolling on the blacktop and firing back. Ms. Bunchwick swerved and ducked in the air, each shot barely missing her.

Emma climbed over the cemetery fence and grabbed Tommy's hand, pulling him toward the church.

Ronan and Vince were close behind her, but I had a plan to stop them.

I pulled the ropes hard to the left, steering the elephant

toward them. Then I yanked back on the ropes, so hard that the elephant's head arched up and his front feet sprang into the air, kicking in a circle and then landing between them.

Vince screamed and curled into a ball, covering his head with his hands.

Emma opened the church door and pushed Tommy, Wilson, and Juan inside.

The elephant jumped again and landed, Ronan and Vince rolling to avoid its monstrous feet.

"Don't hurt us, Duncan!" Vince screamed. "We're just hired help."

"Then leave! Get out of here. Now!"

Ronan stood cautiously, watching the elephant's movements, then grabbed Vince's hand and pulled him up, running down the street and through an alley until they were out of sight.

"Traitors!" Seamus screamed at them.

"They left you," Ms. Bunchwick said. "You're all alone now, Seamus, and we got you outnumbered. Give us the wand."

"Never," he growled.

Ms. Bunchwick shrugged at me.

"It was worth a shot," she said, and continued firing.

I whipped the ropes again and the elephant charged at Seamus.

Seamus ripped a metal spike from the cemetery fence and flew into the air, shooting bolts at the elephant's side, scorching its lumpy gray flesh.

"Keep moving, boy," Ms. Bunchwick said. "It's only a rock, remember? Can't feel real pain."

"Are you sure about that?"

The elephant twisted in circles, squealing and moaning, then bucking back and forth. I held on tight, trying not to be thrown to the ground.

Ms. Bunchwick flew around me, deflecting Seamus's bolts and firing back at him.

Sirens sounded from up the hill, and the flashing lights of cop cars lit up the buildings, coming closer, but always a few steps behind us.

"About to have some real trouble if we stick around," Ms. Bunchwick yelled, waving her hands at me. "This way, boy! Keep it moving."

I turned and saw Emma watching us from the front door of the church. I waved goodbye, wondering if it would be for the last time.

EMMA

My lawyer wants to remind you again that I had nothing to do with that giant monster elephant or any of the destruction it caused. Ms. Bunchwick transformed it and Duncan was riding it, so even though I was super jealous of him at the time, I'm pretty sure you can't pin any of that on me.

The worst I did was break that giant piece of glass from the front window of Lots o' Value. I'm sorry Duncan's dad lost his job, but he knew the risks. Anyway, it was Seamus that fired the bolt that did it. And it was Seamus that did all the stuff with the tree and the house. Why would *I* want to destroy Duncan's house? I loved that place.

So yeah, none of that was my fault, either.

I plead the Fifth again (because I'm still a little confused about how many times I have to do that).

Anyway, when all that stuff with the elephant was going on, I was hiding in the church, watching from the small window above the holy water font with Tommy, Wilson, and Juan.

"Did it work?" Tommy said. "Do you think we fooled him?"

"No," I said. "Not at all."

"Bummer," Juan said. "Do you think they could, like, die or something?"

"What do you think?" I said, and watched as another wave of bolts hit the elephant and sparkled in the air around Ms. Bunchwick.

I joined Duncan's dad at the front door and we opened it a crack, enough to see that things were going pretty bad for them.

Seamus was attacking faster, and the elephant twisted and lurched, powerful in size, but too slow for Seamus.

Duncan pulled at the reigns, directing its movement and ducking to avoid the blasts. I have to say, in hindsight, he looked pretty cool. He waved goodbye to me and I gave him a thumbs-up.

"What next?" Duncan's dad asked.

"Can I see your phone?"

He handed it to me and I dialed a number, watching as the elephant ran down the street and turned the corner, heading back toward Duncan's house.

"Hello?" a voice on the other end said.

"It's time."

DUNCAN

The front of the church was a burning battlefield, every inch of road destroyed and smoking.

"Follow me! Quick!" Ms. Bunchwick said, and we turned down the street, going back in the direction of my now-destroyed house, swerving through intersections and narrow side streets.

The elephant ran, its hulking body shaking the earth with every step.

I bounced up and down, never staying in any spot for more than a millisecond. That was a good thing, too, because Seamus was close behind, firing hot light at me, and each shot that hit the elephant made it move faster.

"Turn!" Ms. Bunchwick said, and I directed the elephant onto my street.

The large tree was lying across the road, roots and all, surrounded by a pile of things that used to be in my room.

In the middle of the road was a torn cardboard box with the words *Little Houdini's 101 Tricks to Fool Your Friends* printed on the front.

It was my very first magic set, full of tricks like a cut-and-restore rope, cups and balls, a marked deck, and a transforming hanky.

I felt a sick twisting inside me, like something was lost that I'd never get back, and I wanted to explode.

Cold rain hit my arms and lightning cracked overhead.

Seamus landed in the middle of the road, arms held up to the sky as the black clouds twirled above him, his whole body glowing.

His face grew and morphed, stretching and pulling, coarse hair sprouting from his head and neck. His arms transformed into thick hairy claws and he landed on all four feet, a golden lion with a black mane.

"Careful!" Ms. Bunchwick screamed. "Don't reckon the elephant will like that very much."

Seamus roared and snarled, jumping up onto the fallen tree and then lunging toward me.

The elephant made a screaming sound and reared back, spinning to avoid the lion's snapping jaw. The attacks happened fast and the lion sunk its teeth into the elephant's flesh, dashing from leg to leg.

"Time to get down, boy," Ms. Bunchwick said, sending a shield of bolts around me. "The elephant's job is done. This is between us now."

I pulled at the rope, unraveling it from around the elephant's head as it bucked and jumped to avoid the clawing and snapping lion.

I wrapped the rope a couple times around my wrist and then slid down the elephant's side until the rope was tight, then ran toward its tail.

The lion transformed into Seamus, and he hit the elephant's stomach with a gigantic blast of light, strong enough to send shock waves down the street, stripping the few remaining leaves from the trees. The elephant reared again, standing on its hind legs and moaning.

I ran farther down its back, dangling from the rope, at least ten feet from the ground.

"Jump!" Ms. Bunchwick screamed. "Now!"

I let go of the rope, and fell to the ground, rolling on the wet pavement. I pushed my hair out of my eyes and smeared blood across my face. My hands and knees were cut from the fall, and my back felt like it had been snapped in half.

Above me, the massive shape of the elephant moved, silhouetted in the clouds. Between its legs, I could see Seamus whipping the wand like an evil circus trainer, hitting the poor animal over and over, a nasty smile pasted on his face like he enjoyed seeing a creature in pain.

"Enough!" Ms. Bunchwick screamed. She hit Seamus in the ankle with a sparkling blue bolt and he fell to the ground, cursing at her.

"Your job is done, big fellow, and we thank you for your service," Ms. Bunchwick said, bowing. She pointed her wand at the elephant and held out her hand, lifting it above her head, her whole body trembling with the effort.

The elephant levitated a few inches from the ground,

enough to glide over the street and up the sidewalk, toward the hole in my yard where my house used to be. It squirmed in the air and thrashed its feet, looking down, confused by what was happening.

"Best if you . . . *grrr* . . . get out of . . . *ahhh* . . . our way now," Ms. Bunchwick said, releasing it right on the pile of broken wood and bricks. "Sorry to wake you up from your slumber."

The elephant sat down and tilted his head, then raised its trunk and blew a final trumpet sound before transforming back into a giant rock, taller than the surrounding houses and every inch as wide.

"Thought that spot looked a bit empty," Ms. Bunchwick said. She turned toward Seamus, wand out, and her hand was shaking.

"Ms. Bunchwick, are you all right?" I asked.

"Oh, fine, fine," she said. She circled Seamus, matching his every move like a sword fighter, preparing to strike. "Bit exhausted, is all."

Her knees wobbled and she tripped on the fabric of her dress, stumbling a bit.

"You and me, all alone," Seamus said.

He fired a bolt at her, but she threw a card and hit back, the light colliding in the air and exploding into a flash of fire and smoke.

"This night will end with the wand in my possession. You know that's the truth."

She smiled and fired back.

He deflected and jumped, sending back two quick shots.

Ms. Bunchwick hit one in the air and fell to the street, rolling to avoid the other. Her whole body shook, and she was barely able to push herself up. She lay on her back, crawling away from him, her hands tangled in the wet strands of her long gray hair.

"We've been marching toward this conclusion for decades, Edna. Did you ever see it ending any other way?"

"I was hoping you'd choke on a piece of roast beef, if I'm honest."

She fired back, but her shots were slow and easy for him to block.

"It's time we stop this," Seamus said. "It's quite sad. You're too old and weak, Edna. And haven't you done enough damage?"

Ms. Bunchwick's hand dropped to the ground and her body slumped like a deflated beach ball.

Another step, then another, and Seamus was right above her, the wand fixed to her forehead. She wasn't fighting back. She wasn't even trying anymore.

"Ms. Bunchwick," I said. "What's happening?"

"I admit, perhaps it was foolish to think we could beat you," she said, rolling the wand around in her hand. "Time we face the facts, ain't it? Who was I to think I could beat you? I was only your assistant. You were always the star, Seamus. Forgive me."

She held the wand in her opened palm and lifted it toward Seamus.

"No, Ms. Bunchwick, you can't!" I yelled, and hot tears

streamed down my face, mixing with the cold and heavy rain. I pushed myself up, ready to run and knock him over, but she waved at me to sit down.

"We tried," she said, looking at the wand one last time. "No one can say we didn't."

She held out the wand, and he reached for it, his long fingers quivering in delight.

"All I ask is when you find the tree, you promise me you won't do anything *too* evil with it. Minor felonies, perhaps. No murder, you hear? And leave the kids alone. They were only helping on my orders."

"Whatever you want," Seamus said, and his eyes widened as the tip of his wand glowed a bright red color. "As long as you believe it, darling, I'll tell you anything."

His fingers moved closer and closer to the wand, but stopped when Emma's voice came from the rooftop, breaking the silence of this horrible moment.

THE END

EMMA

"Hey, you're not *really* going to give him the wand are you?" I shouted from the top of a house on Duncan's street. I had climbed the latticework by the back porch and could see the whole scene from that height. By the looks of it, I was just in time.

Seamus was standing right over Ms. Bunchwick, his hand closing in on the wand.

"*You*," Seamus growled. He turned and pointed at me, then yelled, "I won't spare you because you're a child. You and the boy both deserve *everything* that's about to happen."

He turned back to Ms. Bunchwick, but she was on her feet now, running toward me, her arm arching down and then springing up before Seamus tackled her to the ground.

The wand flew up, through the rain and flashes of lightning, coming toward me.

DUNCAN

The wand twisted unevenly in the air, spinning in slow motion.

She'll never catch it, I thought, but the one thing I've learned lately is to never underestimate Emma.

My heartbeat pounded in my ears as the wand got closer to her. I wiped the water and blood from my eyes, and an unnatural sound came from the pit of my stomach. The wand was higher than the house now, arcing down toward her open hand.

Emma stood, frozen in place.

Another crack of lightning ripped through the sky and her hand closed around the wand.

I jumped to my feet, screaming for her to fight back, and in a puff of smoke she disappeared, teleporting behind the elephant rock.

"Emma!" I yelled. "Throw it here!"

She glared at me and then teleported again, this time appearing down the street in Mrs. Benner's rose garden.

Seamus shot another bolt but it was too late—she was already gone, teleporting fifty feet behind him in the middle of the road. He screamed and spun around, unleashing a wall of light toward her. Emma ran and jumped, doing a midair flip and then tucking into a ball, rolling toward the houses and vanishing into smoke.

"Do it!" Ms. Bunchwick screamed. "Now!"

"Almost," Emma said. She was back on the roof now, aiming the wand at Seamus's hand, but there was no time to strike.

Seamus flew into the air and fired, spinning in place. The bolts came at a rapid-fire rate, unpredictable in their movement. They lit up the street and knocked the bricks and siding off the nearby houses.

"Get down!" Ms. Bunchwick yelled.

There was a loud scream and Emma fell backward, clutching her side and gasping.

She was hit.

She teleported behind me and grabbed my shoulder.

"It . . . hurts . . . so bad . . . Duncan," she said, buckling at the knees.

Seamus landed, smiling at her pain.

"Give me the wand," I said, grabbing Emma's arm and pulling her up. "I'll finish this."

She shook her head and pushed me away.

"No you won't. She will. Trust me, Duncan."

I looked in her eyes, but something was very different. She seemed far away from me, staring into the sky.

"What's going on?" I asked, but she didn't answer. "What are you doing?"

She pushed away, limping toward the houses, then she teleported again, to another rooftop, and then to the end of the street. She grabbed the stop sign and pulled herself up, her knuckles white on the metal pole.

The wand hung loosely in her other hand, and she lifted it up, pointing it toward Seamus.

He pointed his wand and walked slowly toward her.

"You're badly hurt, child. Give it here and I'll heal you. I'll do anything you want."

She shook her head and pulled her wand back.

I held my breath, waiting to see who would strike first.

It never happened, because a shadow leapt from behind the house on the corner and grabbed her.

EMMA

Quinton's arms wrapped around my shoulders, and he pulled me down to the ground. I kicked and snapped my teeth at him, but there was no escaping.

He grabbed the wand and I tightened my grip and thrashed around. There was nothing else to do.

He pulled at my fingers and pried them apart. The wand began to move, slipping out of my palm until the last twisted knot passed through my knuckles. From there, there was nothing to grab onto, nothing left but smooth bark.

And then it was gone.

Quinton stood in the rain and jumped and cheered, pumping the wand up and down in the air.

"I got it, Pop! I got it!"

"Well *done!*" Seamus said, extending his hand. "Bring it here."

Quinton spun the wand in his hand and rubbed its rough side, like it was the most amazing thing he had ever seen.

"*Quinton,*" Seamus said.

"Don't rush me, all right? I'm savoring the moment. After all this work, all the sacrifices we've made, we finally have it."

"Yes, yes, it's ours. There will be plenty of time to stare at it later. Give it *here*."

Quinton walked toward Seamus, removing the small, dangling piece of wand from his necklace and holding the other half in his palm.

From the sidewalk, Duncan yelled, "Ms. Bunchwick, what's happening?"

But she didn't answer.

I ran to Duncan and pulled him toward her. It was like we were invisible to them, part of a world that no longer existed now that the whole wand was in their hands.

Together we sat on the road and watched as Quinton handed the wand and necklace to Seamus.

"All the power in the world is waiting, son," Seamus said, placing his hand on Quinton's shoulder. "All for us."

Seamus held the pieces together and pulled a roll of tape from his breast pocket. He wrapped them together and lifted them in the air, closing his eyes and whispering a curse.

The tip of the wand glowed and lit up Seamus's face like a jack-o'-lantern. He continued chanting, levitating off the ground, his arms raised high.

The rain stopped, and the clouds rolled in waves, as black as ink, swirling around him like a tornado. A strange light formed in the center. It was too bright to look at, and my eyes felt like they would burst.

Ms. Bunchwick wrapped her arms around us and we fell to the ground as a giant bolt came from the clouds and down to earth, covering Seamus in light.

DUNCAN

Seamus glowed from the light and raised higher into the sky, the wand held above his head, waiting to see where it would point him.

Quinton watched from the ground, knocked over by the powerful force. He laughed and clapped his hands.

"This is it, children," Ms. Bunchwick said. "Cover your eyes."

But I had to watch, even though it was so bright that I thought I might go blind.

The light roared and crackled, changing colors, first green, then blue, then red.

The wind whipped heavier, sucking everything toward the light. Trash and leaves spun around us.

"I'm so sorry," I said, but Ms. Bunchwick didn't answer. She rubbed my head and pulled it to her shoulder.

Emma grabbed my hand and squeezed.

And that was the end.

The explosion started above the clouds, and then shot to the ground like a bomb had dropped in the middle of the road.

The wall of light expanded, illuminating the entire town

in a flash of daylight and then vanishing. The clouds rolled away, spreading out over the sky in a thin mist of gray. The moon and stars shined above us, and everything was deathly quiet.

Then there was a cry, a slight moaning at first, and then a pained scream.

Seamus lay on the road, his clothes burnt and smoking.

"What . . . did you . . . *do*?" he asked.

"No!" Quinton screamed, running to Seamus's side and helping him sit up.

Seamus was old now, like the very first time I had seen him. His skin was wrinkled and drooping, and his thin gray hair barely covered his splotchy skull.

"Use the spell without the real wand and the worst thing you can imagine will happen to you," Ms. Bunchwick said. She was on her feet now, and she pulled half of the wand from her dress and pointed it at him.

"This is the *real* half," she said, tossing a card and transforming it into a bolt to prove it.

"I wondered what the wand would deem a fair punishment for someone so despicable. It searched your head for the worst that you had. You've always lusted for power and youth, Seamus, and now you ain't got either. You'll live the rest of your days old and weak. Shame that *that's* the worst thing you can imagine."

"But . . . how?" Seamus asked, looking at Emma. "Her piece was real. I saw it."

"You know better than to trust your eyes. I tried to tell

you that the world doesn't need real magic. The magic created in here," Ms. Bunchwick said, pointing to her forehead, "beats anything else."

He examined the pieces of wand in his frail hand and pointed it at her. It shook as he whipped it back and uttered curses, but nothing happened.

"You're powerless, Seamus," Ms. Bunchwick said. "The worst thing you could ever imagine. I'd reckon the wand has marked you so you can't ever use it again."

Seamus dropped his hand and the wand rolled down the street.

Ms. Bunchwick picked it up and unraveled the tape. She threw the fake half away and attached her half, and the whole wand glowed in her hand.

"I should have known that dying with the wand wouldn't solve any real problems. Not with the tree out there, waiting to be found. I should have passed it on ages ago. Never thought I could find a magician honest and true who was worthy of it. And certainly never thought I'd find *two*."

She turned to us and smiled as the police circled us on the street, sirens wailing.

"It's yours now, children, if you want it. Take it, along with all the pain and responsibility that goes with it. I'm sorry to do this now, after all this trouble."

She dropped the wand and rolled it toward us.

"It's been ages since I've said these words, but I love you kids, and all your fighting words and annoying ways. I'm so happy you broke into my house and ruined my life."

"Stop right there!" a police officer yelled. I looked over and saw a line of police cars with their doors open. Officers stepped out, guns pointed at us.

I raised my hands, preparing for my second arrest, and said, "I still don't understand. How did you do it?"

Emma grabbed my shoulders and helped me up, staring into my eyes.

"I'm special," she said. "One of a kind."

And then everything made sense.

THE REVEAL

Magician's Code

♠ ♥ Code ♦ ♣

OFFICIAL CO____ CONTRACT

1. *Consectetur adipiscing elit. Mauris aliquam odio lorem, ac varius odio blandit at. Curaequam, nibh ligula. Quisque fringilla, ante et consequat vehicula, lectus metus tempus ipsum, laoreet urna risus metus velit, ut finibus velit velit ac purus. Aenean sapien nibh, feugiat id feugiat nec, consequat maximus, sapien mauris rhoncus metus, et tristique ipsum lacus et orci.*

2. *Sed sagittis ullamcorper massa eu consectetur. Maecenas finibus lacinia arcu, bibendum egestas ex. Cras feugiat bibendum sollicitudin. Sed sed velit eu. Curabitur sit amet arcu mi. Sed dictum. Donec vel fringilla sapien eget sollicitudin odio. Praesent erit odio, varius.*

3. *Phasellus at sem nisl. Nam tempus erat erat. Nullam gravida odio consectetur text. Integer ornare quam eu lacus. Maecenas eget aliquam ante pretium vel. Maecenas ullamcorper, elit et quam pulvinar, ut purus, faucibus consequat velit ornare ultrices. Vestibulum pellentesque vel tincidunt et augue sagittis convallis. Donec risus purus at mi faucibus condimentum. Integer ultrices eget metus a aliquam. Pellentesque et risus massa ut neque vestibulum diam. Morbi lectus elit, auctor ac ornare quis, sagittidis ultrices at.*

4. *Cras vel tellus posuere, finibus odio ut, dapibus luctus. Pellentesque id dui vestibulum varius ut amet. Etiam congue, augue sed vulputate eleifend, odio est dapibus urna, integer blandit euismod ante ut auctor. Duis posuere molestie mauris, a tincidunt sapien rhoncus enim, et faucibus erat placerat in. Quisque vitae magna aliquet, rhoncus neque sollicitudin fringilla dui vel fermentum.*

5. *Cras vel lorem tellus. Ut an sapien quis orci facilisis facilisis. Mauris nonsed in amet vestibulum sit amet, euismod sit amet nunc. Aenean gravida ante tellus, ac dictum. Sed massa dui, semper eu uces ac, molestie lobortis metus. Sed eget orci s.*

Duncan Reyes

Duncan Reyes

...tristique nibh erat. Sociis id gravida vitae laoreet a quam. Nam scelerisque elit, eget dignissim posuere sem eros sit amet nibh. Vivamus ullamcorper, tortor ac ullamcorper cursus. Phasellus sit amet nibh. Etiam tristique ut risus quis vehicula. Fusce molestie, ligula varius ne venenatis nisl.

...blandit lacus convallis sit sem. Mauris magna leo, tortor at justo vel, auctore. Donec dapibus maximus metus. Duis congue lectus eu arcu ullamcorper, at viverra sapien, suscipit aliquet urna. Curabitur metus justo an vestibulum maximit.

Phasellus felis turpis, sodales auctor ligula vel, euismod pellentesque dui. Quisque consin tempus, mattis diam pretium ante, nan faucibus odio libero vel magna. Etiam suscipit ut est eros. Curabitur id nec aliquet, interdum leo sit amet, blandit nisl. Aenean pellentesque dui vel nunc. Nulla in mauris laoreet, hendrerit quam ut, ullamcorper sem. Pellentesque is blandit accumsan lacinia sed ac nunc. Phasellus erat risus, dignissim nec fermentum vel, ullpias.

...ullam, elementum ipsum id, imperdiet lorem. Vivamus mollis ornare nulla, eget dignissim velit, vel vehicula clem felud a magna. Nulla laoreet ullamcorper lacus, vel gravida augue varius ad amet. Nulla molestie eget velit ac pulvinar. Mauris duis turpis orci. Nunc laoreet sed eleit, convallis quam. Donec est erit, aliquet id dignissim non, consectetur a neque. Nulla.

...Morbi dapibus lorem at fringilla. Donec et commodo ligula. Sed quam dorm, sollicitudin ac pel mauris egestas orci. Curabitur tincidunt orci purus, eleu commodo mauris sollicitudne rhoncus ne suscipit porttitor vel nec leo. Quisque in odio porta, imperdiet eget ut, eleifend lorem.

Emma Gilbert

Emma Gilbert

EMMA

"Don't shoot!" a voice yelled from behind the police cars.

Officer Ralph came running down the street and stood between us.

"They're the good guys," he said. He pointed at Seamus and Quinton. "That's who you want."

Seamus lay on the wet road, snarling. Quinton curled up in a ball, crying like a little baby. Ms. Bunchwick was beside him, cradling his head in her arms and rubbing the tears from his eyes.

The police moved in and handcuffed them, then put them into the back of a car.

We were also taken down to the station, and they wanted to know everything that had happened.

I mean, we kind of destroyed half of the town and miraculously moved a giant elephant shaped rock to the spot where Duncan's house used to be, so I guess everyone deserved an explanation.

And that's what we've been doing for the last week. A police escort follows us around all day at school (for our protection, they say) and then takes us to the station at night. Then they interview us for hours and have each of us write down a full account of what happened, starting at the very beginning and going right to the end.

It's not the worst punishment in the world, actually. I kind of like writing. It's a lot like doing magic. You know the ending before anyone else does, so you can hide important parts from your audience, adding flourishes here and there that misdirect them from the truth.

So what is the truth anyway?

How did we defeat Seamus, saving the world from possible destruction?

Have you figured it out yet?

DUNCAN

You're probably wondering how she did it.

How did Emma convince Seamus she had the real wand, when it was really still tucked in Ms. Bunchwick's dress?

It wasn't until I looked into her eyes that I understood.

It's not a great trick, really. In fact, it's probably the oldest one in the book, but Emma doesn't know magic history as well as I do.

Anyone that knows her well enough would *never* even think to consider this. It would be too obvious.

So obvious that I even missed it at first.

I really shouldn't reveal the secret, but I'll give you a hint: three Emmas.

EMMA

Aren't you one of those Gilbert girls? Tommy's dad had asked. You better believe I am.

Anyone that's spent any time in Elephant knows about the Gilbert triplets. Normally, I would never even think to use my sisters in a show, because everyone would figure it out.

Ms. Bunchwick didn't learn about them until she was in my house and saw our family portrait on the wall.

Something special, she called it, but it didn't always seem that special to me. More like a curse. I've always considered myself a pretty original person, so I never liked having two people that looked exactly like me around.

Never know when duplicates might be handy, Ms. Bunchwick had said. She slipped me half of a fake wand and told me to let him have it.

At the time, I thought it was one of her old lady expressions that meant I had to attack Seamus as hard as I could, but that wasn't it.

All I needed to do was convince Seamus I had the real wand, and then let him take it from me.

When times are tough, your sisters will be there for you.

Right before the police took us down to the station, Duncan figured it out.

"Dark green," he said.

"Yes."

"Anna's eyes are a little more blue."

"They are."

"She's a really good actor."

"There's a reason she gets the lead role in every production she auditions for."

Anna stepped out from behind the Elephant Rock and bowed.

"It was her idea that we pretend to get hurt."

"Wendy gets shot by an arrow in *Peter Pan*," Anna said, clutching her side and falling to the ground. "I had a lot of practice with stage falls."

"I really thought you were dying."

"Thanks, Duncan."

Jenna appeared at the end of the street and yelled, "Hey, are we done now?"

"I should have known when you flipped in the air," Duncan said. "You would have broken your neck."

Jenna did a cartwheel down the street. When we were younger my parents enrolled all three of us in gymnastics. Four hospital visits later it was decided that I wasn't very good at it.

"I just can't believe you got them to help," Duncan said. Anna and Jenna have always thought Duncan and his magic tricks were really stupid. They'd hide their faces every time I performed so no one would confuse them for me. "Vanishing the Statue of Liberty would have been easier."

"That's *exactly* what I said!" I yelled.

From the police car, Seamus looked at us, his eyes darting back and forth between me, Anna, and Jenna.

He may not have been fooled by my other tricks, but it looked like *teleportation* was a huge success.

And that was all that mattered.

Convincing them to help wasn't that hard. They may have been a little embarrassed by me, but it turns out they didn't actually want me to get hurt. I mean, I still had to promise to fix up their destroyed rooms and do their chores for a month, but it was worth it. I figured I'd either be dead or have a magical wand that could do the work for me. Problem solved one way or the other.

Anna, Jenna, and I worked out a routine to make it look like we could teleport anywhere we wanted. A pocket full of smoke bombs for each of us, and we could switch spots over and over.

When we weren't visible, we would run to our next location, making it look like we could be in a dozen places at once, seemingly at random.

Then, right at the end, when I was clutching onto the stop sign, I saw Quinton in the bushes, crawling toward me.

He was about as stealthy as a buffalo in roller skates.

I pretended not to see him, looking straight ahead as Seamus came toward me, wand raised, ready to strike.

Quinton grabbed me, and I fought just long enough that it

didn't seem suspicious.

Let him have it, Ms. Bunchwick's voice repeated in my head. *Let him have it.*

Oh boy, did I ever.

After it was over, our parents were there with Tommy, Wilson, and Juan.

"Duncan, you rode the Elephant Rock!" Tommy yelled. He pointed at the giant rock that was sitting where Duncan's house used to be. "And . . . whoa . . . your house."

"You guys are *awesome*," Wilson said.

Tommy looked back and forth between us.

"I'm impressed . . . I mean . . . wow . . . and then you did all that flying . . . and . . . wand stuff. Can you teach me?"

"Sure, Tommy, but maybe we should start with something smaller," Duncan said, smiling at me.

I bent down and picked up a magic kit that had fallen out of Duncan's bedroom. "How about I teach you that card trick now?"

"Yeah," Tommy said. "I'd like that."

DUNCAN

So the story ends in a pretty standard way: the good guys win, the bad guys get locked up, and the bullies befriend the bullied.

But that's okay. I think magic works well with standard things. It takes things you've seen a million times and does something different and unexpected.

And this isn't really the end, you know? Because if anyone out there knows the wand exists, they know we have it.

Maybe someone's planning an attack on this building right now.

We've told you everything that happened, because you deserved to know, but don't think for a second that we're completely safe.

You can't protect us forever, and we'll never tell you where the wand is. Emma is too good at hiding things.

If you believe our story, then you have to believe that the tree is still out there, waiting to be found.

And we can't let that happen.

AN EXCERPT FROM RALPH NEALE'S ANNUAL REVIEW

Ralph Neale
ANNUAL REVIEW
Property of Elephant County Police Department

TOP SECRET

REVIEW #LG108412

Ralph: Do you know what I keep thinking?

Interviewer: No.

Ralph: Two hundred thirty-seven dollars and sixty-two cents. I keep saying that number over and over in my head. If I had just paid to replace Duncan's books, none of this would have happened.

Interviewer: What do you mean?

Ralph: I don't know. Maybe it would have been better if we had left her alone. But I didn't believe Duncan. Come on, a witch and a magic wand? That's ridiculous, right? Only it wasn't. I should have believed him.

Interviewer: I see.

Ralph: You believe me, don't you? I'm not crazy. Look at all the damage that was done. Do you really think that could have happened without magic?

Interviewer: I don't know.

Ralph: I could have stopped it if I had just paid the money. I didn't handle the situation well. I regret that.

(uncomfortable pause)

Interviewer: Mr. Neale, I feel like we're avoiding the real question here.

Ralph: Oh yeah, what's that?

Interviewer: Do you know where Duncan and Emma are?

(muffled laughter)

Ralph: I thought this was a review, not an interrogation.

Interviewer: I'm compelled to ask. I feel like you're avoiding it.

Ralph: I'm not avoiding it. I've been asked that by everyone here and I've told you that I don't know anything. They were in your custody for a week giving statements, and when they were done they were sent home with around-the-clock security. After a while you started phasing it out. Too expensive, I guess, and the town is already furious at how much money this whole thing is costing.

Interviewer: Do you think it was a bad idea to remove their security?

Ralph: I don't know. It wasn't my choice. I'm suspended without pay, remember? Anyway, you couldn't guard them forever, I get that. And no one suspicious showed up in town. I was watching. As far as I know, Seamus and Quinton are still locked up, and those two guys that were helping them haven't been seen since that night. Maybe no one else even knows about the wand.

(rustling papers, something mumbled inaudibly)

Interviewer: You're a police officer, Ralph. It will be much worse for you if we find out you're lying.

Ralph: I know.

Interviewer: No one's been able to locate Ms. Bunchwick, either.

Ralph: What can I say? If she doesn't want to be found, she won't be found. She hid from her own husband for decades.

Interviewer: Where do you think the kids are?

(silence)

Interviewer: Take a guess.

Ralph: Well, there are really only two options. Either someone kidnapped them, or they left on their own.

Interviewer: Why would they leave on their own?

Ralph: You read their statements. The tree is still out there, and they have the key to finding its location. But that's crazy, right?

Interviewer: I don't know. Is it?

ACKNOWLEDGMENTS

There is a group of people behind every book, and I would like to thank the entire team at HarperCollins Children's Books for their hard work. Special thanks to my editor, Christopher Hernandez, for pushing me to make the book better. Thanks to John Hendrix for his amazing work on the jacket art and Jenna Stempel-Lobell for the jacket design. And of course, giant, elephant-sized thanks to my agent, Alexander Slater, for his support, encouragement, and believing in this book.

I'd like to thank my early readers for their comments and ideas. Thank you to Kelley Rose Waller, Robert Swartwood, and Amanda Lighty. Your help was invaluable.

In the course of writing this book, I became fascinated with the history of magic, and I'd like to thank Jim Steinmeyer for writing some of the best books on the subject. If you have any interest in the history of stage magic, I can't recommend his work enough.

The illustrations in this book were made in Photoshop and on an iPad Pro. I would like to thank the team at Procreate for making my favorite art software, and Kyle T. Webster for making some extraordinary brushes. While I am thanking software developers, I would be remiss not to mention the team behind Scrivener for creating the best writing software on the planet.

Thanks to my mom and dad, Allen and Marilyn Perry, for their constant love and support, and my grandparents, Leon and Marian Scott, for buying me magic tricks and pretending to be fooled. Last, but certainly not least, my wife, Andrea, and sons, Wyatt and Everett. I love you all.

THAT NIGHT'S TRAIN

THAT NIGHT'S TRAIN

by

Ahmad Akbarpour

Translated by Majid Saghafi

Groundwood Books / House of Anansi Press
Toronto Berkeley

Groundwood Books / House of Anansi Press
110 Spadina Avenue, Suite 801, Toronto, Ontario M5V 2K4
or c/o Publishers Group West
1700 Fourth Street, Berkeley, CA 94710

We acknowledge for their financial support of our publishing program the
Government of Canada through the Canada Book Fund (CBF).

Library and Archives Canada Cataloguing in Publication
Akbarpour, Ahmad
That night's train / Ahmad Akbarpour ; illustrations by Isabelle
Arsenault ; translated by Majid Saghafi.
Issued also in electronic format.
ISBN 978-1-55498-169-4 (bound).—ISBN 978-1-55498-170-0 (pbk.)
I. Arsenault, Isabelle II. Title.
PZ7.A275Th 2012   j891'.5534   C2012-902202-0

Groundwood Books is committed to protecting our natural environment.
As part of our efforts, the interior of this book is printed on paper that
contains 100% post-consumer recycled fibers, is acid-free and is processed
chlorine-free.

Design by Michael Solomon
Cover and interior illustrations by Isabelle Arsenault
Printed and bound in Canada

ONE

"No, no," said Grandmother, and the little blue-eyed girl didn't say another word. She knew that if she upset her grandmother, she would have to fetch her pills. And then when she went out to get her some water — or anything else, for that matter — walking down the train corridor would bring back old memories.

She was five years old now, but she could remember being on the

train with her mother when she was three. She still remembered the flowers on her mother's shirt, and how she had jumped into her arms, and they bumped heads pretty hard.

The train went *clickety-click, clickety-clack* and entered a tunnel, and everything went dark.

The young woman sitting across from them closed her book. The little girl thought, If my mother were alive, she would be reading a book, too.

And her grandmother, who had a good idea what the little girl might be thinking there in the dark, said, "Your mother is in heaven now, Banafsheh."

The train went *clickety-click, clickety-clack* and came out of the darkness.

The young woman opened her book

again. Just before she turned the page, she turned to the little girl and smiled.

"If my mother were alive, she would be reading me a story now," Banafsheh said.

Her grandmother gave her a kiss on her cheeks.

"Not all books are story books, you know," she said. "Some are for studying, too."

The young woman closed her book.

"I wish I had a story book with me," she said.

Then, as though she had just remembered something, she opened her purse and searched inside.

"I usually carry one or two of my books with me. This time, though, I think I left them all back in the vil-

lage." She opened her arms. "Come over here, baby girl..."

"No, no," the grandmother said, and she patted Banafsheh's legs. "She would interrupt your reading."

The young woman put her book back in her purse.

"Children belong to everyone, you know," she said.

As if she had been waiting for those very words, Banafsheh threw herself into the woman's arms, and the woman gave her a kiss on the forehead.

Banafsheh glanced at the woman's lips. When their eyes met, she thought, My mother's eyes were much prettier.

"You see how kind this lady is?" her grandmother whispered, leaning closer. "She is just like your mother."

They could hear children playing in the train corridor.

"Are you coming into town, too?" Grandmother asked the young woman.

"I'm getting off in two stops," she answered, as she ran her fingers through the little girl's hair. Then she smiled. "I'm a writer, but I also teach at two villages on opposite ends of the train line."

Banafsheh stared at the woman's fingers when she raised her arms to point to opposite ends of the train. She imagined going to faraway places.

If she were a teacher in my town, she thought, I would see her again.

Grandmother smiled. "You mean you always have to travel from one end of the line to the other?" She pointed

to both ends of the train, too, but now Banafsheh stared at her grandmother's fingers and imagined faraway places that were strange and shadowy.

The teacher smiled. "No. On holidays I come to town." And this time Banafsheh smiled, too, and the train gently sounded *clickety-click, clickety-clack* and stopped at the next station.

There was an announcement that the train would leave again in half an hour. The teacher held Banafsheh's hand as they left the compartment.

"Won't you come with us?" she asked the grandmother. "You'll be bored here by yourself."

The grandmother grinned as she lay down on the seat.

"The only thing walking does for

someone my age is start a pain that will linger in my back and legs and arms," she said.

There were lots of people at the station. The sun had already set, and night had come.

As they walked together, the teacher reached into her bag and pulled out two pieces of candy. She offered them to the little girl, but Banafsheh only took one.

They stood at the guard rails at the edge of the station. A vast, dark desert lay before them. Banafsheh's blue eyes caught sight of a faint light shining in the distance. It seemed very far away.

"Are you going there?" she asked the teacher shyly, pointing at the light.

The teacher smiled and thought

about writing all this down. Then she took Banafsheh's hand again, and they started to walk.

"Three days a week I go there, and three days a week I go back there," she said, pointing to the tail end of the train. "But on Fridays I come into town. I'm sure I'll see you then."

When she comes to town, I am going to give her a kiss, Banafsheh thought, but she was too embarrassed to say it.

Instead, she asked, "Will you tell me a story?" The teacher sat down near a tree and turned to her. Banafsheh remembered how she would lie in her mother's arms and pretend to be asleep when her mother read her stories.

"Of course, I would love to come

and tell you my latest stories," the teacher said. She stood up, took her hand and started to walk back to the train.

The train lay there like a dragon in a fairy tale, with no ends in sight. The teacher thought about fairy tales, and how some of them were real, and some were imaginary.

Suddenly, she remembered the little girl. She turned to her, squeezed her hand tightly, and said, "I will call you and come on Friday. Definitely."

"When the phone rings, I will pick it up myself," Banafsheh said happily. "Most of the time they want to talk to my father, or sometimes to my grandmother." But she couldn't remember the phone number, no matter how hard

she tried. "I forget one of the numbers, but there are two fours and a five and a nine in it."

The teacher smiled. "When you go to school next year, you'll be able to write everything down yourself."

The loudspeakers called the on-going passengers to get back on the train. Banafsheh thought that the teacher would get off at the next station, and that her grandmother would probably fall asleep.

When they boarded the train with the crowd, she held the teacher's hand tightly. Banafsheh's hands felt warm. So did her head. She felt a little diz-zy, too. When the passengers rushed to the door, the teacher held her hand even more tightly and noticed that the

girl's palm was warm and sweaty. Her hands felt like a fairy tale.

She wanted to tell the little girl once again that she would come and read her stories, but there was too much noise. After they squeezed onto the train past the flow of people, they turned to each other and smiled.

The grandmother was sound asleep as the train went on its way. *Clickety-click, clickety-clack.*

The little girl tapped her grand-mother's shoulder — gently at first, but then a little harder.

"It's a good half hour before we get to the next station," the teacher said. "I'm sure she'll wake up by then."

Better sooner than later, Banafsheh

thought, and she yelled, "Grandmother!"

Her grandmother straightened her neck a little and asked sleepily, "What do you want, dear?"

Banafsheh leaned over and whispered in her ear, "Phone number for the teacher. She is coming on Friday." Grandmother groaned and rubbed her lower back. The train passed over a gorge full of strange trees.

The little girl tapped her grandmother's shoulder once more.

"Our phone number," she said again loudly. "She's getting off at the next station."

"Okay, okay." And the grandmother mumbled, "Four, four, nine, two, five." Her eyes suddenly popped open.

"Sorry, sorry. Four, four, nine, five, two."

Banafsheh watched the teacher write something down in the dim light. She decided that she wouldn't go anywhere on Friday.

The teacher was thinking of that night's train, and how the strange feeling in her heart was different from all other nights' trains and all other feelings.

Banafsheh was only thinking about Friday. She imagined that the teacher would call while they were having breakfast. Her father would be away then, and it would take her grandmother a while to get up off her seat to pick up the phone.

So she would just run to the phone and pick it up herself and say, "Hello,

Teacher." But the thought of saying that embarrassed her a little, so instead she thought she would say, "Hello, who is this? Who would you like to speak to?"

The loudspeakers announced that the next station was five minutes away. Banafsheh stood up to look out the window. Darkness lay over the desert. It looked back with its own eyes, like the pale glow of a few distant lanterns.

She gathered up all her courage and asked, "When you come, what story are you going to tell me?"

The teacher stood up to pack her bag. She smiled as she thought about her answer.

"What story would you like me to tell you?"

Banafsheh didn't answer. She looked out again into the darkness, whose eyes seemed closer and brighter this time.

The train gently sounded *clickety-click, clickety-clack*. The teacher sneaked one last peek at the little girl's blue eyes. They seemed to be hiding a secret.

Banafsheh was thinking, I won't cry until after she leaves.

At the station, the teacher and a few other passengers got off the train. She waved back at Banafsheh.

"I'll come for sure," she said as she walked a few steps alongside the moving train. "For sure."

Banafsheh didn't want to go back into the compartment. So she just walked up and down the corridor. She

walked until she felt dizzy. She imagined the teacher really coming to visit and how she would talk to her easily and openly. She would say, "I knew God would send me a mother." She might even say, "I want to tell you a story, too."

She was telling the teacher the story in her mind when the conductor grabbed onto her to keep her from falling.

The train made a one last *clickety-click, clickety-clack* sound and woke up the passengers so they could go home.

~∘~

The next day, Banafsheh played outside her house, but every half hour she

would ask her grandmother if anyone had called.

On the second day, she stayed home all morning. She only left the house to play for one hour all afternoon.

On the third day, she stayed home all day to wait for the following day, which would be Friday.

On the fourth day, Friday, she stayed so close to the phone that she could have answered it on the first ring at any time.

Even though she had decided she would wait for it to ring three times before she picked it up.

TWO

The children listening to this story were in the fifth grade. The last bits of winter snow were falling. The children's eyes were glued to the lips of the teacher, who was warming her hands over the classroom heater.

"Excuse me, miss, but what happened next?" one student asked.

With the exception of one child in

the back row, everyone else repeated, "Yes, what happened next?"

The teacher walked over to the window and looked out at the snow covering the bare branches of the trees. She was quiet for a few minutes, thinking of the one student who wasn't interested in the rest of the story.

So she turned to her and asked, "Seti, don't you like the story?"

"It's good, but..."

The teacher felt a chill on her shoulders. She started to walk back to the heater.

"Everybody must express their opinions. Don't be shy, children." She turned to Seti. "But what?"

"Excuse me, miss, but the ending is obvious."

"Excuse me, miss," another student joked. "Let her tell us what happens, then."

"Yes, he's right," said the teacher. "Tell us the rest."

It was hard to tell if Seti's cheeks turned red then because of the cold or because she was nervous.

"I don't know the rest," she said. "But it's obvious that the teacher is going to call the little girl and go to meet her and tell her stories."

The children turned to Seti and listened carefully. They were nodding.

But then a boy raised his hand. "Excuse me, miss."

The teacher stared at his raised hand for a while, but her thoughts were far away.

{29}

The children looked back and forth from the teacher to the boy's hand. Even though the teacher was standing next to the heater now, she still felt cold.

Suddenly, as though waking from a daydream, she said abruptly, "Go ahead, Asima, tell us what you think."

"You would only tell a story with such an obvious ending to kids much younger than us. In this story, surely something not so obvious is going to happen."

"Like what?"

The children turned back to Asima.

"Maybe the teacher will never call the little girl, or she'll lose her phone number."

The teacher hesitated. Then she said, "Maybe the grandmother was so

{30}

sleepy that she gave the teacher the wrong number."

She walked back to the window. Many hands went up, but just then, the bell rang, and they were all lowered to pack their bags.

"We'll leave it until the next class," the teacher said. "I want you all to let me know what you think. Don't be afraid to say whatever is on your minds."

~⌒o⌒~

When she left the school that day, the teacher saw the children playing in the white snow that made the village look brighter than ever. She followed their footprints, stepping very gently on the snow.

The village men sitting out in front of the shop rose to their feet to show their respect.

As she greeted them and went on her way toward the alley, she heard one of the men say, "Many have come and gone, but this one is different."

Another man said, "God didn't create all humans alike, just as he didn't make your five fingers the same." And he held up his own hand to illustrate the point.

Yet another man smiled. "The ones who should like her — the children — love her like honey."

The teacher continued on her way, exchanging greetings with the women she passed. As she walked back to the room she rented in the home of one of

her students, she was still deep in her own thoughts.

THREE

The phone rang. One... two... three rings.

Banafsheh was so excited that she didn't even know what to say.

"Hello," she said. She was sure it would be the teacher, who would say, "Didn't I tell you I would call? Didn't I tell you?"

When no one answered, the little girl said again, "Hello...?"

"They'll call back," her grandmother said. Banafsheh could tell from the hissing noises that it was a long-distance call.

Then she recognized her father's voice.

"Banafsheh?" When the connection improved and they could hear each other more clearly, her father told her he would be flying home that very day. As Banafsheh passed the phone to her grandmother, she thought how amazing it was that both the teacher and her father would be coming on the same day.

She could hear children playing outside. Her grandmother reminded her that she still needed to help clean the vegetables and water the flowers.

"I'll water the flowers later," Banaf-sheh said. She set the vegetables down next to the phone and started to sort them.

Her grandmother tried to think of other things she could do to keep her mind occupied. And she thought about the teacher herself. She wondered why Banafsheh liked her so much.

She remembered her dark eyes, her long nose, and how you could only see two of her teeth when she smiled.

She was really quite ordinary, the grandmother thought. But then she remembered the mysterious way the teacher would stare into space after she wrote things down.

She told Banafsheh to turn on the television so she wouldn't be bored.

Then she tried to change the subject again.

"What is your father going to bring you?"

Banafsheh had forgotten to ask him. All she could think was that her grandmother really talked too much, and that soon she would be seeing the teacher with her father.

Around noon, she picked up the phone to make sure it was still working.

Ring-ring...ring-ring. The bell at the gate sounded.

She was happy her father was home, but she didn't budge from her spot near the phone.

"Didn't you hear the bell?" asked her grandmother.

Banafsheh carried the phone with her to the door, but the cord only reached the middle of the room, so she had to leave the phone there. Her grandmother thought that was very funny, but she knew better than to laugh.

Her father only had eyes for his little girl, but as soon as her grandmother came to greet him, Banafsheh ran back to the phone. He watched his daughter's hair swinging as she ran.

"She's waiting for a phone call," Grandmother explained. "Otherwise she would have stayed in your arms all day."

"Are her friends calling?" he asked as he took off his glasses. He was still a young-looking man.

"No, not a child. Someone she met on the train."

Probably some old man or woman, he thought.

"This time you will like her choice. She met a very wholesome young woman."

And Banafsheh's father smiled and went inside.

~⟡~

"Banafsheh, what does this teacher lady look like?" her father asked at lunch.

She wanted to say, "Just like my mother," but she was too shy. So instead she said, "She looks just like me." Her father put down his fork and picked up his glass of water.

After lunch, before his afternoon nap, he called her.

"Banafsheh, come here." When he didn't hear anything, he called again, "Banafsheh, I want to read you a story."

Grandmother pointed at the phone and smiled. Banafsheh's father didn't say another word. He went to his room, put on his glasses and started to look through the story books that he had bought for her.

Banafsheh was still awake an hour later. Eventually her eyes felt heavier and heavier until she fell asleep right there next to the telephone. She had a dream about her grandmother, her father and the teacher.

"Don't you want to go to the park?"

her grandmother asked later that afternoon.

"No," Banafsheh said.

Her father stayed home that evening, too. Banafsheh remembered her dream, but she felt a little embarrassed to tell them about it. Maybe she would tell her grandmother later.

That night, they stayed up until late and waited. But no one called. At bedtime, Banafsheh lay in her father's arms, and he read her a story.

Once upon a time, there was an old man who used to go to the same park at the same time every day. He would always sit on the same bench in the same corner of the park. He was used to that bench. If anyone else was sitting on it when he arrived, he

would walk around nearby until they left. Then he would put his hat down on one end of the bench and sit at the other end with his newspaper.

The old man was used to one other thing, too, and that was the little girl who would come and sit next to him whenever she got tired of playing.

Then he would put away his newspaper and say, "Hello, little one. Tired, are you?" She would laugh and ask strange and funny questions, like how did one's hair turn white, or whether it was true that when your hair turned white you wouldn't be able to play anymore.

Sometimes the old man would leave his newspaper and hat on the bench, and they would go for a walk.

One day, the old man waited a

long time for the little girl to get tired of playing and come to talk to him, but she didn't. He didn't like to keep looking over and around his newspaper at the playground. So he thought of something funny. He poked two holes through the newspaper with the pen that he used to do the puzzles. Looking through the holes, he could see the little girl talking to her friends.

A little later, he noticed her pointing him out.

Then she ran over to him. She didn't ask him any strange questions that day.

Instead she said, "Tomorrow I'm moving to another town with my family."

"Banafsheh, are you still awake?"

"Yes." Banafsheh was sure that the

little girl would give the man her new address.

The old man took out his pen, tore off a corner of his newspaper and wrote down his address. He put the piece of paper in the little girl's pocket.

"You won't lose it, will you?" he said.

"No, I won't lose it, but I don't know how to write yet."

The old man smiled. "Not now. Not even when you are in the first or second grade. But when you are in third or fourth grade, promise you will write me then."

She saw the two holes in the newspaper as she was making the promise, and that almost made her laugh.

"You mean the old man was going to wait for the little girl to go to school and learn to write before she would write him back?" Banafsheh asked.

The old man waited a few years and calculated that by then, the little girl would be in the third grade. He waited yet another year, but he never received any letters. Just to be sure, the old man waited one more year. He waited until she would be in the middle of fifth grade.

Then, when he had lost all hope, he made a strange decision.

Banafsheh thought the old man was probably angry with the little girl. He had probably decided that even if he got a letter, he wouldn't answer it.

Maybe he would never even open it, or he would tear it up.

"Banafsheh, are you sleepy?" her father asked.

"No."

So he continued to read.

By then the old man was much older and weaker and couldn't travel anymore. He decided to write to all the schools in the town where the girl said she had gone and send them his address. He sent about thirty letters — one to each school.

Banafsheh's father paused.

"What next?" she asked. "What happened next?"

Her father was quiet. She reached over and tapped his shoulder.

"What next?"

Her father seemed to be dozing off.

"Oh, yes," he continued. "A few days after he sent the letters, the old man got sick and went to the hospital. And right there on the hospital bed, alone, the poor man…"

Banafsheh struggled to keep her eyes open. She wasn't listening to her father anymore. She was thinking about how the teacher was still young. She thought about the old man in the hospital bed who might still have been thinking about the letters just before he closed his eyes forever.

She was thinking that next year, she would be going to school, too.

And then she fell asleep.

FOUR

"Quiet now. Quiet," said the teacher, and she started the math lesson. The children knew then that they would have to wait until the end of the period to hear the rest of the story. These students usually found math easier than other subjects, but today they were in no mood for things like adding and subtracting.

The teacher wiped the chalk dust

off her dress. Then she stood by the heater and called one of the students to the blackboard. The children were whispering to one another, and the classroom was filled with noise, but no one was saying anything aloud.

One of the children threw a paper airplane at the student who was standing at the blackboard. The rest of the class burst out laughing.

"Quiet." The teacher had planned to give the student a math problem to solve, but she realized that the class was not in much of a mood to study math. So instead of getting upset about it, she smiled and waved the boy back to his seat.

She imagined what an uproar there would be if the class knew that she

hadn't called Banafsheh in nearly three months.

The class clown raised his hand. She always made him sit in the front row so she could keep a close eye on him.

"Excuse me, miss." But even before he said anything, the class burst out laughing again.

"Be quiet, children. Sadeqi might not always be joking, you know."

Sadeqi turned around and stuck out his tongue at the laughing students.

When he turned back to the front, he said, "Excuse me. But I think in this story, the little girl is probably going to die."

Outside, in the snow, a crow landed on a branch right beside the classroom window. The teacher's throat felt

dry. She asked one of the students to fetch her some water. She walked toward Sadeqi's seat, feeling a little dizzy. She leaned over to ask him why he thought that, but she was at a loss for words.

Instead she said, "In some stories, maybe nobody dies. Okay, children," she continued. "The teacher doesn't lose her phone number, but she doesn't call her for a few months, either."

The crow flew from the window back to its old spot. Asima put up her hand. The teacher stared at it blankly.

"Go ahead, Asima," she said finally.

"Excuse me, miss. I think it is probably going to end up like your last story. I mean, either the teacher or the little girl is going to die."

This time the teacher laughed out loud.

"No, this story is different," one of the other children said. "In the other story, the man was very old, but the teacher and the little girl are not old."

Seti said to the teacher, "Tell us the rest yourself, please. I am sure something unexpected happens so that the teacher cannot call her."

The teacher made her way to the window. She looked out, watching the crows peck through the snow.

"Well, children, the teacher does not lose the little girl's phone number, nor does anything unusual happen to her. She doesn't phone Banafsheh for nearly three months. And then one day, she finally decides to call her."

"Maybe the teacher lost her mind," Sadeqi said. "Just like Bibinaz does." The children all burst out laughing again.

At first, the teacher laughed, too.

But then she said, "Bibinaz is really not all that unusual. She just gets lost in her own thoughts sometimes."

After class, the teacher thought about the train ride as she went into town. It seemed like everything was coming back to life again — the grandmother, Banafsheh, and the feeling of the little girl's sweaty palms.

FIVE

The phone was ringing.

Banafsheh heard it from her room, where she was drawing. Her grandmother heard it, too, and called out for someone to pick it up. But Banafsheh wouldn't pick up the phone on Fridays anymore.

Still, she walked over and stood behind her bedroom door and listened.

Banafsheh's father was in the kitch-

en. He wiped his hands and headed for the phone.

"Hello." After a short pause, he said, louder, "Hello, who is this?"

It must be for him or for Grandmother, Banafsheh thought. She wanted to go back to her drawing, but for some reason she kept listening.

"Yes, yes, I have heard a lot about you." Her father sounded very happy. Grandmother stuck her head out her bedroom door, and she was listening curiously.

"Ahhh," she said. She looked at Banafsheh's door as she walked into the living room.

"Yes, of course she's here. She's in her room drawing. Could you please hold for a moment?" He put the phone

down. "It's the teacher. Banafsheh's friend," he said happily, as he went to call her.

Grandmother picked up the phone and greeted the teacher. "Banafsheh has been thinking about you a lot these past three, four months," she said.

When her father came into her room, Banafsheh hurried back to her drawing. He kissed her and noticed that her face felt a little warmer than usual.

"The teacher has finally called," he said.

Banafsheh didn't say a word. When he took her hands to lead her to the phone, he noticed that her palms were sweating. He thought she must be sick, or she would surely be much more excited.

"I don't want to talk to her."

"A few words. Just a few words, and then I'll take you to the doctor."

"I am not sick, but I do not want to talk to her!" Her cheeks were red.

Her father left the room, disappointed. Banafsheh ran behind the door to listen again.

"Would you excuse me, please?" Grandmother said, just before she covered the mouthpiece. "What is it?" she asked Banafsheh's father quietly.

"She won't talk."

"Oh, dear. Now what do we do?"

"I think she's a little sick. She'll probably be okay later."

Grandmother got back on the phone. "Banafsheh isn't feeling very well. Otherwise she would talk to you."

Banafsheh was listening behind her door.

"No, no, it's nothing serious. You shouldn't worry about her. Just a few hours ago she was playing out in the yard." Grandmother sank wearily into the chair next to the phone. "Believe me, nothing has happened ... All right, okay. I'll try to get her to say a few words. Could you hold on, please?"

She put down the phone and whispered, "The poor woman is so worried now. She thinks something bad has happened."

"I couldn't convince her. Maybe she'll listen to you," Banafsheh's father said.

Banafsheh quickly jumped onto her bed as her grandmother slowly opened

her door. She took Banafsheh in her arms.

"Oh, dear. You're running a fever. The teacher is worried about you, you know. She thinks something bad has happened to you."

Banafsheh started to cry and hid under the sheets. Her grandmother went back to the phone, feeling helpless and disappointed.

"Please don't worry about her. She's just feeling a little under the weather. That's why she can't talk. We'll take her to see the doctor just to make sure." She smiled. "Of course you're welcome. Certainly, we would love to have you. Please come, any time."

From behind the door, Banafsheh

could hear her grandmother giving the teacher the directions to the house.

After her father finished washing the dishes, he took Banafsheh to the doctor.

SIX

Now, before we proceed any fur-
ther with our story, let us think
about the teacher, who is overcome by
a very strange feeling as she hangs up
the phone.

You might think that she would be
upset because the little girl didn't want
to talk to her. You might also think
that she would be angry at herself for
taking so long to call.

Or perhaps she is confused because she can't figure out how to end her story.

What is important to her is that she finds a clue in some conversation or between the lines of all these various tales that could explain why she is feeling so strange. Even more important, she must be able to carry on with her story. Another thing to consider — even though some might find this quite upsetting — is that she is capable of anything, no matter how cruel, if it will make a good ending for her story.

A story must be eventful and exciting, either good or bad, she thinks to herself.

Now, everyone should be very concerned about the feelings of the teacher, who is at this very moment looking

in a bookstore window staring at some books — a few of which she has written herself.

And she narrows her eyes and makes a rather risky decision.

Alas, she decides she has to somehow get rid of the little girl. Her hands tremble as she takes out her pen. She makes a small note on the corner of her notebook. Her heart is beating so fast, and her handwriting is so bad that if you saw it, you would never believe it could be an author's handwriting.

She is not in the mood for her publisher to spot her. But he does, and he catches up with her just as she is about to leave.

"Please, come in. You have finished your latest work, perhaps."

He explains how well her books have been selling, especially *The Old Man and the Little Girl*.

But she is deeply absorbed in her own thoughts.

Writing a book is so complicated, she thinks. There is no doubt that she likes the little girl, but she is willing to let her die, just to make her story more exciting.

Of course, up until this point in the story, the child's illness is quite minor. So it would not be very convincing to the reader that she would just die without a good reason.

Then, suddenly, the woman thinks of this. The father takes his little girl to the hospital. Although her ailment is not serious, the nurse gives her the

wrong injection, and right then and there...

"Please, sit down." Her publisher explains that many people have called to praise her most recent book, and one young girl in particular has written her a personal letter.

"Thank you very much. I appreciate it," she says as she takes the letter and absentmindedly tucks it away in her purse.

"You haven't said a word about your latest book. If you don't mind me saying, you look a little worried. Is there a problem? Anything I can do?"

She smiles and tries to answer calmly. "No, no problems. I expect to finish it soon. Just a few chapters to go." If she can't finish it, she thinks, she'll rip

it all up and throw it away. All of it. The little girl, the grandmother, the father, the students.

She says goodbye to the publisher and starts to cross the street to catch a taxi. She is so deep in thought that she doesn't notice the car speeding toward her. It is so close that she can't react fast enough. Her mind goes blank. So she closes her eyes and gets ready to die.

Now, opinions about death can be very interesting indeed. Old-timers may say that death is a bitter experience, but how bitter depends on the circumstances. For example, let us examine how people will feel if this author dies. People will be saddened by her death, but only to the extent that they knew her. It is fair to assume that

some might blame her death on her own carelessness, and yet be saddened by it to a certain extent as well. Still, although people know that this very author has been the instigator of many harsh events herself, they might be too sad to continue reading her book, at least for a few days.

Then there are those who may not necessarily be happy about her death, but are not altogether sad about it, either. They would argue that there is no point mourning the loss of a person who would be so cruel as to let the little girl die in the hospital because of a wrong injection.

Anyway, let's get back to the author. The speeding car passes by so close that it knocks off her purse and scatters

the contents all over the road. A young boy at the corner watches the scene in shock and disbelief.

Still shaking, the author picks up the pieces, repacks her purse and crosses the road.

The boy notices a letter she has left behind. When he goes to pick it up, a car passes over it so fast that the letter flies up in the air and lands near the curb. He picks it up and runs over to the woman, who is still shaking after coming so close to death.

"This is yours. It fell out of your purse."

The author starts to shove it back into her purse, but a mysterious feeling stops her.

There are various opinions about

the nature of this mysterious feeling.

Some attribute it to her fatigue, and liken the opening of the letter to ridding her body of this fatigue. There are also those who would argue adamantly that some supernatural force has compelled her to read the letter.

Either way, what is important is that most readers are curious about the contents of the young girl's letter and would like to find out about it as soon as possible.

Maybe it is this same mysterious feeling that has made the author pay closer attention to the letter. So much so that she sits on a bench at the first bus stop and carefully opens the letter to read it.

Dear Author,

I remember feeling so happy the first time I noticed the book The Old Man and the Little Girl *in the bookstore window. I could hardly speak. The shopkeeper must have said a few times, "The money, the money," rubbing his fingers together. I had forgotten that you had to pay for books, too. I seemed to have lost my mind. I was thinking that books should be just like the water that runs in the creek. Free. Then I thought of water fountains, and meanwhile the shopkeeper was still rubbing his fingers together.*

I didn't go home straight away. I just sat down on the bench at the first bus stop and started to read the book.

Dear Author, when I was halfway through, I thought that maybe you had

written a different story, because so many things in the story had changed. But I will never forget the holes in the old man's newspaper. I cried. It drove me crazy. I thought he would always be there, like the big old trees in the park.

I read the other half of the book at home. I couldn't believe that you said I never wrote to him. I sobbed. I showed the book to my mother and cried.

Dear Author, I never lost the old man's address. Quite the opposite. I wrote to him as soon as I could, with my mother's help. I got a letter back about a week after the end of first grade. I was playing in front of the house with my friends. I still re-member the postman's skinny face and shining eyes.

I have kept all of the old man's letters.

In the last one he wrote: I might be going on a long journey, very long. Don't write back anymore. Of course, when I come back, I will write you again myself.

I cried then. I was in fifth grade.

My mother asked if I wanted to go and visit him. "He must be lonely in that hospital," she said.

The next morning my father bought tickets for our trip. We got on the bus just before noon and arrived there around sunset.

Dear Author, I have kept all of the old man's letters, and if you want to publish them, I'll send them to you. I cannot write about our visits in the hospital, because it would drive me crazy again. I only remember that his hands were like

bark — like the bark of the old trees in the park.

A few buses had gone past, but the author was still sitting there. She was getting ready to read the letter again when another bus arrived. The old lady sitting next to her at the stop led her onto the bus. She climbed on board without thinking, not even sure about the route or the destination.

She looked out at the streets through the bus window. Everything seemed new to her. It was as though she was seeing the trees leaning over the walls onto the street for the first time. She could see the children so much more clearly. She saw how marvelous and amazing children were.

They seemed to be so much more sensible and aware than adults.

She didn't realize that the old lady sitting next to her was calling her, waving her hands in front of her face.

"I'm sorry. I wasn't paying attention. Yes?"

"You don't seem to be feeling all that well," the old lady said in a motherly voice.

"No, no, I'm fine."

"Perhaps you have a little one at home."

"No, I'm not married yet." And she thought, If Banafsheh makes up with me, I would love to be her mother.

Everyone was getting off the bus at the last stop. The author had no choice. She got off, too. She missed

the little girl. She thought she must be back from the doctor by now, and she looked at the little crumpled piece of paper in her hand with Banafsheh's address on it. She realized that she was quite far from home. So she immediately crossed the street and waved her arms to stop the first taxi.

A taxi stopped. She got in, shut the door quickly and handed the crumpled piece of paper to the driver.

SEVEN

*R*ing-ring.
Banafsheh's father and grand-mother were out in the yard. Banaf-sheh was watching television. Her father, who was watering the garden, opened the front gate.

Banafsheh walked over to the window. She was not too surprised to see the teacher.

She could hear her father saying,

"No, no, it was nothing serious. She's feeling okay now." He stood very politely at the gate as the teacher walked into the yard. Banafsheh watched her grandmother and the teacher greet and hug each other.

As for the teacher, she could see the main character of her story behind the window. She thought the little girl seemed to have lost a bit of weight.

Banafsheh ran back to the television, but she didn't turn it off. She looked at the phone and went to pick it up, even though it wasn't ringing.

She didn't know what to do, and she didn't want to cry. So she ran into her room and shut the door behind her.

But she didn't go to bed. She stood just behind the door.

The teacher walked up to her bedroom door.

"Hello, Banafsheh."

Banafsheh could not bring herself to say anything, no matter how hard she tried. And so she only said hello in her mind.

"Are you upset with me?"

All the kids on my street knew you were supposed to call on Friday, Banafsheh thought.

"I know you're upset. But when little ones make mistakes, grown-ups forgive them. Now it's your turn. You have to forgive me."

Banafsheh said nothing.

"Look, look at this. I didn't call you

{81}

all this time because I was writing this. It's the story of that night we met on the train."

Banafsheh looked out through the keyhole. She could only see the teacher's hands holding a stack of pages with writing on them.

I waited for you a long time, she thought. I didn't even go out to play with my friends.

"Please make yourself comfortable," her grandmother said. "She'll come out eventually."

"Tea is ready," Banafsheh's father said. "Would you like some?"

"I would like that," the teacher said, and as she spoke, her lips reminded him of what Banafsheh had said, about how the teacher looked just like her.

Banafsheh probably doesn't remember, he thought, but the teacher looks like her mother, too.

Moments later, Banafsheh stood on her toes and looked out the keyhole again. This time she could only see her father's hands and the tea tray.

"Go ahead, please help yourself," Grandmother said. "And I am sorry I wasn't feeling well that night, so I couldn't really talk to you very much. I ended up troubling you with Banafsheh, too."

"Oh, no, not at all," the teacher said. She turned to Banafsheh's father. "Perhaps you read stories to Banafsheh?"

"Yes, sometimes. Her grandmother tells her stories of the old days, and I read her children's books."

The teacher thought it was a good time to take out the three books of her own that she had brought.

Banafsheh looked out through the keyhole, but she couldn't see anything. It was all very quiet out there.

Her father placed *The Old Man and the Little Girl* to one side.

"I bought this one for her myself. I've already read it to her, too," he said.

The teacher was glad to hear that.

"I would never have thought, never …" she said, as she took the letter out of her purse and gave it to him to read. Grandmother was peeling fruit for everyone.

Banafsheh's father was very moved by the young girl's letter, but at the same time he seemed happy to learn

that the teacher had written the story. When Grandmother found out she was the author of the book, she got up and kissed her on the forehead.

"I'm really sorry," the teacher said. "I'm going to try again. Maybe she'll make up with me this time." And she walked back to the bedroom.

"Thank goodness she is so smart and understanding," Grandmother said. "She seems caring and kind, too. And she likes Banafsheh."

Banafsheh's father was reading one of the books. He turned a page and said calmly, "I am praying that she comes out." Grandmother wanted to say something more, but instead she just looked at the teacher, who was standing outside Banafsheh's door.

"Banafsheh…"

There was no answer. Banafsheh was trying very hard not to cry.

The teacher was thinking that this had turned into a complicated story. There was no way it could end up having a good or decent ending.

Aloud she said, "Banafsheh, if you come out, I will go outside with you. I want to play with the other children, too."

Banafsheh peeked through the keyhole again and saw the same pages in the teacher's hands.

The teacher is lying, she thought. Otherwise she wouldn't be holding those papers. And although she had sworn not to, she started to cry.

Grandmother sighed as she got up and went to the teacher.

"Won't you please come and sit down?" she asked. "I'll talk to Banafsheh myself."

So the teacher returned to her seat. She was furiously rolling up the pages in her hand when the father said, "I see you've written something new."

"Yes, but it's not finished yet." She was thinking that it was not a good story at all. It had caused all these troubles.

And all of a sudden she made an extraordinary decision.

Grandmother came back and whispered, "I think she may want to come out, but she feels a little shy."

Banafsheh's father smiled. "I'll see what I can do." But the teacher stopped him before he could stand up.

"No, wait. Let me try again, a third

time." And right then and there, in front of Banafsheh's father and grandmother, she ripped up all the pages. All of them.

A mound of shredded paper now sat on the table in front of her.

The teacher walked over to the bedroom. Grandmother started to pick up the pieces of paper, but Banafsheh's father stopped her.

"Please, wait."

"Banafsheh, look," the teacher said. "Do you see?"

Banafsheh stood on her tiptoes one last time to peek through the keyhole. She could see that the teacher's hands were empty. Those hands reminded her of that night back on the train. She remembered her own small hands, too,

and how they were sweaty when the teacher held them.

I knew God would send me a mother, she thought.

"Banafsheh, I can hear the children. Let's go and play with them."

Banafsheh wanted to laugh out loud. She looked through the keyhole again. The teacher's hands were empty, empty.

She thought, We will play outside a little and then we'll come back into the yard. She imagined the other children would probably want to come back into the yard, too.

But she would really rather be alone with the teacher.

Author's Note

The first time I walked into the Story Writing for Children class in the summer of 1997, I was quite nervous, even though I was twenty-eight years old. Masoud Nasseri had told me the children were talented.

"I have never had any doubt about the children," I said.

So why was I so nervous?

Maybe my main worry was that I didn't know what approach I should use to teach "story writing" to children. How much could I teach them, anyway?

Even more important, how could I make friends with the children?

Things all changed in about two months.

I do not mean to exaggerate the children's talents, but what amazed me so profoundly was their superb imagination. Just as interesting were the topics they selected for their writing — topics that adults would never imagine in their wildest dreams. And perhaps most important was my friendship with the children. Maybe the story of *That Night's Train* can shed some light.

The main reason I wrote this story is because of what had happened to Banafsheh Zarrin, who was in second grade. Her mother told me how Banafsheh had met a young woman on a train, and how she had stayed so faithful and dedicated to that friendship.

Of course, it goes without saying that many things are always changed in stories, but Banafsheh's story inspired me to write some things and read them to the children.

Seti Atashzaei, who was in the sixth grade, commented, "Some of the plot is too predictable."

So I fixed some parts, and on the day it was my turn to read, I read the story to the children again.

Arash Akhtaran, who was in the fourth grade, said, "There's too much clickety-clack in the first chapter."

"On the contrary," said Payam Ibrahimi. "It's very nice. In fact, let's call the story *Clickety-clack*."

Arman Asgharloo would not say anything.

"How do you like it?" I asked him.

"It was good, sir," he said.

To which I replied, "Thank you very much, but that doesn't help with the story. You must say something more specific, such as what you think about the character of Banafsheh." Everyone in the class turned to Banafsheh and laughed.

Banafsheh opened her blue eyes wide.

"It has nothing to do with me," she proclaimed seriously. "I don't even like the Banafsheh in the story."

I am still not really sure whether or not she was telling the truth.

Nonetheless, I dedicate this story to all of those children.

....

About the Author

Ahmad Akbarpour is a novelist, short-story writer and author of children's books. He has won the Iranian National Book Award and was selected for the IBBY (International Board on Books for Young People) Honour List in 2006. He is the author of the picture book *Good Night, Commander*, illustrated by Morteza Zahedi.

Ahmad Akbarpour lives in Shiraz, Iran.